RIDLEY SPEAKS

BOOKS BY KIRK WARD ROBINSON

······

NOTES FROM THE FIELD SERIES

Notes from the Field:
A Diary of Journeys Near and Far

More Notes from the Field:
Southbound on the Appalachian Trail and Other Journeys

Final Notes from the Field:
Northbound on the Appalachian Trail

THE SPEAKS SAGA

Timewall Speaks

Blaize Speaks

Ridley Speaks

Priscilla Speaks
(forthcoming)

FOUNDING SERIES

Founding Character:
Documents that Define the United States of America and its People

Founding Courage:
Courage and Character in the United States of America

NOVELS

The Appalachian

The Latter Half of Inglorious Years

STORIES

August Roads

Life in Continuum

A Robin Waits

NONFICTION

Hiking Through History:
Hannibal, Highlanders, and Joan of Arc

ridley
speaks

A NOVEL

by

KIRK WARD ROBINSON

HIGHLAND
HOME

Nashville

Ridley Speaks
A Novel

A Highland Edition

Copyright ©2024 by Kirk Ward Robinson

All rights reserved, including the right of reproduction in whole or in part in any form.

This is a work of fiction. With the exception of public areas of Nashville, Tennessee, any resemblance to real people, places, or events is entirely coincidental.

Designed by Victoria Valentine

Printed in the United States of America

HighlandHome Publishing
Nashville, Tennessee
37215

ISBN: 979-8-9886815-1-9
Library of Congress Control Number: 202490604

Visit www.kirkwardrobinson.com

Author's Note

......

Human trafficking in some form is going on all around us. We need only peer into the margins to see it.

The town of Bilbo is fictional, although it is based upon a real town—which will remain unnamed—that lies somewhere along the 2200 miles of the Appalachian Trail.

prelude

......

THE TWO BROTHERS HOPPED from boulder to slick boulder as the slanting rain stung their bare backs, chill gusts threatening to send them aloft at a misplaced step. Neither complained or hurled curses. Nature was what nature was, and a storm was as much a part of it as a warm sunny day. The tree line ahead would offer some cover soon enough, but more importantly, would bring them within a hoarse-throated shout of their destination.

The brothers were twins, almost seventeen years old, with identical high cheeks, full lips, and jet braids that lofted with each gust, flinging spray into the torrent. Their breechclouts and leggings were sodden and heavy, their beaded moccasins now like sopping sponges beneath their feet.

Wayah was the first to call out.

"Blaize!" he hollered into the tree line, his voice snatched and carried away on the wind. Nene came up beside him and leaned in close, squinting against the needles of rain.

"They cannot hear us over this, *Agidoi*. We need to get into the trees." Nene had to holler to be heard above the din, using the Cherokee word for sibling, the inside way the twins referred to each other.

Dense spruce and hemlock, their crowns a mystery shrouded in mist, shunted the wind and the velocity of the rain but did nothing to lessen the downpour. Fat drops splattered against the brothers' coppery skin, drizzled off their noses and braids. They splashed through the forest, each keeping pace, until they spotted the brushy lodge that they had hurriedly built in similar weather more than a month ago.

"Blaize!" Wayah hollered again, coming to a pause as he took in the site.

Nene held position at his brother's shoulder. With despair, he could sense the emptiness of the place. "They are not here," he said abjectly.

"They must be," Wayah insisted. "Where would they go?"

It was damp inside the lodge, dark and with a permeating chill. Mice were nesting somewhere. The reek of their urine limned the air. Blaize's tired little suitcase was gone, along with her field bag and cradle board. Wayah squatted in defeat, wringing the wet out of his braid as a distraction.

"The hearth is cold," Nene commented, running his fingers through the ashes.

"They have gone," Wayah returned dismally.

"But why? Where?"

Wayah stood and sighed. "To find out what happened to us. We were gone too long. I was afraid of this. But where could they go?" He shook his head at his own question. "It does not matter. We cannot track them now anyway."

"They must have hiked out the long way, to the interstate," Nene said, his voice skeptical as he added, "If we go quickly we could catch them in a few days."

"No." Wayah's shoulders slumped, more resignation in his expression than he would have revealed to anyone but his brother. "They will be too far ahead. Once they leave the forest, there is no way for us to find them."

"We could try," Nene pleaded even as he knew that the effort would be futile. He pushed back against a vision of sensitive Jocela, struggling through a world that was infinitely more dangerous than the forest.

"No, *Agidoi*, we must return. There is nothing we can do. And *Etsi* still needs us."

Nene pondered, worried by the conclusions he drew. "What will happen to them if we do not try—and to the babies? How will they survive? Our mother can spare us for a few days."

"Blaize will take care of them," Wayah said with a note of pride. "She is *Ghigau*. War woman. She cannot be conquered."

He scanned around, his features hardening at the injustice that had befallen them all, the intrusion into their peaceful mountain hold by the Feds, Blaize forced to give birth to Ridley during their flight from the mountain. Wayah thought of Blaize and Jocela as *Agilvi Usdi*, as his little sisters, in spirit if not in blood. Nene felt the same, although his concern for Jocela seemed to reach deeper still.

Wayah went to his brother, identical in every way although Wayah had always seemed the older of the two. He took Nene by the shoulders, looked deeply into the mirrors of his brother's eyes, and said, "It is now for Blaize to find us."

······

BLAIZE LOWERED HERSELF from the cab of the eighteen-wheeler and dropped the last few feet to the pavement, landing in a puddle that splashed to her knees. The door slammed shut above her, without even a parting comment. The rain had finally stopped, at least there was that, but then she might have preferred the rain. The drumming of it on the cab's roof had been loud and numbing, like a cloak of unreality between her and what she had to do, as if someone else were lying under that smelly truck driver. Her leather shirt and leggings were still damp from her trek through the forest, but now with a sticky warmth that seemed to cling filthily to her skin. The cold spring rain could have washed that away, leaving her shivering but clean. She shrugged. There was nothing to be done about it.

It was deep into the night now, the air soggy and heavy and an effort to take in. The files of parked big rigs resembled giants at slumber, ominous and quiet save for the tinkling drips here and there. The truck-stop store shone across the way, beyond the diesel pumps, white light, too bright, a welcome beacon for some, too penetrating for her, like an X-ray that could expose her most guarded secrets.

She splashed toward the light, hobbling and sore, but forced herself upright and steady when she spotted Jocela sitting with the babies on the bare cement under the awning on the side of the store, her back against the wall so they were below the view of those inside. Jocela was smoking a cigarette and looking off toward the shrouded mountains as if she had left something behind that she would never be able to retrieve.

"I thought you stopped doin' that," Blaize said as she approached.

Jocela studied the end of her cigarette as if entranced by the curl of smoke. "Only sometimes," she said distantly. She flicked the cigarette into a puddle, listened indifferently as it hissed, then said without turning to Blaize, "Ridley's hungry."

Blaize dropped against the wall, loosening her top. Jocela passed Ridley over without meeting Blaize's eyes. Nineteen-month-old Tommy, Blaize's first child, was sitting pressed into Jocela's side, asleep, his fair hair damp and pasted to his forehead. Ridley was fussing a bit more than usual, but settled down immediately once she found her mother's breast.

Blaize was a small girl and always would be, with a pretty, delicate face, honey hair in a tight rope braid, and probing green eyes that seemed darker in the night. At fifteen years old, she resembled a schoolgirl playing Indian, much too young to be nursing an infant, even scandalously so. She had taken the name Blaize, though, and it fit. Her years as an orphan in foster care, and juvenile detention later, had provided her with more experience than her age would suggest, as well as an explosive ferocity that had cowed civil servants, child abusers, and mountain men alike.

She sat back and sighed.

"Why are ya out here?" she asked Jocela. "Why didn't ya stay inside?"

Jocela was also fifteen, tall, beautiful by anyone's measure, with pale skin, dark hair also in a long braid, and fragile in some undefinable way. The two friends, who first met at the girls' group home when they were six, were exact opposites, but their bond transcended blood. Nothing would ever part them.

"Everybody was starin' at us an' I couldn't stand it no more," Jocela said, "so we came out here ta wait."

Jocela lit another cigarette, blowing a cloud of smoke that lingered in the thick air. The cigarette trembled between her fingers. "You were in that truck," she said.

Still looking away, she didn't catch Blaize's startled reaction.

"I was just gittin' outa the rain," Blaize offered unconvincingly.

"You were in that truck for a long time."

Now Blaize looked away. "It ain't nothin', Joss."

"Did you git us any money?"

"Yeah."

Jocela went silent, puffing her cigarette until the cloud enveloped them all. They had been trekking through the forest for more than a week, leaving behind the sanctuary of their hastily-built lodge to find out what happened to everyone after the Feds raided the encampment. The storm had blown in late in the day as they topped their last mountain. A light in the distance had guided them through the chilling rain to this truck stop, where they had arrived penniless. It had fallen to Blaize to find them some money, and she had. Now Jocela was struggling to suppress how Blaize had done it.

"Do those really work?" Blaize asked, gesturing at Jocela's cigarette even though Jocela was looking the other way.

"They work for me."

"Gimme one then."

Jocela finally looked over, her expression warring between despair and denial. "You sure?"

"Yeah, I'm sure."

Jocela handed Blaize the pack, her hand trembling as she did so.

Blaize tapped out a cigarette, hesitated, but then put it between her lips. "You got somethin' ta light it with?" she asked, the cigarette bobbing as she spoke.

"Yeah." Jocela handed Blaize a little blue lighter.

Blaize had seen this enough times, so she knew what to do. She lit her cigarette, took a tentative puff, and then a deeper one that sent her into a fit of coughing that dislodged little Ridley. Blaize gasped for air, brought to only as Ridley began to squall.

"Ya gotta go easy at first," Jocela said.

"Yeah," Blaize coughed. "Yeah." She readjusted Ridley, then sat back taking lighter puffs. "I think I'm gittin' it now," she said after a few more tries.

The smoke did make her feel better. It stilled her mind. Most of all it did that. She began to savor each puff, pausing to cough now and then but not as violently.

"So what are we gonna do now?" Jocela asked after a while. Blaize had by then lit a second cigarette and was handling it shakily.

"First we gotta git some street clothes. They'll have 'em in the truck stop."

"We got enough money for that?"

"Yeah." Blaize exhaled some smoke. "We got enough."

"Then what?"

"Then we gotta go ta Johnson City." Blaize felt a little dizzy now, a languid kind of dizziness that could lull her to sleep right where she sat. She would welcome that, sleeping it all away until the clean light of morning.

"Why Johnson City?" Jocela asked, her gaze once again lost in the dark forest.

"'Cause of that guy," Blaize said drowsily. "What's his name? Terrance. Yeah. He knows everybody. He'll know what happened."

"How are we gonna find 'im?"

"I don't know, but we will," Blaize managed to answer as she nodded off.

Her chin fell and she was at last free of the night.

chapter one

......

My name is Ridley Speaks and I was born in the wilderness, under a tree during a howling storm.

At least that's what Aunt Joss always told me. Mama would never talk about it, as if it were a deep family secret, or a scandal of some sort, although I can't imagine why either would matter more to her than to Aunt Joss, inseparable as they are.

When I was a young girl, I spun this into a fairytale princess origin story, incorporating my big brother Tommy, since we were so close. Tommy didn't know where he'd been born. Aunt Joss said she hadn't been around then, and of course Mama wouldn't offer Tommy any more detail than she would offer me. So Tommy and I took our mysterious origins and elevated them with childish imagination and perhaps longing. I was the princess, he was my brave knight, and we would do battle with the evil forces we perceived in every musty corner and dark closet.

We were living in the Blue Place then. That's the only name we ever had for it, and we were young enough when we left it that neither of us has any notion where it was. What I remember most is the dust and the bare cement, the rusty metal doors that banged and screeched, and the desolate alleys between corrugated buildings of chalky blue, where weeds grew through cracks in the pavement, and where pick-up trucks driven by surly men would sometimes back in through the big door to load or unload while Tommy and I played outside.

And I remember the man. I didn't like him. It's not that he scared me, although he looked scary enough, it was just that everything he said to Tommy and me seemed disingenuous, as if he had to pretend that he was nice or else he might get in some kind of trouble. He was a sickly-looking man who had more gray hair on his face than on his mottled scalp, and teeth that no smile could make pretty. And he had a smell, like something from a bottle under the kitchen sink. Mama and Aunt Joss worked for him in some manner. Mama would take off for a day or two here, a day or two there while Aunt Joss kept watch over us, and when she returned she would smell like something from under the kitchen sink, too.

Mama never told us that she loved us, as if her lips couldn't form that word, but she was always happy to see us again. She would bend down and smile, take us and hug the breath out of us while we wrinkled our noses against the smell, then she would sit and read aloud to us, book in one hand, a cigarette in the other. She would read for what seemed hours, until our eyes stung from the cigarette smoke and we were too sleepy to pay attention, and I might nod myself awake and she would still be reading. Mama loved to read. She taught Tommy and me how to read when we were very young. That's what I always try to remember the most.

Anyway, at some point after Robbie was born I discounted my wilderness origin story as just something Aunt Joss made up to amuse a child. My origin was no clearer to me, but it certainly hadn't been in the wilderness, not considering our surroundings and the traumatic arrival of my younger brother who, like Tommy and me, had no father, and who, unlike Tommy and me, shared no resemblance whatsoever.

Robbie was a disagreeable baby who did not improve with age. He bawled constantly, which was heretical from our point of view because crying was something Mama absolutely forbid. Why I do not know, but I never saw her cry, not once. Still, Mama doted on Robbie. She cradled him, nursed him, and read to him even before he spoke his first word. But his black hair and stocky features...he was like a changeling, not like Tommy and me in any way.

I look like Mama, although I'm a lot taller. A *lot* taller. I have her light hair, her pert nose and sharp chin, and before she lost her front teeth, I had her smile. My eyes are blue, though, not green, and Tommy's eyes are blue, and his hair is light and he's tall. He doesn't look as much like Mama, but he looks enough like me that you can tell we're brother and sister. We were always close and connected that way, and no one, not even Robbie once he was older, would ever dare to cross us.

Except Mama, of course, who never shied away from crossing anyone.

So that was our new fantasy, that Tommy and I came from the same father, that we were the special two, unique in a family of mongrels that Mama would birth every few years. Well, that's not a fair thing for me to say. Robbie was a mongrel for sure, but Timewall, who came next, was sweet, a real Boy Scout, so earnest in everything he did, and so afraid of Mama. Then came Priscilla, bitter from early on and I don't blame her. As for the baby Mama was pregnant with when I left, I don't know anything.

I've gotten ahead of myself. It's hard to put it all in order, that this led to this, which led to this. There was so much in so short a time. I had most of it written down in my diary, day by day by day and it all seemed to make more sense that way, but Mama found my hiding place while she was searching every cushion and corner for money one morning, and she read it and she was so angry. She wouldn't give it back, and I fumed, and then I turned eighteen and I left.

You see, you didn't stand up to Mama, to Blaize. It was futile. You couldn't win. You couldn't intimidate her with fury, with size, or even with queasy intimations of violence. She would only stand her ground, glare you down, and dare you to do your worst. Tommy and I figured this out early on, so we knew better. Don't even go there, just keep it passive-aggressive until you're old enough to leave, then put her so far behind you that you could finally gloss it all over.

But that's for later. For now, writing this down is the only way I can get that therapist to leave me alone. He wanted to talk—of course he did—talk and talk and talk until I would be, in his estimation, good in the head, fully reconciled, and ready to be let out of this place. But I don't want to talk. Not to him, not to anyone. This is imprinted. You have to try to understand.

Mama had a mantra that she repeated so often as we were growing up that it burrowed deep into our psyches. "Don't you talk ta no strangers," she told us over and over. You have to hear this in Mama's accent, a twang like a cat in heat dangling by a single claw from a high E guitar string. It's an Appalachian accent, a mountain hollow accent, like listening to a

Grand Ole Opry show from the 1960s on an old tinny radio. I have an accent too, considering that I was raised in the South, but mine is more of a drawl and my voice is husky and that's why I was always reluctant to sing, until recently when someone told me I had a "raw, authentic sound." But then, someone else told me that I was "no Loretta Lynn, so lose the hick accent." I don't know what to make of it.

About not talking to strangers, this is the most exposition Mama ever gave me on the subject. I was in middle school and there was this counselor named Mr. Sternman whose job it was to look in on the more (by his reckoning) challenged kids. He wanted me to talk, and in my breast I really wanted to, perhaps needed to, but when Mama found out she sat me down, red in the face, and exclaimed, "Didn't I always tell ya not ta talk ta no strangers?"

"But he ain't a stranger, Mama," I pleaded.

She pulled back with a haughty expression. "He ain't, huh? So how old is he, then?"

"I don't know, Mama."

"Is he married? Does he have kids?"

"I don't know, Mama."

"So where was he born? Where'd he go ta school? Does he have brothers and sisters?"

I was by now losing patience. I jumped up, towering over Mama, parked my fists on my hips and shouted, "I don't know!"

Mama eyed me back into my chair with that way she has, lit a cigarette, then went on heatedly, "That's right, ya don't know. Ya don't know nothin' about this guy. But if ya talk to 'im he'll know everything about you. You'll be givin' 'im power over ya, and ya won't never be able ta git it back."

Mama was right, of course. She knew things from a place so tightly concealed that none of us could even imagine where that place was. Even though I was never as paranoid as she and Aunt Joss were, I didn't talk to Mr. Sternman. So I won't talk to the therapist here. Simply won't do it. He suggested with exaggerated disappointment that I write it all out instead. I can write. I can write pretty well. Tommy taught me how when I was five, and I would write little stories, nothing special, but coherent stories that had a beginning, a middle, and an end. Then, in the third grade, I started writing poetry. I wrote this little poem about an old alley cat we had, and my teacher was so impressed that he asked me to get up and read it to the whole class, which embarrassed me because my voice was already rough by then. The poem went like this:

> *I have a cat named Andy*
> *He always comes home sandy*
> *His hair is all curled*
> *He's out of this world*
> *He's my cat, his name is Andy*

It's silly, I know, but I was only eight or so at the time. For some reason, though, my teacher loved it. He encouraged me and I kept at it. Still do.

So I'm writing this out. If I'm diligent, I can spare myself from that nosey therapist for however long it takes. Of course he doesn't know that I'll never let him read it. Not—going—to—happen. And I'm not obligated to stay here anyway. I can walk out any time I want. But I feel an odd duty to stay, to validate their efforts, nauseatingly attentive as they are most of the time, as if I were a broken bird in desperate need of their care. Emotional detachment isn't a behavioral abnormality, it's a survival skill, something these people would know if they hadn't been catered to all their lives. And besides, my bed is soft, my room is private, and the food is free; and except for that therapist and the odd visit by the police, no one bothers me. I don't mind taking advantage of that for a while.

Oh, and something else: The accents back home are as twangy as I've already described, with g-dropping, double negatives, and all the rest. I work hard to keep from doing it myself, but that's the way everyone else talks. It gives me a headache trying to write all of that out, so whenever you see an "is not" or an "am not," think *ain't*. Can't is *cain't*, get is *git*, nothing is *nothin'*, because is *'cause*, you is *ya*, and is *an'*, to is *ta*, your and you're is *yur*, "should have" is *shoulda*, "used to" is *useta*, and so on. If you've read Faulkner, then you know what I'm talking about. If you haven't read Faulkner, then you should have.

chapter two

......

MAMA NAMED ME RIDLEY. Aunt Joss said that when I was born, Mama just seemed to know that this would be my name. We don't know where she got it, not even Aunt Joss. We don't have any family except us, no photos, no scrapbooks, nothing handed down, so I doubt it's a family name. Aunt Joss said she'd never known anyone by that name before. My name is a riddle wrapped in a mystery that Mama keeps hidden away like everything else. I do like my name, though, so I'm not complaining.

As for our lack of lineage…well, you don't ponder that kind of thing when you're a kid. Mama was all we knew and needed. We trusted her in our very cells, to keep us safe and fed and cared for. Nothing scared us back then, not with Blaize Speaks in the room. It wasn't until we were older and met other kids, kids who had moms and dads, grammaws and grampaws, and family photos around Christmas trees and turkeys that we began to wonder if there wasn't something wrong with us. By the time I started high school, I knew absolutely that there was something wrong with us.

We'd been living in Bilbo for so long by then that it had become our de facto hometown. The Blue Place and the mountains and the scattering of accommodations afterward were too far back to grasp as more than flashes of memory. Bilbo—isn't that a ridiculous name for a town? Here's what I learned about Bilbo in my history class: Bilbo was founded before the Civil War by a rich Southern planter named William "Bill" Borton, who named the town Bortonville. William Borton built an ostentatious mansion right in the middle of town, a mansion that held prominence over the shanties of people whose envy grew with every view of that mansion through their unglazed windows. The people began to call the town Bill Bortonville as a jibe at the old man; then after Borton died and the war was lost—and a few generations went by until no one remembered anything about it—people just naturally shortened Bill Bortonville to Bilbo.

So there you have it.

We lived in a white single-wide trailer across the tracks from town. All of us. In a trailer. I wasn't aware of any stigma associated with trailer life until a girl I knew at school let it slip one day. For us it was just the way it was, no better or worse than any other place we'd ever lived. Mama was there, that's all that mattered; and as far as that girl was concerned, I gave her Mama's look and told her to mind her own business, and she did.

Aunt Joss was living somewhere else by then, with her daughter Lainey, who was Timewall's age. Aunt Joss would come by to visit almost every day, seeming to get bigger and heavier at every visit until one Christmas the redwood deck out front collapsed under her. That wasn't as funny as it sounds. Poor Aunt Joss was lying down in all that broken wood, the sky a chilling gray and threatening to drizzle, unable even to roll herself over; and Lainey was screaming for help and Mama couldn't get out the door because, small as she was, she would have fallen far enough to break an ankle.

Timewall helped me get Aunt Joss up, jumping in as if the accident had been his fault and all that weight was on his shoulders. I don't think he was even nine years old at the time. Tommy was out with friends, Robbie was off being Robbie, Priscilla was too young to help but wouldn't have helped anyway, so it was just Timewall and me, trying to get underneath Aunt Joss so that we could lift her, Mama watching helplessly from the doorway and more rattled than I'd ever seen her.

But we got Aunt Joss up, who did cry, she and Lainey, while Timewall and I stood back dumbfounded, which left the matter of what to do next, Mama stranded up there, Aunt Joss beached down here and so ashamed she couldn't look us in the eyes. It was Timewall's idea to drag some cinder blocks over and stack them into steps. Afterward, we pushed and shoved and got Aunt Joss inside and that was more or less the end of it. Over the next day or so, Mama tugged all that broken wood into a pile that was still there when I left.

Mama and Aunt Joss had been clean for a while. I could just about believe that things were normal, that our lives weren't so different from everyone else's, that the future held nothing but good things. Tommy wasn't as reconciled. He wouldn't confront Mama—he knew better than that—but I could see the reproving look in his eyes, and something wounded in hers, as if he were betraying her in some primal way, as if she'd had some sense in her heart that Tommy would never, ever, hurt her. Not Tommy, not her boy. Of all of us, not *him*.

And then when Tommy turned eighteen he left. Just left. I don't know who this hurt worse, Mama or me, but I know who showed it the most. I don't think Mama understood what Tommy meant to me. His words that day were clumsy, full of regret, but, he added, I was old enough now to hold my own against Mama. He didn't have to worry. No, I'm the one who has to worry. Tommy's in Afghanistan. How could I not?

I blamed Mama. I worked hard to keep it concealed, the way Mama would, but that bitterness gnawed at me, desperate to get out; and then Mama came home one day and told me that she was pregnant again, news I took with a huff and a glower and a slammed door. I was eighteen years old, graduating in two months, and I was done. The look in her eyes was something like what she'd given Tommy.

Mr. Sternman was now my high school English teacher. He saw promise in me, he said, and helped me personally with my writing. I got an A+ in his class. When I told him I was leaving after graduation, he went white with disbelief and sputtered, "But—but Ridley, what about college? You have the grades."

"I don't want to go to college."

This seemed to confound him so deeply that I felt as if I'd just plunged a knife into his chest while he was offering me cookies and milk.

All he could come back with was a bewildered, "Why not?"

"Because it takes too long, it costs too much, and I'd have to pay people to teach me what *they* want me to learn, not what *I* want to learn. I won't give people that kind of power over me."

I meant that, still do, and this wasn't a last-minute decision. This had been percolating in me for a while, I just hadn't had the courage to tell him until that day, the day I'd become so disgusted with Mama.

"But Ridley," he pleaded, "you can't make it in life without it."

"Wanna bet?" I said.

I hate it that I shattered someone else's dreams for me, but then they were his dreams, not mine.

Timewall was twelve then and took it the hardest, about as distraught as I'd been when Tommy left, as if poor Timewall's very last salvation was walking out the door. Robbie was out breaking and entering somewhere, Priscilla was down at the old abandoned depot so she wouldn't have to listen to any of it, and Mama was in her chair in the other room, puffing furiously and not about to capitulate to anything.

Timewall had a cowlick that wouldn't stay down. I dabbed my tongue and patted his hair into place, then held my fingers to his cheek for a moment. I think Timewall actually loved me, and what do you make of that? Timewall didn't see what I saw, that Mama would knock every brick from under every foundation before she would yield. I was only doing what she would have done.

"But where will you go?" Timewall asked shakily.

"I'm going to California," I answered with a firmness of resolve that would brook no other outcome.

"Why California?"

"Because it's the farthest place I can get to from here."

......

THERE IS LITERALLY only one street in Bilbo, Main Street. We call it Only Street because that's really what it is. Anyway, houses and businesses poke out from it like thorns on a rose, while down at the twisted stem, where Only Street crosses the railroad tracks and turns to gravel, lies the trailer court, an old abandoned rail depot, and a similarly decrepit mill. Beyond all of this are dense woods that eventually become a national forest; and cutting through these woods is the Appalachian Trail, famous to the thousands who hike it every year, but infamous in Bilbo.

I don't know why that was. The trail certainly didn't bother me, but it sure seemed to bother just about everyone else in that town. Robbie was especially cruel to the hikers who came through. The hikers had to leave the woods and cross the railroad tracks in order to rejoin the woods on the other side, so they were out in the open for those few minutes. Robbie and some other boys would throw rocks and trash at the hikers, and sometimes water balloons filled with pee. I caught them in the act a couple of times and ran them off, but they would just swarm back after I left. There was a little clearing a few steps down the trail and off to the side that had a wooden bench, where I often went to escape our crowded trailer. I met a lot of the hikers there, so I'd come to know quite a bit about the trail, that it led to places far from Bilbo, but more important to me at the time was that it passed under the interstate only a few miles ahead.

I left the trailer the morning after graduation (which, surprisingly, Mama did attend, Aunt Joss squeezed in on her left), carrying my guitar and a purple daypack that contained a change of clothes, some snacks, a bottle of water, what money I had saved, and my phone. It was the last day of May, a Saturday morning that was remarkably cool and pleasant, as if even the weather were an ally in my escape. To reach the bus I'd have to walk all the way through town to the highway, which would expose me to the eyes of nosey townsfolk, and even—just possibly, because she would do it—Mama driving by and pretending not to notice me. I didn't want to start out that way. This was my business and no one else's, and if Mama didn't want to say goodbye to me in the trailer, I surely didn't want to see her driving by and acting as if it were nothing.

So I took the trail, where in an hour or so I would reach the interstate and could flag a bus. Priscilla ignored me that morning, just turned over in her bed across from mine and pulled the covers over her head. Robbie was still out breaking and entering somewhere, and Mama wouldn't come out of her room. Only Timewall was there to see me off, with a look on his face that I wish I could forget. Why do we have to hurt others just to live our own lives?

I liked walking the trail, all green and full, with birds flitting everywhere. I didn't see any hikers, but then none of them would dare sleep anywhere near Bilbo so they were all either well behind or well ahead. I reached the interstate much sooner than I expected, only one mountain in the way, which I took at a breathless pace that had me panting at the top. There was a view from that mountain, a pretty view of undulating forest green, as if the forest were forever and Bilbo just an aberration; and when I made it to the interstate I did give some thought to just going on, taking the trail wherever it led, but that would have left me too close to Bilbo after a hard day's journey, as if I hadn't made any progress at all, while a bus could whisk me across several state lines during the same amount of time. So I climbed the embankment, walked to the next exit, and waited for the bus.

I do sometimes wonder, though, how differently things might have turned out if I'd just stayed on the trail, experienced the freedom that so many of the hikers had described to me. Maybe it would have been better, maybe worse, so really not worth contemplating.

At this point you need to know that in my entire life I'd never been much beyond Bilbo. The Blue Place? The mountains? They seem far continents in my memory, but they're probably just around a corner I never needed to take. Beyond that it's all been repetition: up Only Street to school, down Only Street to the trailer, a monthly trip down the highway to Hampton, where Mama paid her utility bills, and bi-monthly trips to the Walmart going the other way. I'm not even sure where Aunt Joss lived since we never went there to visit. I'd never seen an ocean, a sand dune, or a sail boat except on TV. I'd never seen an airplane that wasn't high in the sky, or a building tall enough to be called a high-rise. I'd never been to an amusement park or a music concert. I'd never swum in a swimming pool.

So I kept my nose pressed to the window as we rumbled up the interstate, every sight a new and wondrous revelation. I couldn't bear to miss any of it, and could scarcely imagine what I might see out west.

There were tangles of interstate highway at the bigger towns, twining like snakes into cloverleaf configurations that could have swallowed Bilbo whole, with cars flowing like corpuscles along the ramps below us, sometimes stacking up for a mile or more, glass towers glinting in the sun, some with mirrored windows, some with bronzed windows, and I wondered if people just stood behind those windows to watch the traffic go by. I would have, I think. It was all too fascinating to overlook.

So I had little time to mull the momentous decision I'd made. Should I be sad? Should I feel loss or homesickness? I didn't feel any of that. I felt excited, bursting at what lay ahead. I was eighteen years old and beholden to no one, free in a way that made me giddier than sips of hard cider at a homecoming party.

And then a memory flared up. The view beyond my window went to blurred forest greens and concrete grays dappled by the sun, and I was in my head even though I didn't want to be. It was my earliest memory, just snatches of images and sounds that I talked over with Tommy when I was older, to confirm that I was really remembering and not just conjuring something I'd seen in a book or on the TV. Tommy had been old enough to remember much of it. His memories fill in those early years for me, until now his recollections feel as if they were my memories all along.

It was Mama's eighteenth birthday.

Of course, to me, Mama was always what she is now—she was Mama, an adult, but really she was only a girl who had just turned eighteen. This was more than a birthday for her, it was emancipation, released at last from a fear that I couldn't grasp until I was old enough to do the math, that she'd been underage with two babies and no legal guardian.

Aunt Joss threw Mama the party, which was held somewhere that neither Tommy nor I could ever figure out. There was a jukebox with colorful lights, like candy on display, and a ball that turned and glittered near the ceiling. There was music playing, loud music, bold and rhythmic notes, with lyrics that repeated and reverberated over and over, something about clover. I remember liking the sound of it even though it hurt my ears, because Mama was there, smiling and even laughing, and I remember smiling, too, there with Tommy holding me in his little arms in a corner out of the way.

Then that song ended and another began, a hard thumping of drums and guitar that rattled the glasses on a shelf above us. *"That's my song!"* Mama shrieked, darting to the center of the dance floor, under the glittering ball, her hips rocking, her bare arms held high, fingers feeling the notes. She was wearing jeans and a pink halter top, and cowboy boots that propped her up a bit higher. *"Ch ch ch ch ch ch Cherry Bomb!"* she sang through her still-perfect teeth, and I was clapping my own little hands and grinning because Mama was happy, and cherries were sweet and maybe this meant that Mama was going to give us some.

I know that song now. I can even play it, although my voice doesn't do it justice.

Hello world I'm your wild girl, I'm your ch ch ch ch ch ch Cherry Bomb!
Mama rocked her hips in time with the beat and belted out this line—
Have ya and grab ya until you're sore
—and the trouble started.

Mama wasn't dancing with anyone but herself, alone in her own happy place, encircled by a raucous crowd that clapped and hooted and hollered for more, some of the men doing lewd things with their hips. Tommy and I could see most of it between the legs of the partying people, Mama jumping up and down, her hair flying and wild, and then a man stepped in and took her by the hips.

"C'mon baby, give me some of that," he said through a grin that wasn't nice. He had long dark hair and a bristly face. Mama only stood as high as maybe his breastbone.

"Get off me!" Mama hollered, going from fun to fury in an instant. She shoved him, sending him back maybe a step, then stood there with a look of venom. I can still feel the smile slipping off my face, feel Tommy holding me tighter.

"Hey, baby, don't be that way," the man said with drunken contrition.

"How I am isn't up to you!" Mama spat at the man

"Why, you little c—" the man spat back. I'm not going to write the word he used. You know what it is.

You wouldn't have thought that Mama could have gotten any madder. She turned purple with rage, and in one lightening motion, she jumped as high as she could and rammed her fist into his face. The man stood there for a second as if he couldn't believe what had just happened, and Mama was back on her feet, her nostrils flaring, right in his face if she'd been tall enough for that. The music came to an abrupt stop, all the pretty lights going out on the jukebox. The man rubbed his chin, turned red even through his whiskers, then pulled his hammer of a fist back. Mama didn't flinch, didn't blink. She defiantly raised her chin to the man, her own fists bunched; then a woman named Charlie stormed in with a baseball bat and a look of fury that would have sent a mama grizzly bolting for the woods—and the man thought better of it and stalked away, muttering curses as he went.

Afterward, the music started up again, everyone smiling, including Mama, and that's all I remember of that night.

I took my guitar down and strummed that song as the mountains went to hills and the traffic got heavier. I didn't sing, just strummed the song in lighter notes, wondering what I would do if something like that happened to me. The people sitting near me seemed to appreciate the diversion, so I switched to Country music—I'm better at that—and played them a Miranda Lambert song I like, the one about the small town, which was ironic considering that I'd just left a small town but that's not where my head was just then. I was only reminiscing with music, entertaining people and passing time, and then the sun was low, casting us all in a warm orange hue. Buildings rose tall above the interstate, and we wheeled into Nashville.

Nashville was my first-ever city, a real city, with more people just right there around the bus station than lived in all of Fuller County back home. I came off the bus a little dazed by it all. I had plotted every leg of my trip using the computers at school, so I knew that I had to change buses in Nashville. I coughed at the diesel exhaust as I crossed the bus lanes, coughing harder before I could make it to the lobby. I put a hand against a sooty brick wall, bent over, and concentrated on my breathing, in through the nose, out through the mouth, calmer now. My throat tickled—more like itched—but I'd stifled the coughs.

A scrawny guy with the red eyes and blemished complexion that I'd come to know too well sidled up next to me, leaned against the wall and crossed his boney arms.

"You just get in?" he asked.

I eyed him with loathing and didn't answer.

"Hey, I'm just being friendly," he said, acting offended. "Where are you from? Small town, I bet."

His eyes darted as if he were evaluating every inch of me, pausing on my daypack, which was grasped in my free hand, on my guitar, which was slung on my back. I was wearing a denim skirt and a white T-shirt, with suede calf-high boots and a thin black jacket that did more to keep the sun off than any cold out.

"If you need a place to stay, I know where you can go. C'mon, I'll show you."

He turned as if to go, but when he saw out the corner of his eye that I wasn't following, he whipped back around with a smile that he probably thought was reassuring.

"I even know some people down on Music Row," he went on. "That's why you're here, right? To spread some CDs around, get an agent? I can help you with that. I know people."

This guy had the beginnings of a dip in his lip, the way Aunt Joss's had started. He was wearing a yellowed T-shirt, ratty jeans cinched tightly to hold them up, and sneakers with holes big enough that I could see his ugly toes. I gave him my most incredulous look.

"Really?" I said. "Really? Does that actually work on people?" I might be from a hick town but I'm not a hick and I'm not stupid.

"What—hey, I'm just being nice."

"Then go be nice to somebody else." I shouldered past him and went inside.

There was a line waiting at the ticket window, disheveled people of all kinds who looked either too weary of life or too anxious to rip someone off. People were jostling and bumping into me. I kept a tight grip on my daypack as I took it all in. The place was dingy, gray, with flickering fluorescent lights in a stained ceiling, and a sickly reek of body odor mixed with stale cigarette smoke. The floor was gritty beneath my feet, as if someone had spilled salt on it. I shuffled forward and finally made it to the window. The woman behind the window was black and infectiously cheerful.

"Well, how are you, hun?" she asked with an animated smile. "Where you headed today?"

"I need to go to Memphis next," I told her, feeling buoyed by her energy. "And then to Little Rock."

"Sure, hun. Let me just punch that up for you." Some tickets popped up out of a machine. "Yeah, we got you covered. That bus goes in about an hour. I need to see some ID please."

I reached into my daypack and showed her my ID card. I didn't have a driving license. I've never driven a car. I don't have a birth certificate either, just a paper that Mama had to sign so I could go to school.

"That's good," she said, sliding my ID back. "Now just sign these tickets right here, and that will be forty-nine dollars."

I dropped my ID in my daypack, parked my daypack beside my knee, signed the tickets, and when I reached down for the money, my daypack was gone!

At first I couldn't accept it. I shuffled left and right, as if my daypack might be hiding behind my other leg. I backed away from the counter, checked behind me, checked the man who was standing behind me.

"Did you see anybody—?" I asked him but didn't finish the question.

"Hurry it up," someone said from farther back.

I turned to the woman behind the window. "My pack," I said in a fog. "It's gone. Did you see anybody?"

Her smile flattened and she pulled the tickets back suspiciously. "That's forty-nine dollars, hun. C'mon, people are waiting."

"But...but..."

"Listen girl, I don't wanna miss my bus," the guy behind me grumbled.

I backed away while the woman behind the window shook her head, as if she'd caught me running a con. The man behind me pushed forward, and then the rest of the line, and now I was off to the side, searching every corner, under every chair, as if I'd simply sat my daypack down and forgotten to pick it up again even though I'd never been anywhere beyond that line. We delude ourselves easily when we suddenly become desperate. I even went in to check the women's room, although I knew that I hadn't gone in there.

By the time I accepted the situation and gave up the search, all of the people who'd been in the lobby had cycled through, replaced by people who looked no different than their predecessors. I went outside in a haze of denial. The sun was very low, not even bright enough in the reflection off the glass towers to hurt my eyes. It was warm, but the air carried a chill.

The street was dizzying now, too much to take in. I had to stop and bend over to catch my breath. Cars zipped past. Crowds of people came and went in suffocating clusters. There were grungy people sitting on the curbs holding up handmade signs, *Help a Vet, Spare Change, God Bless*, and looking about as pathetic as Uncle Bates, Bilbo's resident drunk. Sirens warbled and reverberated between walls of brick and stone, nowhere in view but jarring just the same. I wanted to run as fast as I could, find a park, a stand of trees, any place to escape the chaos.

And this was where I was stranded, without money, identification, or even a phone.

chapter three

······

MAMA TOLD ME ONCE, in her no-nonsense way, "Ridley, feelin' sorry for yurself don't do nothin' but make ya miserble, an' everybody around ya, too." I had to write that in her accent (with a chuckle) because that's the way I best remember it. Mama said she learned this from an old mountain man who was now long dead, shot in the head.

Out on the curb, as the sun met the sidewalk, I went through the stages, reaching anger soon enough and stopping there for a long visit. It was the red kind of anger, Blaize anger, the kind you don't mess with. I could envision it clearly now, that scrawny guy following me in, slinking along the floor like a mangy possum until he could get his hands on my daypack; and if I ever caught up with him, life in the bottom of a busy privy would be better than what he had coming.

I wandered along the sidewalk with my vengeful thoughts, nowhere to go, waited at a crossing light, and a streetwise girl shouldered up beside me. She had dirty blond hair and dark eyebrows, wore a clean white pleated skirt that frilled around her cowboy boots, a bright yellow top, and a hard-ridden look in her eyes.

"Hey," I said. "Is there any place to stay around here?"

She seemed to only just then notice me, looked me up and down as if confirming something, lingering a moment on my guitar.

"You just off the bus?" she asked in a weary twang. The day was going dusky now. I noticed that her skirt wasn't really that clean, and that some of the stitching around her shoulders was fraying.

"Yeah."

She seemed to nod inwardly. "There's a rescue mission just up that way."

That was a term I had no familiarity with. "I don't need rescuing," I said, not meaning for it to come out sounding harsh, but then, yeah, I probably did. "I just need a place to sleep until I can work things out."

"Don't we all," she mumbled. "Well, suit yourself." She started across the street.

"Wait!" I hurried after her. "Is there a park around here or something?"

She turned to me with a look of veteran disbelief. "You mean you'd rather sleep with the homeless people?"

"I'm not sleeping with anybody but myself," I half growled back.

"Have it your way," she said with a roll of brown eyes. "Go back the way you come, over the pedestrian bridge, and follow the river to the right. Shelby Bottoms is that way. Can't miss it."

And then she skipped across without a backward glance.

I turned, looking back past the bus station, shrugged, and went that way. It was fully dark before I made it over the pedestrian bridge. A street paralleled the river, with plenty of lights reflecting off the water so the route wasn't hard to follow. I cleared an industrial area and then the night became darker, with trees closing in above me. Dusky cars with booming bass beats idled past now and then, slowing to a crawl as they went by, as if they were perusing the latest hillbilly wannabe off the bus. I walked forthrightly, head up and with my arms swinging wide. No one stopped to accost me, lucky for me—or maybe even for them, considering the mood I was in. I entered the park, a golf course to my left. I fished a plastic bottle from a trash can, filled it at a water faucet, and continued on until I found an asphalt path that plunged into thicker woods. I followed it.

The night was still, the woods quiet, the air sticky and cool. I saw a light in the woods, worked my way toward it, and came across an encampment of homeless people, with tattered tarps and tents and trash everywhere, as if a storm had blown a landfill into a tree line. Why make such a mess? I backed out and moved on in the pitch black until I felt soft grass beneath my feet. I lay down there for the night, weary as if I were months gone from Bilbo rather than hours, wrapped in my jacket and grateful that it wasn't raining.

The morning rose and I was stiff and hungry and damp with dew. Dull light seeped through the trees as I hauled myself up and went looking for something to eat. A jogger thumped past me as I moved along the path, huffing and puffing and reeking of deodorant, the sickly, suffocating kind that men like to use. I had to cough a few times to get that out of my throat. He said nothing to me, and I said nothing to him, as if the morning hadn't proceeded far enough yet for civility.

I was really hungry, my stomach growling loud enough to startle the birds. These woods were different from the tall forests I knew, scrubbier, with hairy vines and prickly briars and dense spindly trees. I was starting to get anxious, feeling faint, and then I saw what I was looking for. I ran to them, urgently tugging them out of the ground and chomping on them without even washing them off first, leaves, stems, flowers—the roots digested better if cooked, though, so I tossed those over my shoulder as I went.

When I was in the mountains recovering, Mama would take me on walks through the forest, holding my hand as green sunlight flashed in our eyes, patient as I'd never known her, pointing out this plant and that plant, the dandelions and plantains, the ones you could eat. There were other edible plants too, and poisonous plants. She taught me all of that during a month or two of a summer that still feels like an eternity in my recollection.

I was five years old, Robbie was a fussy baby, Tommy had finished the first grade, and we were still at the Blue Place. After bedtime one night, I started coughing and I couldn't stop, hacking coughs that had me doubled over and speckling my sheets with blood. I could taste iron in my throat. Mama came to me, sat at my side and held me, Aunt Joss standing in silhouette in the darkened doorway, rocking Robbie in her arms. Tommy was propped wide-eyed on an elbow on his bed across the way.

"Is it whooping cough?" Aunt Joss asked Mama through the darkness. Her voice shook. "Blaize, we need to get her to a hospital."

Mama pulled me closer as the coughing became a spasm that threatened to rupture my throat, her cheeks trembling around a reassuring smile that must have cost every ounce of self-control that she possessed. I felt so safe, so perfectly safe, even as I couldn't catch a breath and my throat felt like fire.

"We can't take her to the hospital, Joss," Mama said over her shoulder. She brushed the hair out of my eyes, her smile faltering.

"Why not?" Aunt Joss asked with more bite than was normal for her.

"It's okay, baby girl," Mama cooed to me; and then to Aunt Joss, "Because they'll know us then. They'll make a record. And they can still try to take the babies away and I'm not going to let them."

"But—but—you went to the hospital when Robbie came," Aunt Joss sputtered.

"That was different."

Tommy and I both remembered that night too well, all the blood, Mama trying to give birth right there in the Blue Place but something went wrong. I still have nightmares about it sometimes.

"*How* was it different?" Aunt Joss's voice was verging on hysteria, not helped by Robbie's incessant squalling.

"Robbie was stuck. It was an emergency. An emergency room emergency. I didn't have to give real names."

Jocela seemed to deflate. She was still slender at the time, so seeming to deflate took some effort. "So what are we going to do, then?"

"Ridley needs faith."

Even at five I recognized that word, which made no sense to me because we weren't religious in any way and never had been as far as I knew.

"You can't be serious," Aunt Joss exclaimed. "We can't get up there. It'll take too long."

"No it won't," Mama insisted, stroking my damp forehead and holding on to that fragile smile. "Go call Charlie. Call her *now*."

Fever memories, but it wasn't a fever I had. We all bundled into a pickup truck, the adults shoulder to shoulder and me in Mama's arms, her eyes never leaving mine; and the night swallowed us as we sped through it, the tires howling through the floorboard; and then we were bouncing and fishtailing and I was coughing as if my lungs were unattached and time seemed to stretch out into a month of nights with no daylight ever to come, just bouncing and spinning tires and Robbie bawling in Aunt Joss's lap and Tommy looking on as if his heart had been yanked out; and then we slid to a crunching stop and Mama piled out of the truck with me in her arms and hurried me through the chilled night to a warm cabin where we were met by a dark woman with a noble face and a perplexed expression; and she took me and lay me gently down and gave me something to drink that made my throat feel so cool and I don't remember the sunrise.

I heard them talking later, in the other room. It was fully light, late afternoon by the slant of it through the windows, but whether the same day or not I didn't know. I was alone. Tommy wasn't there, and I didn't hear Aunt Joss or Robbie.

"You already know what this is, Blaize," the woman stated with a note of admonishment if not disgust. I learned later that her name was Faith. "She got close to it somehow."

"That can't be," Mama said. "There's no way."

"Do you think a man like Terrance is careful when he makes that poison? And children will get into anything. She breathed it, Blaize. Probably while it was cooking. It has burned her throat, and your cigarette smoke only aggravates it. Why do you do it? Why do you stay there when you do not have to anymore?"

Mama was being scolded and she was taking it, which only drove my curiosity even further.

"I owe him," Mama said weakly.

"You do not owe him your children's lives."

"Yeah." I heard Mama fall back onto a chair. "But I don't know how to do anything else."

"That is for you to worry about later. For now, she should stay here where the air is clean and she can heal. Ask Charlie. She will let you use her cabin. She will not live up here again until Daryl is freed."

"Is there anything new with that?"

"No, it is the same."

"It's not fair. Daryl was never a part of it."

"He was not working for Leslie, but he *did* do favors for Leslie—and he *was* driving the truck when the Feds raided the camp."

"Yeah," Mama acknowledged with a sigh.

So we lived in the mountains now, where every day wasn't sunshine but every day felt special, marked by something that would capture my attention, a bird or a squirrel or a pretty flower. And Mama took me for those walks in the forest, showing me things with a kind of airiness in her voice, as if she were trying to remember something she'd lost.

Once, on a bright afternoon, Mama walked me to a clearing and lay down with me in the cool grass while I coughed croaking coughs. She held me to her and we watched the clouds make shapes in the sky. The air was crisp at that altitude but I felt cuddly warm, interrupted only when Mama lit a cigarette, but she was careful to blow the smoke away from me. And she seemed so old, so sad and worried, and I told her it would be okay, and she looked at me tragically and nodded.

Two men came around sometimes, men with identical chiseled features and long black braids. These were Faith's twin sons, Wayah and Nene. I could never tell the two apart. Mama knew them, and Aunt Joss knew them, and they were nice to Tommy and me. Sometimes they would strip off their shirts, showing their copper backs to the sun, and Tommy would strip off his shirt and the three would disappear into the forest, and Tommy would return with a grin and a little sunburn and with a long feather tied into his hair, which was too short for a braid.

Time went by until the Blue Place slipped into a fog of memory, and the mountains seemed forever. My throat improved, although my voice never did, and cigarette smoke still sent me into spasms of coughing.

Tommy sat with me through the lazy afternoons, under a tree and just at the edge where the shade left off abruptly and gave way to so many versions of brightly lit green that I couldn't count them all. He taught me how to write my name and other words, and before long I could write short sentences and spell some bigger words; and Mama might come up and sit with us as this went on, looking like a little girl sometimes, and her eyes would be damp. I won't say wet because Mama didn't cry, but she could still show you how she felt things. It was an idyllic time, an eternity in my memory but so brief when I think back on it.

Mama and Aunt Joss spent a lot of time with Wayah and Nene. They would couple up and go off together, Mama with Wayah, Aunt Joss with Nene, one pair this way, the other pair that way. Aunt Joss was ebullient, happy in a way that showed how unhappy she'd been before, which we'd always thought that was the normal her but now we knew it wasn't. She seemed as light as air, floating in a dream world, holding Nene's hand and wearing a delicate smile that could lure you to tears for her happiness, even if Blaize was our mother.

Mama went with Wayah, not holding hands but their bodies pressed together, his arm around her, blending into the woods and then gone, as if they were creatures of the forest. Never before or since have I seen Mama actually look content with life.

Mama's twenty-first birthday came, a happy occasion celebrated in Faith's cabin with everyone there, and not nearly as raucous as Mama's eighteenth birthday. We had cake and milk. There was no alcohol of any kind, only cider—regular cider, not hard cider—and Mama didn't even smoke cigarettes for a few hours. The next day, we had to leave the mountain because it would soon be time for Tommy to start school again—and to my surprise, it was time for me to start school as well—but first we all went for a long walk in the forest.

We walked along a rushing stream, where the water gurgled and splashed off slippery rocks, then we climbed through a forest of giant trees that stood like patient guardians of something older than time. We eventually came out onto a wide rocky ledge where Mama and Aunt Joss and the twins sat down with us while Faith walked to the ledge and stood on a high rock. She was wearing a beaded deerskin dress that she'd somehow made white, and beaded moccasins that looked like colorful works of art. She stood in stoic contrast against a blue sky that was as clear as a mountain spring, the wind teasing her braids. And then she took out a willow flute and played, haunting sounds that seemed to belong to the wind; and the eagles came, circling high above us, and you couldn't not believe that you were witnessing something magical. I wanted to stay forever.

Our journey down the mountain in the pick-up truck seemed to take twice as long as our journey up had, but this time I could see everything. I saw misty waterfalls where the water seemed to float off in the air, and ancient grandfather trees with gnarled roots entwining mossy boulders, as if the trees were giving birth. I saw chipmunks and squirrels and bright-colored birds, red and blue and yellow, and on a rock in the sun, I saw a little striped snake.

And then from one moment to the next we were out of that forest magic and crossing a parched field; and then we were on the interstate, speeding along between the big trucks, Mama looking out from time to time as if she might know them. We pulled up to a two-story, blocky red-brick building with identical screen doors and windows evenly spaced along the ground floor. Children were playing on the hard-packed soil of a well-trodden yard, while a few emaciated trees cast limpid shade.

"Where we at, Mama?" I asked.

"This here's Bilbo, baby," she answered with a sigh. "It's where we live now."

Our new home was on the second floor. The inside was starkly white and smelled like fresh paint, the furniture old and scratched and itchy. Tommy and I shared a room, Mama, Aunt Joss, and Robbie the other.

"Public housing's not so bad," I heard Mama comment to Aunt Joss from the other room. "And they say we can get money from the state."

I didn't hear Aunt Joss say anything back.

We settled in. Mama took a job at the Minute Burger, while Aunt Joss stayed home to look after us, and soon enough it was time to start school.

I'll remember that morning forever, Mama with that airy look again, pleased in a crushingly innocent way. She dressed me up in a plaid jumper that I'd never seen before. I don't know where she got it, and every once in a while she would just stop and look at me and go off somewhere until I had to tug her back into the moment.

"C'mon, Mama. We'll be late for school."

Mama took Tommy and me hand in hand and walked us to school. She got Tommy settled in pretty quickly, but I was more of a challenge. What I didn't know until later—and it doesn't matter anyway—is that Mama lied about my age, otherwise I wouldn't have been able to start school for another year. She had to argue with the man who was the principal, a balding man who seemed terrified of her, and then sign a paper, but they got it all straightened out and Mama walked me to a classroom, where I got to sit at my own desk.

Mama stood in the doorway watching me for a time, her expression gone to that far off place again and with a sliver of a smile that seemed ages in the waiting, the last time I can truly remember her with all her teeth.

It was all so new and exciting, and then it all fell apart.

······

THE WALK BACK to downtown Nashville, my guitar slung over my shoulder, was a couple of miles at least, so the morning cool had gone off somewhere to rest and recover by the time I made it to the pedestrian bridge. I trudged up that steep, arcing bridge with barely enough energy to make it to the level center. Raw dandelions will only take you so far, but at least it would be downhill on the other side.

There were a lot of people out, considering that it was a Sunday morning. Tourists, I supposed. The bridge wasn't choked with them, but there were clusters here and clusters there, sometimes the babble of a foreign language. This is what they had all come for, Music City, the Cumberland River below, a giant stadium off that way, a strange sculpture that looked like railroad tracks caught in a tornado and bent into curls; and then looking the other way, towering glass buildings standing shoulder to shoulder, as if crowding out and making quaint the vintage, red brick buildings below. I could see the Johnny Cash Museum from where I stood, and a Hard Rock Cafe, but whatever lay beyond them was hidden between corridors of red brick. If I'd come as a tourist I might have been able to appreciate all this, but I wasn't a tourist and I wasn't interested in Music City. I was only interested in finding a way to get my hands on some money so I could get back on the bus and continue on to California.

And I had no idea how to get my hands on that money, not even a starting place.

There were musicians scattered around on the center of the bridge, some playing to the air and looking forlorn, others drawing smiling interest from a few wandering tourists. Some were huddled against the rails strumming guitars, some twanging fiddles. One boy was drumming a lively beat on empty plastic pails, while a tall old black man in an impeccable black suit with a white bow tie, and in a voice more gravelly than mine, was singing *a cappella*: *I see trees of green, red roses too...* I wondered what his trick was, how his voice seemed to fit so well when mine sounded so awful.

I left them and headed down, made a right and a left and started up Broadway. It was all dizzying to me, made worse because I felt faint. Tourists were bumping shoulders, clotting the sidewalk, taking it all in with an enthusiasm I couldn't share. I saw the Ryman Auditorium, pondered it a moment then moved on. It was hotter now, sweat beading on my forehead. I could smell the hot dogs from a vendor across the street. My mouth watered and I grew dizzier, just plodding along, absently crossing streets, and then I sighted a McDonalds. Tommy used to go through the dumpsters out back of the Sharpe Mart in Bilbo looking for food. I thought I might do the same here, but first went inside to the ladies room to wash up.

You can do a surprisingly thorough job of it in a public restroom, I just hate it when they have the hand blowers and not paper towels. This one had the hand blowers. I worked at myself as women came and went, some throwing judgmental glances at me even though I didn't look that bad. I just needed to wash my face and under my arms, and comb my hair out with my fingers. I got that done and appraised myself in the mirror, and yeah, I looked okay, no worse than any of those ladies with their gossipy eyes.

And then I looked down and I saw the purse. The toilet stalls had partitions that didn't go all the way to the floor. The woman in there had set her big black purse against the partition. It bulged out a little and I could see right down into it, glasses, phone—and a billfold! I didn't spare a moment to think about it, to mull the morality of it. It was just the two of us in there at the moment. I tossed my water bottle into an empty stall as a distraction, then I reached down and snatched that billfold.

I hustled out of there, the woman in the stall completely unaware as far as I could tell, rounded some corners into an alley and only then paused to take a breath. There were only two twenties in the billfold. The credit cards were useless to me, and the photo on the driving license looked nothing like me at all. I took the cash, dropped the billfold in a mail box, then waited a while before going back. Feeling edgy, as if every eye were on me, I ordered a burger and fries and a coke, gobbled all that down and headed out.

Only then, with my stomach full and my blood charged up again, did I feel it—more shame than I had ever felt in my life. Mama and Aunt Joss did a lot of bad things when they were in the worst of their addictions, but I never knew them to steal. I felt so disgusted with myself that I wanted to go throw up that burger, to purge it from my system as if that might purge my conscience as well. Of course it wouldn't and couldn't.

All I could do was swear that this would be the first and only time—but I would be hungry again tomorrow, and the day after that, and after that, so what would I do then?

Still early in the day, with no destination and no idea, I flirted to get a few empty black trash bags from a boy cleaning tables in the McDonalds, then turned back for the park. Along the way, I passed more people performing on the sidewalks, some looking ragged and street worn and probably stoned, others bright and chipper and twanging out tunes, their empty guitar cases speckled with quarters and dollar bills, sometimes even a five or a ten.

I went past them, made my way to the park, and in the light of day found a better place to set up, secluded in some trees and soft underfoot. I sliced those trash bags apart with the knife I kept in my boot, tied them to some spindly little trees as a rain cover, then lay another underneath on the ground. No one could see me in there, and I wouldn't leave any kind of a mess. Mama had always been fastidious that way and so was I.

We kept our homes clean, desperate as they might have been, and this would be my home until I could find enough money to get away.

chapter four

......

SOMETIMES THE DAYS just seem to race by, while at other times they limp along like they'll never get there. It all depends on what you're doing, I guess. Whatever the reason, those next days in Nashville weren't out to set any kind of record, they just drug by from one hour to the next and with nothing to show for it. At least the weather held, growing warmer each morning until my daily walk over the pedestrian bridge became a bit too sticky for woodland hygiene, not that I'd let anyone get close enough to sniff me out anyway. Still, you have to keep yourself up when you're living rough, otherwise people will set themselves against you and just make everything harder. That's something Uncle Bates told me once. He's that town drunk I was talking about.

I can't say that Uncle Bates practiced what he preached, and he wasn't my uncle. I don't know whose uncle he was because he was as tight-lipped about it as anything you might try to get Mama to spill. I guess he must have been a hundred years old—well, maybe fifty or sixty but he looked a hundred—with jowly gray cheeks and a belly that stretched his shirt buttons to their limit. But he had a twinkle in eyes that seemed too blue for the rest of him, the kind of twinkle that made you feel special. He wasn't a stranger because Mama knew him somehow, so I could talk to him without feeling bad about it. I liked talking to Uncle Bates, even if he did smell bad most of the time.

I would often find him sitting on the curb out front of our building, sometimes bent over like a bag of dirty laundry, belching and blabbering at his feet, his face purple and swollen. Other times he'd be sitting there looking up at the sky, smiling off distantly and appearing as nothing less than the jolly grandfather some of the kids at school had. He was always around somehow, out the corner of an eye or in plain sight, as if he were keeping watch on us in some way. Mama must have been mad at him because she wouldn't deign him a look if he were standing right in front of us. Tommy kept his distance because of that, but I liked Uncle Bates all right. Something about him being around made me feel better, I don't know why.

Back to Nashville, though, I did work to keep myself up, washing every day at the McDonalds. I even applied for a job there. They said they weren't hiring anyway because, as it turned out, the national economy was in the process of collapsing just then. Some said another Great Depression was on the way. A man named Obama was running for president and promising to fix everything. I knew nothing of this beforehand, and looking around at the crowds of tourists, and the long lines to get into this place or that place, nothing seemed out of the ordinary to me. Collapsing economy or not, there was plenty of money on parade, just not into my pocket. No, the problem was that I didn't have a Social Security card, not because my daypack had been stolen, but because I'd never had one.

This first came up when I applied for my first job back home. I was in the eleventh grade, already thinking about leaving and going somewhere, and the bus after school could shoot me right up to the Minute Burger on the interstate. Mama hadn't lasted a week in the place, but I didn't have her temper so thought I might do better. The job application asked for my Social Security number, something I'd never even heard of before. I brought this baffling problem to Mama, who only shrugged and said, "So what? Just make something up."

So I made up a number, got the job, and saved enough money to get myself stranded here. The problem I kept running into now was that every place I applied wanted to see an actual card, actual proof. They said it was the law. What could be overlooked in dusty old Fuller County just couldn't go unnoticed in dandy old Nashville.

I still went through the motions, over the bridge every morning, rejection after rejection after rejection, over the bridge again in the evening and try again tomorrow. Over the days since Sunday, I'd snagged more trash bags and had expanded my makeshift home well enough with a roll of duct tape to almost seal out the mosquitoes, and between the grocery stores and restaurants across the bridge, finding food was easy. It's really amazing what those places throw away! I found salads still in the plastic boxes, baked baguettes tossed out like kindling, and lots of doughnuts and cookies.

None of that, however, would get me to California. My two twenties had dwindled to a five and a few ones, and those would be gone by the end of the day because I needed things, necessary things...hygiene things. Now it was another Sunday, and for the first time I began to despair just a little.

I kicked at those thoughts as I went up the bridge, thinking I could throw myself on the mercy of the police or something and get myself transported back to Fuller County. That idea was acid in my throat, real acid up from my stomach, and I had to bend over to cough it out.

"Martin Junior," a gravelly voice sounded from a viewing area off to my right. "Well isn't that something?"

Huh? I straightened and looked over and saw that it was that black man, still impeccably dressed in black suit and white bow tie, grinning brightly enough to light a moonless hollow and looking right at me. He nodded at my guitar.

"Oh, yeah," I said. My guitar was a Martin Junior, not the expensive instrument that Martin was known for, but it made a warm sound nonetheless.

"Do you play it well?" he asked me, and without a hint of condescension.

"Yeah, sure," I said.

"Well then let's hear it," he grinned. "I love the sound a Martin Junior makes, kinda warm and honest, like it's not trying to show off or put on airs."

"Oh, I don't know," I said self-consciously, lowering my eyes to my feet.

"Oh, c'mon girl. This here's Music City. What better place to bend some strings and make a little music?"

No one else on the bridge was following any of this, but I still felt as if every eye had found me through the crowds; and the old man was looking right at me and grinning so earnestly that I felt as if I'd be letting him down if I didn't do something, so I gave him a kind of mumbled okay and nervously went through a Blues shuffle that a guy named Cockadoodle had taught me years ago, adding licks from the scale as I went, bending the strings for some extra flavor.

"Well my my," the man said with an even wider grin. "The lady knows some Blues."

"Yeah, a little, I guess."

"So go ahead on and put some words to it now."

I stiffened up as if I'd been baked in mud, his request beyond any earnest grin or even gunpoint.

"No, sorry." I started edging away. "I can't sing."

"Sure you can," he said, bending back with his hands on his hips as if to give a good laugh. "I hear your talking voice, and I bet your singing voice is like angels in the manger."

That got my heat up, got my Blaize on. It couldn't have been a sincere comment, he had to have been patronizing me all along and I'd been foolish enough to fall for it, like what Mama told me one time, "You trust people too much, Ridley."

He noticed the shift in my demeanor, but rather than break out in laughter he gestured me over with what was now a grandfatherly look, or a look I think a grandfather might have given, like Uncle Bates if he was sober and dressed up nice.

"Looky here," he said gently. "We'll do a little call and response. You know what that is, right?"

I nodded warily. Cockadoodle had taught me that, too.

"So I'll sing a line and you just sing it back. Nobody's looking at us, just you and me."

I toed forward, unsure, and then he sang in his fulsome gravel, bouncing his eyebrows at me as he went, "*I see trees of green...*"

"*I see trees of green,*" I mostly mumbled, which made him grin even wider and invite me closer.

"*Red roses too.*"

"*Red roses too,*" which came out a little more audible.

"*I see them bloom, for me and you.*"

"*I see them bloom, for me and you.*"

I really wasn't singing, I was mostly just repeating each line in my normal speaking voice, but he must have taken this as progress, affirmed by a blazing grin as he gestured me to lift my voice higher.

"*And I think to myself.*"

"*And I think to myself.*" I did kind of sing that line, resisting the urge to cringe at the sound of my own voice.

"*What a wonderful world.*"

"*What a wonderful world,*" and I was actually smiling a little by that last line, his warm gargling voice seeming to temper the sand in mine and making it all come out okay. A few people had begun to gather. I kept my eyes on him and off them.

"You see?" he said with that exuberant grin of his. "You sing just fine. Now I bet you could strum that Martin Junior and we could make some nice honest music for these folks."

I was much more comfortable with that proposition. I picked at some chords until I had the gist of it, and then I strummed as he sang, easing into the mood of it, and then he said as if his voice hadn't left the song, "Now call and response with me, and keep that up;" and I just did it, not even thinking. I played and I sang, seeing skies of blue and clouds of white and people going by. What a wonderful world.

And when the song was over we were in the middle of a crowd of clapping, cheering people who were showering money onto a swatch of black velvet at the man's feet, and I felt as if I'd taken a turn through the clouds, the whole world below me, and everything in it was right and perfect.

The old man seemed pleased in a way that struck all the self-consciousness from me. He bowed to the crowd, so I did a kind of bow as well. After the crowd filtered away, the man bent down stiffly and scooped about half the earnings from the black velvet at his feet.

"Here you go," he said, holding the money out to me. I jumped a bit, startled.

"But that's your money," I objected. "I didn't do anything."

"You were right there with me, girl, and those folks liked your sound. They put half of this here for you, so go on and take it."

I accepted the money reluctantly, looked around for a place to put it, and finally stuffed it in my boot. My remaining other money was in my cleavage, and I wasn't about to go there in public. I didn't count what he gave me because that seemed rude, but I got the sense that I was suddenly in the possession of twenty or thirty dollars. I looked at him when I was done with that, thinking he might be giving it second thoughts but he seemed as pleased as peach pie.

"What's your name, anyway?" I asked him.

"My friends call me Mose," he beamed. "What do your friends call you?"

"They call me Ridley."

"Well, that's a fine name for a fine musician. So where'd young Miss Ridley learn a Blues shuffle like that?"

People were walking past us now, just another stroll on the bridge. I toed the ground, thinking back, half my life back so I had to sort through a lot of clutter. I looked up at Mose and said, "Cockadoodle taught me."

"*Cockadoodle?*" he bellowed brightly, bending back again with his hands on his hips, his grin glinting off the dull iron work. "Now that's a Blues name if I ever heard one."

"It's Disney, actually," I said, and then I was back there as if it were yesterday, every sight, sound, and smell.

I was nine going on ten, we were living three to a room in the trailer, and I was on the cusp of accepting the reality of what Mama had become. The trailer was much too small for all of us, Lainey, Priscilla and me in one room, Tommy, Timewall and Robbie in another, and Mama and Aunt Joss in the third, with towels stuffed under their door. It had been an exciting time when we first moved into that trailer, but that time had passed.

We were crowded but Mama kept the place clean with the discipline of a drill sergeant, even when she wobbled and stumbled and could barely hold her head up. We made our beds first thing every morning, regardless what Mama and Aunt Joss might be doing in their room. We washed our dishes and put them away, kept our clothes folded and in the chest of drawers, and we wiped out the tub after every bath. No one could walk in and say we weren't clean, but then they might notice that it was dusky inside, that there were newspapers taped in every window. This was Mama's thing and she never explained beyond a cryptic, "Windows aren't for just looking out, you know. They're for looking in, too." I have some ideas what was behind it all, but that's not the point, only that I was getting old enough to know that this wasn't normal.

I knew to leave the trailer whenever I started coughing, worse than just Mama's cigarette smoke. There was a help center across the tracks where Mama sometimes worked, and they had a thrift store where people donated things for resale. That store was packed to the rafters with all kinds of things, interesting things that could keep me occupied until the air cleared back home. There were racks of old clothes, some looking like costumes from a 1930s musical, shelves of porcelain dishes that had once served fine Thanksgiving dinners, crates of old books and magazines, Hardy Boys, Nancy Drew, and National Geographic—and then one day, hanging in the front window like a candy cane meant only for me, a guitar.

I knew nothing about music, not how to make it and certainly not to sing it. At school, the other kids got up on stage to sing their songs, while the teachers discreetly gave me a pass. Music was not a theme with any of us, but something about that guitar grabbed me and held on, and I thought that this was a way to make music and not have to sing, to be able to get up on stage with the other kids and not embarrass myself. The little price tag on the string said one hundred dollars, though, enough money to make us rich if we'd had it. It was more than I could imagine, so far out of reach that I just slumped my shoulders and turned dejectedly for the door with its jarring cowbell.

"We can let you have it for seventy-five," a lady said from back there somewhere. I spun around, startled, but then slumped again. Seventy-five dollars was as far away as a hundred.

"Thanks anyway," I mumbled, and clanked on out.

I did bring it up to Mama. It was later that evening and I wasn't coughing, so all of that was over for the time being. Mama was making mac and cheese for dinner. Lainey and Timewall were toddling around and getting into everything, while Aunt Joss was lying on the couch, both sagging in the middle, one arm over the side, knuckles dragging on the floor. Tommy and Robbie were in their room, Priscilla was in her crib next to Aunt Joss, so I stepped up to Mama in our little kitchen nook and hurriedly said, "Mama there's a guitar at the help center I like and can I have it for my birthday?"

Mama looked hung and worn that night, didn't seem to have heard me, but then she turned to me wearily and asked, "What would you want something like that for?"

That was a rhetorical question that didn't require an answer. Mama returned her attention to the mac and cheese, and I went to wash up for dinner.

When my birthday came, though, I woke up and found that guitar in my room! I danced on my mattress I was so excited; and I wanted to rush to Mama and hug her like I did when I was little but her door was closed and Aunt Joss was on the couch and someone was snoring in there and Mama didn't snore, so I got ready and went to school and saved all of that for later.

That guitar was so pretty and shiny, with a cream soundboard and a body the color of maple syrup with streaks of honey, and a dark neck and bridge. I couldn't play it except to make noise, but I would sling it over my back by its strap like armor and wear it to school, feeling as special as any of the other kids as long as I had it with me, never out of my sight, and never with a fingerprint smudge to mar the surface.

Weeks and weeks went by. One of my teachers wanted to give me lessons after school, but Mama said we couldn't afford it. And then one Saturday morning I woke up coughing and I knew there'd be towels stuffed under Mama's door, so I dressed and went on down to the bench in the woods to wait it out.

I was just sitting on that bench, making noise under the trees with my guitar. The day was nice, a little warm, and the breeze was as soft as early summer. Sometimes a ray of sun would find a way through the trees and flicker on my eyebrows, all else quiet except for some birds up in the tops where I couldn't see them.

Then I heard a thump, thump, thump coming up the trail beyond a screen of bushes. Thump, thump, thump, and a man under the weight of a bright orange backpack that was so big that I could have fit inside it came lumbering into the clearing and plopped down on the bench right beside me.

He sat leaning forward, catching heavy breaths between his knees, his backpack still on his shoulders and seeming to be pressing him in half; and now I was faced with a conundrum I couldn't resolve because I wasn't supposed to talk to strangers but here was one sitting right next to me and something was going to have to be said sooner or later, and I didn't know what that would be or what Mama would do if she found out, so I just said, "Hi."

He pushed up against his knees, wiped his brow with the back of his hand, and said to the air in front of us, "Man, that climb was hard."

"I like to climb," I said.

"Well," he turned to me and sighed, "you can do a lot of it about a mile back."

"I've never been that far," I said.

"I don't blame you," he said.

Now that the newness had worn off, I didn't feel shy about giving him a good look-over. He was wearing olive shorts, and a black T-shirt that was ringed with a necklace of sweat salt. He wasn't old, I didn't think, maybe as old as Mama but that's about it. He had short brown hair and kind hazel eyes and a five o'clock shadow that was almost a beard; and when he noticed me looking him over he snorted and smiled a thin-lipped smile, and he seemed too nice to worry about so I didn't.

Then I noticed the guitar neck sticking out the top of his backpack, and for a second I couldn't catch my breath.

"Are you hiking the trail?" I asked him. This was well before Robbie was old enough to harass the hikers, but we all knew what the trail was. In Bilbo, you could be too dumb to zip up your own pants but you still knew what the trail was.

"Yes I am," he answered in a mild accent that was a world away from Bilbo.

"Do you play guitar?" I asked with rising hope.

"I do," he nodded. "And I guess you do too."

"No," I shook my head forlornly. "I don't know how."

"Well that's too bad because you have a nice-looking guitar there."

"Yeah," I said, dejected.

He slipped out of his backpack with a groan, slugged down some water from a bottle, then smacked noisily on a Snickers bar. I sat silently, swinging my legs and trying not to watch him too much. When he got done with all of that, he took his backpack by the strap, made to stand up, but then plunked back down as if he'd left all his ambition at wherever that hard climb had been. He chuckled and turned my way.

"Would you like me to teach you some things on the guitar?" he asked.

"Yes!" I bounced in excitement.

"Okay." He tugged his guitar from the backpack, strummed it a couple of times, then asked, "So, do you know what everything's called?"

"Uh-uh."

"Okay...well, these are the strings, right?"

"Yeah."

"Okay, and they have names. Ready?" I nodded. "So from top to bottom: E, A, D, G, B, and E. Got that?"

"Yeah." I was holding my guitar now, plucking each string as he named it while trying to come up with a rhyme so I could remember them: *Easy E, A like hay, D and G with a busy Bee and another E.*

"Okay, good. Now this part here on the neck is called the fretboard."

"Fretboard," I repeated solemnly.

"And these ridges are called frets. You put your fingers between them to change the sound. Okay?"

"Okay."

"Okay. So now let's try something. It won't be too hard. Put your pointing finger right here on the A string, second fret." He guided my finger to the second fret. "Now just strum the E and A strings, E and A, E and A..."

I did, and made a sound that wasn't just noise.

"Good," he said. "Now move your finger to the D string, second fret, and strum the A and D strings this time."

I did that, too, and made a different sound that wasn't just noise.

"Okay, great. Now we're going to put them together. Watch me first."

I watched him like a revelation in the wilderness, moving his finger from A to D and back again, just strumming and making real music, and it seemed so easy!

"Now you do it," he said, clapping at first slowly then faster and faster, and I hit the strings in time with him and I couldn't believe that I was really playing the guitar, really playing it, and I swear that the trees parted just then and let the sun shine through, that a north wind blew in to rustle my hair, that every breath filled my chest twice as full!

"Okay," he said with a satisfied grin. "That's called a Blues shuffle and we can do things with it. Watch me."

And he started playing, just what we'd done before but he was adding things, and going slow enough that I could follow.

"So," he said after a minute of that. "I'm doing the shuffle that we just did, but in between I'm going up and down the scale. Here's how it works: first you hit the E string open, then you put your finger down on the third fret and hit it again. That's called open-3, okay?"

"Okay," I said, transfixed.

"Then you go open-1-2 on the A string like this." He demonstrated then continued: "Then open-2 on the D string. You see what we're doing?"

"Yeah," I nodded excitedly.

"Good. So next is open-2-3 on the G string and then open-3 on the B string, and you finish with open-3 on the low E string. That's called walking up the scale. You wanna try that?"

"Okay," I said, biting my lip and trying to remember it all. He reached over to help me put my finger in the right place when I got confused, and I just kept repeating and repeating until I had it all memorized and he didn't have to help me anymore.

And then, in another revelation, he started playing the shuffle and told me to walk up and down the scale, and I did and only made a few mistakes; and I felt as if I'd been transported back to the mountains on a streak of light, with Faith on a promontory playing her Indian willow flute, suspended in a sky of nothing but blue and the eagles came, and I knew that magic was real.

Cockadoodle finally let up and set his guitar down. "You were very good," he said. "Uh—what's your name, anyway?"

"I'm Ridley."

"Well, Ridley, I'm Cockadoodle."

"*Cockadoodle!*" I exclaimed. "Uh-uh."

"Yeah, that's really my name," he laughed.

"I don't believe you."

"It is. It's my trail name."

"Trail name?"

"Yeah. It's what we're called when we're hiking."

"Why?"

"I don't know. Because it's fun, I guess. It's the name the other hikers gave me."

"Why did they do that?"

"Well, because I have my traveling guitar with me, and, well...did you ever see the Robin Hood cartoon, the one on Disney?"

"Uh-uh."

"Well, uh, okay—but in that cartoon there's a rooster that plays a traveling guitar like mine and, well, rooster? Cockadoodle? Get it?"

I laughed then. "Yeah, I get it."

"Okay." He settled back to his guitar. "Now let's try something else. This is called call and response. What it means is I'll play something, then you play it right back to me. Think you can do that?"

"Maybe," I said doubtfully.

"Okay, well, let's try anyway."

So he started out on the A string, and I copied him, then he went to the E string and I copied him again, and after a little while of that, he said, "Now I'm going to walk up the scale, and you do it right after me."

And suddenly we were making the kind of music you could hear on the radio and all I wanted to do was keep playing and playing until the sun set, not to get away from the trailer but just to play, but finally Cockadoodle got up, put his guitar away, and said, "That was fun, Ridley, but I better get going now."

"Aw. How far do you have to go today?"

"A long way." That seemed to burden his shoulders, even more when he got that big backpack on. "You just keep practicing like I showed you, okay?"

"Okay."

He turned for the trail. "Bye, Ridley," he said.

"Bye, Cockadoodle."

And then a few footsteps later he disappeared into the trees, going along until I couldn't hear the thumps of his footsteps anymore and all I wanted to do was get up and race after him, but I couldn't do that and I knew it, so I just sat there and played the guitar until Mama sent Tommy out to find me.

"Well, Ridley," Mose said, beaming me out of that memory and back to the bridge. "I sing here every Sunday, so you come on back whenever you want."

"I'd like that," I said, surprised that I really meant it; then I made my way over the bridge to look for a job, with the pestering notion that maybe I'd already found one.

chapter five

......

I COULDN'T EVEN GET a job washing dishes. I stuck my head in an open door behind the restaurant, heard the jabber of Spanish over the clink and scrape of dishes, and doubted that any of them had Social Security cards. But they still got jobs somehow, while the manager wouldn't give me the time of day.

I was in a surly mood when I left that place. This was the morning after I'd sung with Mose, all that good feeling seeming as if it belonged to a different era. I felt funky, my clothes were gross, and I'd had just about enough of Nashville—not the give up and go home kind of enough, the get mad and start some trouble kind of enough. It's probably fortunate for me that the very morning I let my Blaize out was when I spotted that scrawny guy.

I figured I'd run into him sooner or later, he being at the bottom of the food chain around there. I was surprised I hadn't seen him already, but then there he was, within a block of the bus station and ambling along with a scrawny-guy friend. I took off after them, and when I came up behind the scrawny guy I just lifted my leg and kicked him in the middle of his back.

He bowed like a bent spoke, lost his footing, and went down hard, cracking the back of his head on the pavement right at my feet. I didn't give him time to yowl or utter a darned thing, I just put my foot in his face and pushed hard.

"What the f—?" his scrawny-guy friend blathered in outrage, turning on me as if he were capable of doing anything about any of this.

"Get out of here," I ordered the guy as a curtain of red fell over my eyes.

The original scrawny guy was jerking under my foot, grabbing at my ankle and trying to sputter something but the toe of my boot was actually in his mouth now.

"The f— I will!"

Without the f-bomb, would these guys have any vocabulary at all? I kicked the original scrawny guy in the head, then threw my fist into the other scrawny guy's face. He backed up, astonished, ran a knuckle across his lip, then came at me with the coordination of a tray of silverware spilling to the floor. I kicked him in his solar plexus, which took care of him for the moment, but the original scrawny guy had managed to get up and was bolting toward an alley. There were only a few people on the street just then, taking in the show as if this kind of thing happened all the time. It was still mid-morning but hot already, the sun practically boiling the moisture in the air. I was sweating, my T-shirt damp around my neck and under my arms, and I'd already washed up at the McDonalds so now I was even madder.

I took off for the alley, boxing the scrawny guy in between a couple of trash dumpsters. The sun couldn't penetrate that dank alley. It was cooler. I took a breath.

"Where's my stuff?" I shouted.

"Man, *are* you?" scrawny guy whined shakily.

"I'm the girl who's gonna kick your butt if you don't give me my stuff." I unslung the Martin Junior and set it carefully aside.

"You aren't kicking sh—" he blurted, trying to put on some kind of indignant courage, so I kicked him in the knee and he went down.

And then the other scrawny guy was on my back, the crook of his arm around my throat, and man, he smelled worse than I did. I wedged my chin under the inside of his elbow, which gave me the leverage I needed, thank goodness, because if I'd had to bite him I would have had his nasty funk in my mouth and I was gagging just at the thought of it. With my chin wedged under his elbow, I stepped back to get him off balance then dipped my shoulder and tossed him off, where he landed in a scrawny heap against a brick wall that smelled like pee.

They were both lying there now, whining and nursing their hurts, and I had to laugh. The two stupids thought they could mess with Tommy

Speaks' little sister and get away with it? Really? Tommy had been so worried about me after I had a scary encounter with some strange men when I was thirteen that he taught me everything he knew, which was more than enough for these two.

I took the knife out of my boot and knelt beside the original scrawny guy, stuck the blade up his nose the way I'd seen in a movie once, and growled, "Where's my stuff?"

"I don't know," he cried. "Really. I don't know. Maybe I threw it in the trash, I don't remember."

"So you *do* remember me, then?"

"Naw, man, I don't remember sh—. You got me mixed up with somebody else."

"Naw, *man*, I don't."

I fished in his pockets, found a little plastic baggie and a couple of dollars. That's all he had.

"One last time," I said, the red occluding everything. "Where's my stuff?"

"I told you: *I—don't—know*."

"Well that's too bad."

I emptied the little baggie while he watched with widening, disbelieving eyes, then I flicked my knife up and slit his nostril and he wailed like a baby and I slung the Martin Junior over my back and walked out of there, the red going to mist and then gone, and suddenly I felt pretty darned good.

In my elevated mood, I made a conscious decision to pamper myself, well earned by my reckoning. I went into a thrift store and bought some jeans, ripped only low on the thighs, not on the butt, a short-sleeved denim shirt that felt crisp enough to be new, some undergarments, a camo daypack that was stained with ink from a black pen, and in a spur of compulsion, a black felt hat with a wide brim. All of that and I still had money left over. People are always looking for sales, for the cheapest deal, but they'd walk right past a thrift store with their noses in the air.

Afterward, I made my way back toward the bus station and came across that rescue mission. I was dubious about this but I wanted a shower, and I was going to get a shower even if I had to sit through a sermon from those people (I didn't). When I came out I felt pink and clean, confident in my new clothes, hat on and the sun out of my eyes, and now it was time for another treat.

I crossed over to 3rd Avenue, turned in the direction of the pedestrian bridge, and went into a popular pancake place, where I ordered pancakes smothered in butter and syrup, scrambled eggs, and glass after glass of orange juice. This took my last dime, but it was so worth it. The two dollars I took off scrawny guy was the tip I left on the table.

Now it was mid-day. I really didn't want to go back to my encampment yet, so I just ambled along absently, loving the feel of clean clothes on clean skin, my stomach so sated that I wanted to lie down and take a nap. I was just ambling along Broadway, all the clubs and ditzy tourist stuff, pausing now and then to listen to people busking on the sidewalks or in little alcoves. Busking is the word for this—that's what Mose told me—so that's what we were doing on the bridge yesterday and that's what these people were doing here now. I was less interested in busking than I was in just sitting down somewhere in the shade and letting all those pancakes digest. I found a shaded spot over by the Nashville Visitor Center, sat with my back against the wall, plopped my hat down in front of me, and closed my eyes.

There were more people out than you would expect, although not as many as yesterday. I listened to them coming and going, heard the quick clip of a professional woman in heels, heard tourists laughing and boasting, then I heard some coins ring on the sidewalk in front of me. Two quarters were on the sidewalk, a third had made it into my hat. I looked left and right for the person who'd dropped them, but no anonymous face was looking at me or taking any notice whatsoever. So I'd managed to busk seventy-five cents with my eyes closed!

I snorted at the comedy of it, started plucking at the Martin Junior, and slid into a song I liked called *Snowblind Friend*, an ancient song by a band called Steppenwolf that I discovered on the internet when I was doing research for a class paper. I liked it because of its slow 4/4 meter and simple chord structure, the hybrid picking, and the key change at the reprise, which lifted those final verses to a heightened sense of despair. I didn't have to sing it, those somber notes translated the meaning of the song all by themselves; and there's no way I *would* sing it, not without

Mose or someone else to give cover to my raspy voice. So I just played and let the lyrics run through my mind.

> *You say it was this morning when you last saw your good friend*
> *Lyin' on the pavement with a misery on his brain*

I was in my own head with this, not paying attention to people or whether they liked the song or not, just playing as if I were in a world apart, remembering Mama in the bathroom that night.

Timewall wasn't born yet but he was on the way, Mama's stomach swelling up way out of proportion to her size. I was in bed, not yet asleep, when I heard her curse in the bathroom, the things on the bathroom sink clattering to the floor. I jumped out of bed and ran to the bathroom to see, then gasped and stepped back because there was blood in the sink, and one of Mama's teeth was lying yellow against the white porcelain.

Mama scooped me up and sat down on the toilet seat, rocking in silence for a minute as if she were gathering herself, then she set me down and said, "It ain't nothin', baby. Go on back ta bed."

I watched terrified from the corner of the door as she gazed disconsolately in the mirror, probing the gap in her gum, and then she just seemed to shake it off.

"I told ya ta go back ta bed," she said when she noticed me there, trying to reassure me with an unsettling smile that would never be the same again. "Sweet dreams, baby."

Then she went past me, being led by her stomach, and on into her room where she closed the door behind her; and I ran to my bed and pulled the covers over my head, and I did not have sweet dreams.

> *He said he wanted Heaven but prayin' was too slow*
> *So he bought a one way ticket on an airline made of snow*
> *Flyin' low*
> *Dyin' slow*

I really didn't mean to write about that. It's funny how thoughts just take off and do what they want.

Anyway, I shook *Snowblind Friend* out of my head and played Clay Walker's *Fore She Was Mama*, another good guitar song and probably some kind of Freudian thing for me but I didn't pick up on that at the time. More money had landed in my hat, all coins, not enough to get me to California if I did this for months, not even a start. I went through a few more songs that I could play pretty well, then I started picking and humming, running words in my mind for a poem I'd been thinking about.

I hadn't written a new poem since first semester English last year, but this one popped in my head every now and then and I would tack on a few more words and feel for the meter:

> *Mama told me not to cross the street*
> *without looking both ways*
> *And she told me to pay attention*
> *and to make better grades*
> *And she told me that the boys would come*
> *and that they'd gawk and gaze*
> *But Mama*
> *But Mama*
> *You never told me how to love*

Then I got bored with that and just watched the people going by, trying not to think and doing a pretty good job of it. The sun was lowering behind me somewhere, catching a window across the street and reflecting into my eyes. It was a little cooler but still humid. My armpits were damp. I didn't know what time it was. The day hadn't gone dusky but you could tell that it was getting along, and I didn't want to be downtown after dark. Dark was when the dangerous predators came out, not the scavengers like scrawny guy but the people who'd leave you lying and bleeding just because they could. Even way over in the park I could still hear the gunshots at night.

I was about to get up and start the long trek back when a girl stopped in front of me, blocking that reflection from across the way. With her blocking the sun, I could get a good look without having to shield my eyes, and I was startled to realize that this was the girl I'd met at the crosswalk that day, still wearing the same pleated white skirt and bright yellow top. She didn't seem to remember me. Her eyes were on my hat.

"Man, it's really slow today," she said.

"Yeah," I agreed, although I didn't know the difference. She slid down next to me without being invited, and now I had to raise my hand to shield my eyes from that searing reflection.

"Some days it's just not worth getting out of bed, you know?" she said as if we were old friends, or perhaps co-commiseraters.

"Yeah," I agreed again.

"I wish there was something going on. Johnny Winter's gonna be here in a couple of weeks, and Ringo Starr's gonna be here next month. Things'll pick up then, but the CMAs are the best. There'll be money everywhere."

"CMAs?" I asked.

She looked at me as if I had a third eye. "CMAs? *The Country Music Awards?* You've heard of them, right?"

"Oh, yeah," I said.

"That's not till November, though," she pouted. "It'll be cold out, but the streets will be packed with people waiting in lines to give us money."

"Well," I said sourly, "rich people do spend a lot of time congratulating themselves."

She looked at me curiously, seemed about to object but then headed that off.

"But isn't that what we all want?" she asked.

"I guess," I said, when really all I cared about was getting to California, and hopefully long before November.

"I'm Sherri with an *i*, by the way," she said, offering her hand.

"I'm Ridley with a *y*."

"Good to meet you," she came back, not noticing my sarcasm. "So you play guitar?"

"Yeah. What about you?"

"No, I can't play a thing, but I can sure sing."

"Really?"

"Yeah. Maybe we can get together sometime."

"Yeah, maybe."

"Well," she lifted herself and brushed off her skirt, "hope I see you around."

"Yeah, me too."

And then she took off and I wondered if we could duo up, the way Mose and I had, and maybe that way earn enough money to get out of here.

......

MORE DAYS. I saw neither scrawny guy nor Sherri, nor any tourist more than once, and I came to accept the fact that I was busking now. I was a busker, although not a very good one apparently because I hadn't earned enough money to get me across town let alone to California. Now I understood why so many of the buskers looked so ratty, and began to worry if this might be it for me, making just enough money for pancakes every now and then but never enough to get back on the bus. Is this what it felt like to be trapped in a job you didn't care about? And I didn't care, I mean it. I liked playing the guitar, but that was for me. I didn't want to perform. I didn't want to be a musician banging out tunes in smoky saloons, trying not to cough as beer bottles clinked and guys got handsy.

Sunday came around again. I went up to the bridge early to wait for Mose, staking out his spot in that viewing area. The sky was clouding up and looking as if rain were on the way, but there were still a lot of people out. I strummed a few tunes while I waited, all going unnoticed by the passersby. Mose was a little winded when he walked up, immaculately outfitted as always in a black suit and white bow tie. The smile he wore above that could have brought happiness to the world.

"Well, Miss Ridley," he grinned. "I'm so glad you came today."

I went bashful under that attention, even as it felt good to receive it.

"I had fun last week," I said shyly, which was true. I really wasn't there to make money but to have fun, like going guitar-in-hand to the Fuller County Fair and playing songs while having your photo taken next to the Dolly Parton cut-out.

"Well, music is fun," he said, bending back with his hands on his hips and giving me that grin of truth.

He spread out his black velvet cloth and we got right to it, reprising our performance of *What a Wonderful World* from last week, which drew an appreciative glitter of approval. That song was his money maker, no doubt. It occurred to me only then that with different groups of tourists cycling through, he could just sing that song over and over again and no one would be the wiser. But that's not what Mose did. I knew about Louis Armstrong and Frank Sinatra, but I'd never heard of Otis Redding, Bobby Darin or Tony Bennett. We went through songs that were wholly new to me, antique songs that could still carry people away, especially with Mose's warm, pebbly voice, so deep and candid that little old ladies would sometimes tear up.

I struggled with some of the songs. We made fun with that rather than embarrassment, and the people seemed to love it, raining us with largesse until I started feeling uncomfortable about it. This was Mose's place and his earnings, of which he would insist on giving me half even though I was fairly certain that he would have earned the same amount whether I was there or not. So in truth I was taking money from him just to have a little fun, and he was letting me.

We had just finished a song called *Beyond the Sea* when I flipped the Martin Junior over my shoulder and took a step back.

"You leaving already?" Mose asked, looking sincerely disappointed.

"Yeah, I gotta get going."

"Well, you be sure and come again next week."

"I will."

And then, of course, he bent over to gather my part from his velvet cloth, which I accepted reluctantly. He held my hand for an extra moment as he handed the money over, his skin so warm and papery. He looked right at me in that way you can't escape from.

"Ridley, where are you staying?"

I wanted to avert my eyes but couldn't. "Oh, around here," I said.

"Well, you be careful out there," he said, giving my hand a pat.

"You don't have to worry about me."

"Good," he grinned. "Good."

I turned for town, stuffing the money in my pocket, while Mose started from the top and I heard behind me, "*I see trees of green…*"

I went up Broadway and parked my back against a wall around the corner from the Ryman. There was a lot of bustle on the sidewalk, the sky heavy but not smelling like rain. I'd brought my gig bag to keep the

Martin Junior dry just in case. The crowd at the hot dog vendor across the street broke up, so I went over and bought a couple of dogs and a coke, carried these back and sat against the wall to eat. People were walking by, oblivious. Sitting against a wall in a busy downtown...if you were playing then you belonged there, if you weren't then you were homeless and consciously overlooked.

I finished the dogs, unsheathed the Martin Junior and strummed Country tunes, Miranda, George Strait, Brad Paisley. The sun journeyed above the clouds and I hadn't drawn a fraction of what Mose had given me up on the bridge. My butt hurt from sitting so long, and I was giving serious thought to heading back to my camp when a couple settled in just up from me and started playing. There was a guy on a guitar and a girl who sang, and those two were drawing more interest than I was, the guy sitting, the girl standing, bare cheek showing through the back of her jeans. She wore a headband and a frilled leather top, her brown hair 1960s straight and long, as if she were Joan Baez, and he with a silk scarf around his neck as if he were Bob Dylan.

They were so close that we were playing over each other, and I didn't know if there was an etiquette about this kind of thing but it seemed rude of them at the least. This went on and on and my Blaize started to boil. Every time I raised the pitch, they did too, as if they were trying to drown me out on purpose and that's just disrespectful. I forgot about going back to camp, now I was in a competition with those two and there was no way I'd let them win.

But she was singing in a contralto that smothered my guitar play, and I started to see the red, which takes you over without thinking, and I leapt to my feet and hammered a B power chord until everyone was gawking at me, and I let the lyrics fly as if the harshness of my voice would punish them for their blithe indifference:

> Can't stay at home, can't stay in school
> Old folks say, "You poor little fool"
> Down the streets I'm the girl next door
> I'm the FOX you've been waiting for

I wasn't singing, I was shouting, throwing those words out like fists and bloodying every nose in earshot. And there were a lot of them, crowding out those other two and forming a semi-circular wall around me, money falling into my hat like silver rain and green confetti, the people pressing in closer until I could smell the sweat on them, and I gave them more:

> *Hello world I'm your wild girl*
> *I'm your ch ch ch ch ch ch CHERRY BOMB!*

I was so far inside my head by then that I couldn't tell if I was seeing the faces of people in the now or in an old memory of a teenaged girl who still had all of her teeth; and in my mind it was as if I had stopped right there to analyze it all and put it in focus, but I was still singing and my hat was filling, and then I belted out—

> *I'll give ya something to live for*
> *Have ya and grab ya until you'r sore*

—and the trouble started.

Someone grabbed my arm, a young blond-headed guy who didn't have enough tan to be from anywhere worth being from. He yanked me toward him and went to slip some cash into my cleavage, and I slapped his hand away, his face now limned completely in red.

"Hey baby, don't be that way," he said with a smirk. I yanked my arm out of his hand and fixed him with a look that Mama couldn't have matched.

"How I decide to be or not be isn't up to you," I spat at him, and I actually said "ain't" so forgive me that lapse.

He grinned at me, so cocksure of himself, and took my arm again.

My damaged voice was serving me well now because it sounded like something menacing from a jungle.

"If you don't let me go right now," I hissed, "I *am* going to break your arm. Do you believe me?"

He let go with a confounded look, one of his drunken buddies pulling him away, the more innocent in the crowd backing up and then turning in a hurry.

"Good," I spat. "You're not so dumb after all."

"F— you, c—!" he spat back, trying to laugh his humiliation off with his buddies. I don't have to write the words he used. You know what they are.

Their group went up the sidewalk, arms over shoulders and laughing, while the two who had set me in this mood were hastily packing up to leave. I stood there with my nostrils flaring as a girl approached. Sherri. She seemed in awe.

"Man, that was amazing," she gushed. "What *was* that song?"

"*Cherry Bomb* by The Runaways," I said, lips still tight.

"Who?"

"Cherie Currie and Joan Jett."

"Oh yeah, I think I've heard of them. But I never heard that song before."

"It's kind of old." My hands were shaking, adrenalin or some such.

"Well it's awesome. Can you teach it to me?"

She was transfixed on my hat, which might have had enough money in it to get me as far as Memphis.

"I'm hungry," I said. "Let's get some pancakes and talk about it."

chapter six

......

THE PANCAKE PLACE was closed, wouldn't you just know it, but Sherri led us to another place she knew about. By the time we got there I was starving, ravenous would be the word, those dogs I'd eaten earlier burned up in a fit of Blaize.

We took our seats and fished for something to say to each other, as if without sidewalks and music we'd become the strangers that we really were. I focused on the menu. Man, I love pancakes. Even the kind you pop in the toaster will do, and pancakes are not something you usually find in the dumpsters out back. Good pancakes done Southern style will soak up every drop of syrup and butter until they're so heavy they want to fall apart on your fork; and when you get them in your mouth they squish like sponges and all that syrup and butter flows soothingly down your throat.

Sherri played with her hands and then just came out with, "So, where are you staying?"

"Oh, around here," I hedged. "How about you?"

"I got a place off 21st near the Village. Actually, there's like six of us in there, sometimes seven, but it's not bad. One of the guys can burn CDs."

"Really?"

"Yeah. You should come by."

Burn CDs? That's the last thing I wanted to do. It would be as if I were playing at being a real musician.

"Sure—yeah, maybe. But the agencies won't take them anyway, right?"

"Nope. Won't even let you in the door with them, when they let you in the door at all." She frowned. "They've never let me in the door. It's like it's their job to sell music, right? You'd think they'd want to listen to everything out there. Anyway, you burn your own CDs so you can sell them to make a little extra money."

"Hmm."

That ran us out of things to say for the moment, then she asked abruptly, "So where'd you learn that song?"

"Oh, I just heard it around."

"Well, I never heard it. Where are you from, anyway?"

"Back east," I said, dodging particulars; but then added, "In the mountains."

"You mean like the Smokies? That's so cool!"

Sherri was from Murfreesboro, which was just down the interstate from Nashville but the way she talked it might have been three states away. She was twenty and had been bouncing around Nashville for more than a year.

"I tried the Bluebird and the Wildhorse," she said despondently. "I couldn't even get a job at the Opryland Hotel cleaning rooms. I thought if I worked there I could sing in the atriums between shifts, maybe get heard by somebody, but man, you gotta know people to even use a bathroom in this town. I wanna sing, you know? I just wanna sing."

Wanting things a million other people want only makes it easier for other people to have power over you. I didn't tell her that, though.

"You do okay singing on the street?" I asked.

"Enough to pay my part of the rent but that's about it. How about you?"

That I couldn't make enough for a bus ticket? No, I wouldn't tell her that, or about my makeshift camp or rifling trash dumpsters for food. "I've been doing okay," I said instead.

The pancakes came out and that stopped conversation long enough for me to enjoy the sensation of that buttery syrup running down my throat. Sherri started singing between bites, conducting with her fork and hitting high notes that I could only fantasize about. I didn't know the song she was doing but she had a beautiful voice.

And then, because it was inevitable, she set her fork down and her eyes sparkled and she asked, "So, you got a boyfriend?"

No, not for a long time. The boys back home thought I was a prude, protecting my virginity for some future time when I would give it up as if it were my duty to mankind. But then, I'm not a virgin anyway. I like sex as much as the next girl, it's just that the boys seem to want more from me than I want from them. And I don't use curse words either, not from prudishness but because everyone else uses them and they sound like hicks.

And because Mama uses them every other word and I don't want to sound like her either. Sex too, I guess, even though no man ever got the upper hand on Mama and she's had a lot of sex.

Anyway, back to Sherri.

"Not since I left home," I said.

Longer than that, actually. His name was Taylor, Taylor Sharpe, from the Sharpes who lived in the big mansion and all but owned Bilbo. I caught on pretty early that he never came to me, I had to go to him, as if to cross those railroad tracks would mark him for life. I only put up with all that to aggravate Mama, but it was Uncle Bates who really threw the fit, stumbling off spitting curses and shaking his head in disgust. I never learned why, or even why he cared in the first place.

Taylor was so good-looking he could make you squeal.

It all started out innocently enough. We were both seniors in Mr. Sternman's class, and Taylor said he liked one of my poems. That was the only praise I'd ever received from anyone besides my teachers so it was easy enough to overlook our class differences and for me to think that my poetic skill had elevated me in some way.

Taylor drove a Jaguar convertible, the kind with the long hood, and we would power off to some quiet, shaded spot outside of town and I would read my poetry as butterflies flapped around us, and it all seemed so honest and real that I thought his family's reputation must not have been true, or at least that he was the exception. That must have been it because he had a younger brother, Jayson, who was an arrogant brat even at thirteen or fourteen or whatever he was, and their father made my skin crawl, the eerie way he'd look at me.

But Taylor and I read poetry and had sweet afternoons, and then he kissed me and I let him, and I felt that tingle in my belly, and the rest... well, you know biology.

We had a good time, that was enough. I wasn't looking for anything remotely serious, maybe just a friend who understood me, a friend with whom I could take an unguarded breath—and then he started bragging it around school, subjecting my intimate moanings to the cruel ridicule of others.

"You trust people too much, Ridley," Mama told me, maybe even amused by it all.

I didn't cry, of course, but I was low, so low that I let myself go, hair gone oily and I ate chips and cookies and hid them under my bed; then Mama took me aside and told me that bit about feeling sorry for yourself, which got my temperature up, and then she added, "Some people are too soft ta live in this world, Ridley, an' we ain't them. So cut it out an' git yourself together."

Yeah, she said that to me. Can you imagine? But either her words or my simmering reaction to them snapped me out of it, brought me back to who I was before I allowed myself to succumb to sentiment. I challenged anyone at school, boy or girl, to say anything to my back or to my face, and none of them dared; and then Taylor plowed his Jaguar into a tree in an accident that no one can quite figure out, and now he's in the cemetery up by the interstate, with a stone next to his mother's that reads: *Loving Son, Loving Brother.* Uncle Bates was unusually composed on the day of the funeral, as I remember, sober and bathed. I thought he might be planning to attend but he wasn't there.

"How about you?" I asked Sherri because it seemed the polite rejoinder under the circumstances. "You got a boyfriend?"

"Oh, sometimes. It depends."

And so of course I had to ask because she'd left it open-ended for just that reason.

"Depends on what?"

"On whether he gets a gig and needs me to sing with him or not."

That sounded one-sided enough to draw my defend-the-sisterhood face, but she batted that away with her dark lashes and said, "No, it's great. Really. I mean, I should put out a sign, you know? 'Will sing for sex.'"

I blushed at that and she laughed.

"You are so shy about everything," she said playfully. "It's so cute."

"I am not shy," I came back irritably.

"Of course you're not," she said with all seriousness but her tongue was firmly in her cheek. "Anyway, so whaddaya think? Wanna get together out there and see if we can make a little money?"

Her brows dipped when I didn't say yes right away. I had to give this some thought, which wasn't easy under her aggrieved scrutiny, as if the offer were such a slam-dunk that she'd already paid the bill and put it in the mail.

"I don't know," I said, despite the speculation I'd mulled earlier about this very thing. "I mean...I don't know how that would work."

I had complete freedom now, whether it was getting me anywhere or not. If I partnered up with Sherri, I'd no longer have freedom but obligation. But her voice was amazing, it really was, and maybe a little obligation would be worth getting the burden of having to sing off my shoulders. I could just stand there and play while she did all the work, more or less the way Mose and I did, but this would be every day. If I could make that much every day, then I could get back on the bus in a month, maybe sooner, and those were earnings I wouldn't feel guilty about splitting. I made up my mind, but only if...

"I play, you sing, right?" I said.

"Yeah, that's how we'd work it," she said, brightening at the prospect.

"So I don't sing, just you?"

That seemed to throw her.

"I mean," she fumbled, "if you want to sing, sure."

"Oh gosh, that's not what I meant," I said, only then realizing what that question must have sounded like. "It's only...I'm not a good singer."

Her brows bent quizzically. "That's not true! You were amazing out there. I could never sing that song the way you did."

Did she really mean that or was she just being nice? I decided that it was okay either way.

"Sure, okay—let's do it."

"Great!" She was bouncing with excitement. "Wanna start right now?"

I looked through the windows on a waning day. "No, let's start tomorrow," I said. "I don't like to be down here after dark."

"Oh," she brushed that off, "it's not bad until the liquor stores close. If you're off the streets by ten or eleven it's usually okay."

Usually okay, and with a long walk back in the dark.

"I'd rather start tomorrow."

She showed her disappointment but didn't run with it.

"Okay," she said, presenting her hand. "Tomorrow, then."

......

WE MET IN FRONT of the Ryman at nine o'clock. I'd been up since the first murky hours of morning. I was fed, coffeed, and feeling as if half the day was gone by the time Sherri drifted up, looking less than awake and wearing the same clothes, but then so was I. I felt awkward now, like I was on my first date.

"Hey," she announced lethargically, squinting against the early sun. It was a steamy morning with a whitewashed sky. There was a haze in the air that I could feel in my throat.

"So where do you want to set up?" I asked.

"Oh, it's too early for that. There won't be enough people out to make it worth it until the lunch crowd starts pouring out of those offices." She pointed up toward the peculiar tower with two spikes on top, like something out of Batman. "I need coffee and we need to rehearse a little."

We went to a Starbucks and Sherri got her coffee. I passed on the coffee because I was fully awake, and anyway, I was scandalized by the prices. Sherri's coffee cup led us to a park along the river, where we sat on a bench to rehearse.

"So what do you like?" she asked.

I gave her my usual playlist, the Country songs with the good guitar work. She liked Miranda, but shook her head at the rest.

"We gotta play girl songs," she said, then went into *Lucky 4 You* by SHe-DAISY, bouncing her shoulders to the beat. I picked up on that and began to play, finding the guitar work fun, getting caught up in her enthusiasm. Soon I was bouncing my shoulders and playing louder and we had a little show going on. Someone walking along the river clapped.

Carrie Underwood was her real hero, though. We went through that list and Sherri's eyes shined in a dreamy way.

"I love Carrie," she said. "I wish I could get on that show."

Show? Oh, that talent show. Yeah, I'd heard of it. "Have you ever tried?" I asked.

She looked at me deadpan then snickered. "Yeah, about every day."

Once we thought we had enough to work with, we retreated to the Ryman and staked out a spot. Sherri found a bucket for me to sit on. She thought it best if I sat and she stood, and that arrangement did seem to make sense, her voice being the star of our show. I was jealous of Sherri's voice. Isn't that pitiful? I missed a note once just to throw her off, feeling bad about it even as I did it. If it hadn't been for the stuff I breathed at the Blue Place, was this how my voice would have sounded? I shook that off—childish—and played true after that.

We'd only been at it for about an hour when Sherri stepped back and said, "Let's get lunch."

"Already?"

"I'm starving. Aren't you?"

I was always starving, but wasn't about to raid trash dumpsters with Sherri there, so this meant I'd have to spend money that I would rather have saved, each day bringing me one dollar closer and two dollars farther from that bus. I gazed at my hat on the ground at Sherri's feet and noticed that our take was about what I might have made on my own. But now we were splitting it, so even though I wasn't making enough before, that was still more than now.

"Yeah, okay," I said, expectations and obligation, and this was part of it.

We went to an open-air restaurant and sat, people walking past just beyond my elbow, my eyes widening at the menu prices.

"Maybe we should just go get some hotdogs," I said hopefully.

"Aw, heck no, girl. You gotta live, you know?"

I ordered water and some toast. Sherri ordered—a lot. And when she couldn't finish it all, she asked if I would help her out, so I did, pouncing ravenously, and I realized that Sherri was savvier than she let on.

Afterward she was all bustle with a purpose.

"Let's take the bus down to Music Row," she said with unflappable exuberance.

"Why?" I asked, dumbfounded.

"Why not?" she chirped, and suddenly we were on a bus heading somewhere, puffing clouds of diesel at every stoplight. My throat was scratchy.

And then we were on a long esplanade crowded with music shops and studios and scores of tourists, and Sherri was back in her dream as she watched this go by, gazing at doors that only opened for the fortunate few, whose voices or looks or happenstance set them in the improbably right place at the improbably right time and with the improbable foresight to set in motion what a million others would give their lives to experience for a minute—and then to make it seem so preordained. That's not what I wanted. No part of it. Power is never absolute. Fame is always fickle. If you give in to it, there is always someone else who has power over you, and the closer you are to that power the more you have to buckle under it.

What struck me the most was how resolved Sherri was, that somehow, someday, those doors would open for her and she would be beckoned in. It was heartbreaking in its way, but then, what did I really know about it?

"Let's get off here," she said suddenly, jumping up and taking my hand, pulling me off the bus and onto a sidewalk, where we set out away from all the tourist commotion.

"Where are we going?" I asked, resisting the instinctive urge to yank my hand away. Obligation, you know? This was the price.

"I only live a few blocks from here. I wanna show you the place."

We made a couple of turns, putting blocks between us and the clamor of Music Row, and then we were in a quiet little neighborhood populated with cottage-style houses and some really old trees. We walked up to the door of one house and Sherri banged on in.

"Anybody here?" she hollered. No answer. "Well, everybody must be gone," she said, "so come on in."

What struck me first was the smell, musky and dense and limned with stale beer. What struck me next was the disarray, the clothes on the floor, bedding lying out, guitars, drums, and sound equipment against every wall. It was hard to walk through that without tripping over something. Mama would throw a fit if she saw the place. I thought that even during the worst of it, when Timewall and Priscilla and Lainey were little, when the sore on Aunt Joss's lip turned into a hole—even then our trailer never looked this bad.

"Uh," I said.

"I know," Sherri smiled but not apologetically. "We have a lot of people here. It's not so bad, though. It's all about the music, right? And some of the music we make sounds pretty damn good."

"Are you the only girl?"

"Yeah." She fidgeted. "You think you might wanna help me change that?"

I lurched a bit when I caught on to what she was asking. "Oh, I don't know—"

"It's cool," she said with only the barest hint of disappointment. "Just something to think about."

"Yeah, okay."

......

DURING THE JOURNEY back to Broadway, I guessed that Sherri had become my friend, although I kept her one step back in case I'd read this wrong. I shared no confidences with her except obliquely, but she shared with an effusiveness that flushed me scarlet sometimes, especially her rambles and relationships. I couldn't imagine living her life, how I would feel about myself, but she was perfectly at ease with it all, as if hers was the natural evolution of youth and not subject to regret. I wondered which of us was the more free.

Back in town, now late in the day, I started getting antsy. Sherri seemed to know exactly why.

"It's okay," she said. "Like I told you—it doesn't get bad until really late, and this is when you make money, when the rednecks are all drunk and think we're going to sleep with them. The tourists during the day are just being polite with what they give us."

That sounded like a Blaize world of trouble to me, but I was with a girl who had somehow become my friend, and whom I'd have to leave behind if I walked my own walk, or hiked my own hike as the Appalachian Trail guys used to say. It's not so much that I was afraid for my safety as it was what I'd do if someone threatened that safety. As much as I was fully confident that I could take care of myself, I didn't like letting my Blaize out. I didn't like seeing red and going unthinking into violence. Well, most of the time, anyway.

"Okay," I demurred.

"Great!" she bounced.

We set up as the sun went down, soft light reflecting off the towers, the air taking on a touch of cool, dusky shadows reaching for us in lengthening fingers. We went through the Carrie Underwood list, Sherri giving it as much as she might on a stage. The character of the crowds changed, to younger men who weren't as steady on their feet, laughing and gabbing louder as the night deepened but still not drunk enough to try to touch us. You weren't allowed to carry beer around on the street, at least there was that. Police would clop by on horses to reinforce that rule.

And Sherri was right. My hat was collecting money at a noticeable rate. I was starting to feel a little cocky myself, going off on chord variations whenever I could fit them between Sherri's vocals. I was having fun. The money was secondary. The night deepened and I could sense another change in the character of the crowd, more rowdy, less inhibited, beer breaths close enough to wrinkle your nose at. I stood and flipped the Martin Junior over my shoulder.

"It's time to go home, Sherri," I said.

It was as if she'd become drunk on it all, the way she swayed and moved and seemed unsteady.

"Aw, no," she whined. "Just one more."

"It's late."

"It's not that late. C'mon, let's do that one you did yesterday. Let's do it together."

"*Cherry Bomb?* No way. That song always makes trouble."

"No it won't. I mean, there's cops right over there."

A policeman on a horse was sitting saddle quietly at a corner as revelers parted around him.

"Sherri—it's a bad idea."

"Aw, c'mon."

This was why being alone was often best.

"Okay, just a couple of verses and that's it."

"Yea!" she squealed.

My stomach felt off, but I stood and squared myself, cast a look at the policeman, who was still there on his horse, blew the hair out of my eyes, hammered that B power chord, and bellowed:

Can't stay at home, can't stay in school

Sherri sounded off right after me, repeating that line in her higher pitch and I noticed right then that her beautiful voice simply lacked the gravitas for this kind of song.

Old folks say, "You poor little fool"

I was overpowering her with my gritty voice, but if she noticed she wasn't showing it. Instead she was bouncing on her heels as if she couldn't wait to get the next line out.

Down the streets I'm the girl next door
I'm the FOX you've been waiting for

She belted out that *FOX* as if she were challenging every guy watching, and I had to admit that she was infinitely better than me at the showmanship of it, meeting eyes with a lascivious grin and thanking the crowd as even ten-dollar bills were finding their way into my hat. I got caught up in it myself, going on to the line I'd internally promised I wouldn't sing:

Have ya and grab ya until you'r sore

And a drunken guy did make a grab, but Sherri just kicked him back with her booted foot, and he sprawled while his buddies laughed and we finished the song.

The crowd didn't want to break up, egging us on for more, and Sherri seemed as if spotlights were on her, a microphone in her hand, a dream realized, and I hated to be the one to snuff that out but it was really late. I zipped the Martin Junior into the gig bag, bent for my hat, took Sherri by the hand, and pulled her out of the crowd and down the sidewalk.

We fetched up in a diner and ordered coffees, Sherri still buzzed by all the excitement and having a hard time coming down from it. I divided the money, brows arching as I counted it.

"I told you," Sherri said with a mirthful glimmer.

"Yeah, you were right," I had to concede. "But it's still late and we need to get home."

"Yeah, yeah, yeah—so look, wanna go again tomorrow?"

"Yeah," and I meant that. "Same time?"

"No, a little later. Maybe two o'clock."

"Why so late?"

"So we can sleep, for one." She rolled her eyes in a playful way. "And I got an appointment in the morning."

"An appointment?"

"Yeah. An agent. Can you believe it?"

"An agent? When did that happen?"

"Yesterday after you left."

She was sparkling girlishly now, her dreams on a horizon that she could actually see.

"Well...that's awesome."

"Yeah. And if it works out, I'll tell them about you, too."

I stiffened a little at that but she didn't seem to notice. One day at a time, and if anything came from this I could always walk away.

"Cool," I said.

She bent over and hugged me, catching me by complete surprise, her arms around me and I could feel the excitement coursing in her. I gave her an awkward pat on the back, and then we released and I walked into the night, looking back at her, illuminated by a streetlight as if she were on a dark stage, waving at me, her grin like a silver moon. I keep that memory close.

When I saw Sherri again, the sun would hide, the moon would fall, and nothing would ever be the same.

chapter seven

......

SOMETIMES WHEN IT RAINED long and hard in the chill months, Mama would stand in the open door of our trailer and just watch it, her expression worlds away, off in the distance where the mountains met the mist. She was seeing something in the cold drizzle, or perhaps remembering, but what that might have been remained another of Mama's mysteries.

Mama was too complicated to figure out, but I think I have a sense now of what she must have felt because it rained on my camp without reprieve for two days straight.

It started in the small hours after I'd left Sherri, a tap, tap, tap at first, as if moths were fluttering against my plastic walls, then a spluttering in fits and starts, as if the night sky weren't fully committed to anything yet; and then, after what seemed a long sighing breath through the treetops, a raucous deluge descended all at once, pounding at the walls of my shelter as if war were raging all around me.

I jumped up in pulsing fear, clicked a little flashlight I'd bought for ninety-nine cents, and in a panic examined the duct-taped seams of my plastic shack. If water got in, the Martin Junior could be ruined, would probably be ruined, the wood swelling, the veneer peeling, and then I would have nothing, nothing at all. But duct tape saved one of the Apollo missions to the moon, and duct tape saved me. Nothing was leaking, even as my thin plastic walls rippled under the onslaught and I could feel the ground going mushy beneath me. I would have been in worse shape if I'd been in a tent on a camping trip, with sewn seams springing leaks like a rusty hull. Still, not taking any chances, I put the Martin Junior in the gig bag and then put all of that into a trash bag, hugging the bundle to my chest as if I were shielding a baby from the elements.

I didn't sleep another minute that night, not that I could have if I'd tried. The roar was constant, deafening, punctuated by actinic cracks and rips across the sky. The rain continued as black night turned to gray morning. My breath was condensing on the inner walls, tracks like beads of sweat running toward the floor, creating little pools that I mopped up with my dirty clothes. Whenever a break came in the rain, I opened the flap to let the condensation out, sticking my head out as well to see a swampy landscape with water as deep as my ankles; and then the rain would crash down again and I'd button everything up, rocking with the Martin Junior as the day went on, experiencing one interminable hour for every minute passed.

Night came, my stomach rumbled, and still the rain, a ceaseless barrage that had by now left me so numb that I might have been deaf if not for the roar. I snatched perhaps an hour of sleep, the march of time excruciatingly slow, as if daylight had been fractured by a god's hammer and now it would ever be night. The rain eased at some point, which I latched onto with the desperate hope of a sailor in a small boat on a stormy sea.

The rain went on into the day, no longer a roar but a steady tapping and ticking, and if not for the Martin Junior I would have bolted out into it, made for McDonalds, the rescue mission—anywhere. Even though I felt safely camouflaged from any passersby (and who would be passing by in that weather?) there was no way I'd take off and leave the Martin Junior behind. I wouldn't take that chance. So be it if someone stole my clothes and daypack, and the bulk of my money was in a jar buried farther back in the woods, but I wouldn't risk my guitar.

The rain tapered off overnight and I got a little sleep, emerging damp and sticky in the morning with a stomach that was knotting painfully enough to double me over. The sky was heavy, the air wet to breathe, the trees dripping a slow, tinkling beat, quickened when a gust rustled their limbs. I didn't ponder or prevaricate, I grabbed my daypack and my plastic bundle and sprinted for the bridge.

The rescue mission let me shower and do laundry (no sermon this time either). They had food but that was more charity than I could accept.

I felt ashamed enough that I'd come to them a soggy refugee—taking their food would only reinforce that helpless image. I walked quiet streets still slick from the rain, went into the pancake place and took a seat. It took two stacks of pancakes to sate my stomach. I ate the first stack much too quickly, choking on a lump that stuck in my throat. I went slower with the second. Afterward I sat back with a coffee and gazed out the windows at a day so uninspiring that it should have been cancelled at the outset.

It was now a Thursday as far as I could tell, counting back through cycles of light and dark that seemed to have consumed weeks, not days. I had nowhere to go, nothing to do. That inactivity was maddening in itself.

Sherri was probably at home sitting it out. No one would try to perform in this weather, and anyway, no one was out to hear them. It would be so nice if Sherri were here and we could pass the hours with music and gossip—and maybe I would even give her a little of my own gossip. I might go that far on a day like this. I wondered how her appointment with the agent had gone, then realized with a jolt that I didn't have her phone number, not that I had a phone to call her with anyway. And then with an even greater jolt I realized that I didn't even know her last name! It seems ridiculous now, but it never came up. She was Sherri with an *i*, I was Ridley with a *y*, and that had seemed all the introduction necessary.

The thought of having to go back to my camp to sit out the weather made me groan audibly. I ordered another coffee and nursed it, praying they wouldn't throw me out. My thoughts wandered without form, coming to rest on a word or a phrase, and then I was scrawling on a napkin, more words for my poem:

> *And Mama told me*
> *Not to come around*
> *When her door was shut*
> *The towels on the ground*
> *And my breaths would burn*
> *I couldn't make a sound*
> *No food in the pantry*
> *No lights in the house*

> *Winter cold inside*
> *And men came spellbound*
> *And Mama said look*
> *Aren't we living so proud*
> *But Mama*
> *But Mama*
> *You never told me how to love*

I get angry when I think back on all that, I mean nostrils-flaring-fist-bunching angry. It was mostly over by the time I turned thirteen, but I was acting out then, puberty coming on like a stealthy insurgent, and I let Mama have it, blaming her for everything. She trembled with rage, fighting to hold back, and I dared her to do something about it, to come at me with all she had. I was so much taller than she was by then, and I wasn't afraid of her the way Timewall was, or too conflicted to confront her the way Tommy was. Could I provoke her into hitting me? Slapping me? I wanted her to, so that I'd have a justifiable reason to hit her back, to strike a blow that might even it all out.

But there was this about Mama: she never hit us, any of us, not even a pop on the behind. Her weapon was her unyielding intransigence, and as much as my own nostrils were flaring in time with hers, I simply couldn't stand up to that. When she saw that she had subdued me once again, she told me with a steely look, "Ugly times are worse in the rememberin' of 'em, Ridley, than the livin' of 'em was." She was still trembling, still fighting for control. "So git over it." Then she whipped around and stalked off.

Yeah, maybe, I thought to her back, but those had been really ugly times.

Mama never held another job after she got fired from the Minute Burger. Imperious bosses, demanding customers...the least indignity would set her off. So we were on welfare, and Mama would pitch in at the help center sometimes. But none of that brought in enough back then for Mama to buy a car, which we needed because the bus stop was so far away, or for repairs on the trailer or for school supplies or the million other things, so Mama did what she had to do, and the men came spellbound.

And then there was Aunt Joss.

I don't want to say anything bad about her—I guess I would've even loved her if I'd known how—but Aunt Joss was a big walking sack of emotions that Mama managed more patiently than she managed any of us, as if the two were joined together and shared the same arteries.

I'm pretty sure that it was Aunt Joss who started using drugs first, and Mama only did it to keep Aunt Joss happy, or to keep Aunt Joss from feeling alone, or for any of a hundred other reasons that only Mama knows. And yeah, Mama got clean after Aunt Joss left, so maybe I'm right about this.

Anyway, the money would run out and Tommy would be going through the dumpsters looking for something to feed us, or the power would go out and I'd huddle with the young ones to keep them warm while Tommy paced and raged and put his fist through the wall; then Mama would come out, a guy in her room, Aunt Joss on the couch, and bundle us up in her creaky car and drive to Hampton, where we would all be lined up like hillbilly kids for everyone to see while Mama paid this bill or that bill in cash. She never had a bank account because, she told me, they just steal from you; and now there I was and I'd never had one either, wouldn't know how.

It was the summer before Timewall and Lainey started first grade that the knock came at the door. I reached the door first and opened it on a woman dressed in a professional gray pantsuit, her dark hair silken and falling past her shoulders. She smiled nervously.

"May I see Jocela, please?" she asked politely.

I had to stumble over that until I realized that she must have meant Aunt Joss, and this woman was a stranger so there was no way I'd let her in or even say anything back to her, but then Mama came up with a hard look on the woman and eased me aside.

"You can't take her, Tara," Mama said, so hickory stiff that a hurricane couldn't have bent her. "She's grown up now. You don't have a say."

"I know, Blaize," the woman said calmly, "but I hope you'll let me if she wants."

Mama just stood there, her nostrils not flaring but wary just the same, as if she were weighing a trick of some kind. We kids were all together, back out of the way, watching in fascination and all thinking the same thing: Who was this woman? And why did she want Aunt Joss?

"May I come in and speak with you, Blaize?" the woman asked in a benevolent tone.

Mama seemed torn, but she stepped back and let the woman in, who took in the surroundings with brows of surprise, as if she had expected our trailer to be filthy.

"You have a nice home," the woman said after that appraising moment. "I can see how well you look after everything."

Mama shrugged that off, her eyes still hard.

"Why did you come here, Tara?" Mama asked sharply. "You hate me."

"I don't hate you, Blaize. Not anymore. I came to tell you that I understand now." The woman's eyes found Lainey and fixed there for a moment. "I didn't understand before how much she needed you, and that you've been taking care of her since you two were little. That's a lot for a child to take on, but you did it through everything. Now let me help. Let me do what I can. You can use a rest, can't you Blaize? I know how hard it's been."

"It ain't nothin'," Mama said.

"Oh, I think it's something. I know my daughter."

We all mouthed that at the same time. *Daughter?*

"I know how hard it's been." She found Lainey again. "And Elaine needs her mother to be well. That's something I can help with. I promise—you will always be able to see her. You will always be friends. Nothing can take that away, except...how bad is she?"

"She's doin' better today."

"May I see her?"

Mama was grinding her teeth in indecision, looking away as if for an answer to a question none of us could even fathom. I didn't grasp it then but I can see it now. Mama *was* tired, and maybe worried, too.

"Only if she wants," Mama finally answered.

Mama went into her room while we all stared at the woman, at Tara. She knelt to Lainey and reached out to touch Lainey's cheek.

"You're so big now," Tara smiled ruefully. "And you're so pretty. I like the way your hair is braided. Did your mother do that for you?"

Lainey nodded, as wary as the rest of us.

"Do you know who I am?" Tara asked. "I'm your grandmother."

We all kind of jumped in place at that revelation. You mean Lainey had a *grandmother*? We didn't have a grandmother, but *Lainey* did?

Mama came out looking old and used up.

"She says you can come in," Mama said.

Tara dabbed at an eye and went into the room, while Mama stepped outside and lit a cigarette, pacing back and forth through her own cloud of smoke.

Tara was in there for what seemed forever, and when she came out she had an arm around Aunt Joss and a bag in her other hand, and she was walking Aunt Joss to the door slowly and carefully, as if Aunt Joss were too frail to make it on her own, gesturing to Lainey, who gave us a wild look of confusion.

Mama was still outside with her cigarette, her face set in stone as Tara guided Aunt Joss down the steps to her car, which was big and black and shiny and could have fit all of us for a sleepover. Lainey came out like a frightened fawn in a forest, watching as Aunt Joss climbed numbly into the car, Tara adjusting everything for her.

"Come on, Elaine," Tara said. "Come sit with your mother."

Lainey walked to the car, looking over her shoulder at us the entire way, looking at Timewall as if she were begging him to make it all make sense. Aunt Joss's door was open. I saw her heave and start crying, then Mama went up, held Aunt Joss's hand for a long moment, helped Lainey in, then turned to Tara, who cut in before Mama could say anything.

"She's going to be all right, Blaize. I promise you." Mama only nodded. "But what about you?"

"I'm fine," Mama said. "I'm fine as long as she's okay."

"Okay, then," Tara said. She got in the car and backed out while Mama stood there with a look on her face I'd never seen before or since, and then we could hear the car crunching over the gravel and across the tracks.

······

The weather was better on Friday, and Saturday was too nice for Sherri not to be out in it, but I never saw her. I even hung out until after dark, waiting as if we'd agreed to meet, but she didn't show. On Sunday I stayed on the bridge to sing with Mose, those horrible rainy days seeming too long ago to remember.

It was a nice morning, with a puffy sky and clean air, not the least tickle in my throat. Even the river looked clean, reflecting the blue from above rather than its usual green tint. Mose walked up with his dapper look and intractable smile, this time carrying a long, thin, black nylon bag.

"Good morning, Miss Ridley," he said in that wholesome way of his, parking the bag between a couple of tourists at the rail. "What should we start with today?"

There was no need for him to ask that, I knew what it would be.

"I see trees of green," I recited with my own knowing smile, and he chuckled and we got to it.

The playlist was more or less the same as the previous Sunday, some of the lyrics familiar enough that I could mouth along with him as I played, the tourists gathering around us with glowing expressions and singing along to some of the songs. The money, of course, fell at Mose's feet. He acknowledged his thanks with a dip of his head or a flash of teeth while never interrupting his delivery.

I was so into it, having so much fun that I was curled up inside myself, just feeling the music as I played, so much so that when Mose finished the song, I kept on strumming and he had to touch me to bring me back.

"Oh, sorry," I said, a little embarrassed.

"Oh, it's nothing, Miss Ridley," he grinned. "When you feel the music it's only natural. So," he parked his hands on his hips and bent back with a pleased expression, "do you remember *Mack the Knife*?"

"From last week? Yeah, a little."

"Well, I need to rest for a minute. Why don't you do that one by yourself."

I started in place, sputtering, "But...but I don't know all the words."

"That's okay. I got you."

His smile had gone mischievous somehow, no less warm but tinged with mirth. He unzipped his bag and took out a chrome music stand, which he unfolded and set up in front of me, and on it were the lyrics to *Mack the Knife*, the slower Bobby Darin version. I couldn't close my jaw, didn't know whether to be embarrassed or touched.

"So you go ahead now," he said. "Let an old man have a little rest."

My mind was a whirlwind of objections conflicting with a desire to please Mose, and even as I strummed some sample chords I still wasn't sure I could go through with it. And there were tourists around us, clapping me on, and I tried to turn them into a blur in the background, to pretend that it was just Mose and me in a quiet room and no one else in judgment, and I thought back and found that song, bounced my shoulders to that up-tempo beat, unconsciously positioning my fingers for B flat.

And I sang:

> *Oh, the shark, babe, has such teeth, dear*
> *And it shows them pearly white*
> *Just a jackknife has old MacHeath, babe*
> *And he keeps it, ah, out of sight*

People were clapping. Good grief they were clapping, bright grins coming at me from all sides, but most of all Mose, who proved right then that he knew me better than I knew myself; and I fell into it and I loved it, that lightness you feel when you shrug off everything that weighs on you and breaths taste as clean as spring.

And I sang:

> *Yes, that line forms on the right, babe*
> *Now that Macky's back in town*
> *Look out, old Macky's back!*

I punched that last word with a grin of triumph, raucous commotion all around me but with Mose in the middle, shining his smile and clapping with the rest, and I was too elated to take a breath, just stood there in that adulation, and if I'd been anyone else's daughter I would have leaked tears of pride.

Mose gave me half his earnings as always, which I again reluctantly accepted. There was enough money in my hands that, combined with what I had in the jar buried in the woods, I had a real start on a bus ticket, my dream now closer than the horizon. But that came with a pang I hadn't anticipated. If this kept up I'd be leaving soon, I'd be leaving Mose—and Sherri.

"What's that on your mind?" Mose asked me with a single brow dipping. The crowd had dispersed, and those around us now were new and knew nothing of my performance.

"Oh, it's just...that was fun, is all. You hate for it to end, you know?"

"Yes I do," and proving that he absolutely knew me better than I knew myself, he added, "And it won't end. Wherever you go, you take the music with you."

I had to catch myself before a tear could spill out. Mose let me peck him on the cheek, an inexplicable impulse that took me by complete surprise, then he patted my back and I walked off light as air to find Sherri and tell her all about it.

......

I DIDN'T SEE SHERRI that day, and I didn't see her on Monday either. By Tuesday I was concerned. I hung around the Ryman until after lunch, pacing back and forth, and when a bus chugged up I hopped aboard.

I couldn't remember exactly where to get off, and when I finally did, I couldn't remember exactly where to go. I walked streets that had no place in my memory, turning corners and going back the other way, up one street and down another until I'd practically walked far enough to have made it to California on foot. It was getting later and I didn't know the bus schedule. I began to worry that I'd be stranded here, and where *was* Sherri, anyway?

I stopped in front of a house and pondered it long and hard. It had all been so dizzying that day—why hadn't I paid more attention? But this house looked as if it could be the one. So had another house down the way, but this one looked more promising. I went up to the door and knocked, took in some peeling paint and a desiccated plant in a pot, searched my memory for them but couldn't find them.

I heard some noise inside, bumps and slams but no one came to the door. I knocked again, harder this time, heard more bumps and slams, no one coming to the door, and I felt like an idiot just standing out there. I was turning to leave when the door was yanked open.

"Yeah, what's up?" a guy asked, slouching in the doorway with a look of resentment, as if I were intruding upon the seminal moment of his life. He was older than Sherri but not too old, his oily hair long and dark and he needed a shave. I could smell him from where I stood. His T-shirt said *Phish*.

"Yeah, hey," I said. "Does Sherri live here?"

"Sherri who?"

"Uh, just Sherri. She sings."

"Oh yeah, that chick. No, she isn't here."

I brightened up. At least I'd found the right house.

"Oh, so this *is* where she lives?"

"Yeah, I guess."

That guy couldn't string two brain cells together. He was probably stoned.

"So...do you know where she is?"

"Naw, man. She went somewhere."

"Do you know where?"

"Naw, sorry," and he closed the door, slammed it, actually, because the window in it rattled.

I stood there for a minute taking breaths, letting the heat out before it came out as something else, then I picked my way back to Music Row and waited for the bus.

Sherri went somewhere, he said, and all I could think was that the agent she saw set her up with something, something she hadn't made an effort to tell me about. I ground my teeth, fought to keep my Blaize in place. What good were friends if, once they got their shot, they dismissed you and moved on? What did friends do but siphon your energy until they didn't need you anymore? So who needed friends?

I can assure you that I didn't.

chapter eight

......

GET OVER IT, Mama told me when we were having it out that time. That was easy for her to say, she never let her feelings out where they might get stepped on. She never trusted anyone, never left herself vulnerable. Why? Because that trust would eventually be betrayed. It always is. Without fail.

For me, Sherri taking off was like Taylor all over again, except this time instead of being deprived of my self-esteem I was deprived of the opportunity to share something exciting that I'd discovered in myself.

Mose had, with a sly trick, taught me that a voice could fit the right song no matter what that voice sounded like. Now I felt proud and confident out there on the sidewalks, singing and not just strumming. Teaming up with Sherri for a duet would have put a crown on that accomplishment, lifting me so far above Mama that I would be more than her equal, and there would be no ambiguity about who was the better and stronger woman.

Those thoughts taunted me during lonely nights in camp. During the days, I staked out a place and covered Janis Joplin, Dixie Chicks, and Trick Pony tunes, well enough to attract regular deposits into my hat, my bus ticket coming so much closer that I could feel the electric anticipation of it tickling my stomach and coursing along my skin.

Then it was Friday, getting near dusk, and a man approached me.

That day had been long and hot and my throat was sore. I was settled in a kind of alcove in Printers Alley, in a gap between two buildings that had been bricked in but not flush with the facade. Everything was in shadow now, all the neon lights beginning to set the ambience for the coming evening. Foot traffic to the clubs was already starting to pick up, people going by and paying me no notice. My throat was so sore that I could no longer get Janis, Natalie, or Heidi past my larynx, so I sat back to quietly strum, not eager to return to my lonely camp just yet, just strumming and humming and thinking about my poem, what another verse might say:

> *Then those better days when Mama shined*
> *With boots and jeans dancing in time*
> *Motors and men and braids so fine*
> *A tooth-missed smile returned in kind*
> *Mama told me, when so inclined*
> *A new baby was deep inside*
> *Mama you told me all of this*
> *Yes Mama you told me so much*
> *But Mama*
> *But Mama*
> *You never told me how to love*

I was putting this together with the other verses, the meter all over the place but it seemed to work, at least in my head. I strummed and recited the words aloud, humming between verses, drifting into a music theme that tied it all together somehow. In my mind, the first verse started with finger picking at a slow tempo in D minor, taking off in the second verse with a fast and loud 3/4 beat, slowing down in E minor for the third verse, and then a reprise of the first verse but this time in E minor.

I hummed and strummed what I thought the music should be, selecting chords that matched my emotions, plucking and strumming, and then I sang it, not too loud because of my sore throat, but loud enough that I could hear the composition; and it needed work, sure, but it sounded like an actual song and I didn't quite know what to make of that.

"I've never heard that song before," a man said, yanking me out of my head with a start. "Where'd you find it?"

I glared up at the man for intruding when I was in such a personal place. He looked to be in his upper 30s, dressed too nicely for a night out in the bars. He was wearing a white dress shirt, the top button undone, black slacks, and black dress shoes that reflected the neon from the sign above us. He had gold bling on his left wrist, perfect black hair in a professional cut, clean-shaven and angular good looks, and a body that could make a woman his age squirm.

His question seemed innocent enough, so I answered it.

"It's just a poem I'm writing."

"A poem? Really? Then where'd you get the music?"

"I've just been sort of humming it."

"*Humming* it?"

That sounded just skeptical enough to lift my temperature a degree or two.

"Yeah, humming it. That okay with you?"

"Oh, hey, I didn't mean it like that."

"Then how did you mean it?"

"It's only—well, that's the process, right?"

"If you say so."

"You have a raw, authentic sound. Very unique."

"Thanks," I said halfheartedly.

"How long have you been in town? I haven't seen you around before."

"What makes you think I'm not from here?"

Something mirthful glinted in his eyes, but his expression revealed nothing else.

"Just an assumption based on nothing. Most of the musicians I meet are from somewhere else."

"Well, I'm not a musician."

"You sure had me fooled."

"Sorry about that."

I was keeping my tone insolent on purpose because talking to strangers was usually not a good idea, the one lesson Mama drilled into us that actually had some value.

"So," he went on, unperturbed, "do you always play alone, or do you have a band you play with?"

"I'm not in a band," I reluctantly answered.

"I see. So how old are you? What's your name?"

This was the point where I decided that I'd had enough.

"What's it to you? And why are you asking me all these questions?"

"Hey, I'm just making conversation."

"No you're not. You're acting like a perv. So are you gonna leave or do I have to?"

"Hey, don't be that way."

That pretty boy had no idea what a trigger those words were. I jumped to my feet with nostrils flaring. "How I decide to be or not be isn't up to you," I spat at him, and this time I didn't use "ain't."

"Whoa!" He held out his palms. "Look, I'm sorry."

"Well I'm not." I grabbed my gig bag and started putting the Martin Junior away.

"Look—wait, don't run off. I'm not a perv, I'm a scouting agent. I'm looking for someone to sing background and I think you'd be perfect for it."

"Thanks," I said insincerely as I flipped the gig bag over my shoulder. "But I'd rather do my own thing."

"I get it," he said hurriedly, "but this would be a short gig, a few days in the studio at most. Wouldn't you like to be on a record?"

"Why would I want to be on a record?"

That seemed to puzzle him beyond comprehension. I was just about to shoulder past him when he asked, "Well, what do you want, then?"

"About three hundred dollars would do it," I answered flippantly, then I pushed on by and took off up the sidewalk. He ran after me.

"Okay," he said, trotting to keep up. "This gig pays a thousand. A few days for a thousand dollars. Wouldn't that be worth it? Come with me and I'll sign you up right now."

That stopped me in my tracks. I turned to him with an expression that would have scared off a mountain man with a meat cleaver, but he was unfazed, amused even, and that sent the red flooding into my eyes.

"What? You think I'm some stupid hick?" I snapped at him, closing the distance between us but he didn't step back. "You think I'm gonna just go off with a stranger? I'm not stupid, *you* are."

"Okay, okay, I'm sorry. Here, at least take my card."

He did back up then, presenting his card, which I snatched from his fingers. The card was white linen, gold embossed. It felt like a crisp new twenty-dollar bill, and read *Preston Cole, Dardanelle Agency*.

"Just give it some thought," he said, then he turned on his heel and walked off.

Finally.

······

IT RAINED ON SUNDAY. I sat in my hovel listening to the rain drum on the plastic as the day got longer and longer with each passing hour. Most of all I missed my time with Mose. I wondered what he would be doing on a day like this. I wondered where he lived. I wondered if he was thinking about me the same way I was thinking about him. I thought of him as a special man, maybe even a friend, although I knew nothing about him. Did he think I was special in some way? Mama never told me I was special. The only one who ever did was Priscilla, but she meant it as an insult.

It was a little over a year ago, in the morning before school. I was in a rush to make my bed and get the room clean before we had to go, while Priscilla was kicked back on her own unmade bed, tapping her foot and poking at a laptop she'd brought home from one of her classes. I flipped the ceiling light on because it was too dark otherwise, what with the newspaper covering the window.

"Turn that out," Priscilla complained, holding her hand up as if she were being blinded.

"Pris, get up and make your bed."

"You aren't the boss of me."

I could hear Robbie in the other room, picking on Timewall, and I needed to go break that up but I needed to finish this too.

"C'mon Pris, we're gonna be late."

"I don't care."

"Mama's gonna be mad."

"I'm not afraid of her."

"You should be."

"Well I'm not." She pouted a moment, then said, "I can't wait till I'm old enough to get out of here."

She always managed to shoehorn that into whatever she might be talking about. Priscilla wasn't even ten yet, but she was as petulant as a moody teenager and had been since the first grade. Priscilla was strange. Robbie was strange too, but in a mean way. Priscilla was just—different. She didn't look like us. By us I mean Mama and Tommy and me. But she didn't look like Robbie or Timewall either. She was already catching up to Mama in height, with a boyish figure and a boyish attitude. She would only wear jeans and T-shirts, and hadn't been in a dress since the first grade, the same plaid jumper I'd once worn, and which she'd managed to ruin before that school year was half over. Mama was apoplectic, but then Mama was always apoplectic about something. Priscilla was slender like Mama and me, with a hint of Mama's nose and chin, but she had dark brown hair, which she kept short, and dark green eyes that sometimes looked black depending on the light, like evergreens on a gray winter day.

"Priscilla, darn it, get up and make your bed."

I went to take her by the arm but she flung me off as if she were twice her size and age.

"Get the f— off me!" she screeched, another trait she had in common with Mama.

"Don't talk like that, Pris," I scolded her.

"Why not?"

"Because it makes you sound like white trash."

"Well," she smiled evilly, "we *are* white trash."

"No we're not!"

"Oh, you don't think so?" she said with a smugness that begged for a slap across the face. "Who's your daddy, then? Who's my daddy? Only white trash don't know who their daddies are."

I was already exhausted from this, and would have been scandalized if this weren't the same Pris I'd known day in and day out since Mama first brought her home from the hospital. I pushed back against the red and took a long breath. Unlike Mama and Pris, I could control myself—well, most of the time.

"Look, Pris," I said evenly but with teeth clenched. "Just make up your bed so we can go."

"You do it," she said derisively, glaring at me over her laptop screen. "I mean, you're the special one, the fairy princess born in the wilderness like some kinda Lord of the Rings thing. Whadda you need anybody for? You can do it yourself, just wave your hand."

Until that moment I hadn't thought it possible that Priscilla could still find words to shock me, but I *was* shocked, my jaw hanging open.

"Where'd you come up with something like that?" I asked, thrown off balance by such a bald remark.

"Don't be stupid, Riddles. Everybody sees how Mama treats you, even more since Tommy went away. You're her special angel."

"That's not true!" I snapped, blushing at a notion that I'd never conceived while wondering at the same time if Priscilla was right somehow. But she couldn't be. The Mama I knew never treated me like that.

"Whatever, Pris," I said, exasperated by it all and a little shaken as well. Timewall yowled from the other room. "Now I've gotta go deal with that, too, so you can deal with Mama by yourself."

"Just wave your hand, princess," she hurled at my back as I left.

How could a girl Priscilla's age learn to wound so effectively? I tried to shrug it off but it wasn't as easy as that. Some of the things she said ate at me until I couldn't stand it any longer. I went into Mama's room a few days later, softly closing the door behind me. Mama was lying on her bed reading a book, and looked up at me with her brows cocked.

"Hey, Mama," I said, wiping my palms on my jeans and thinking it wasn't too late to retreat while I was still intact. Mama continued to gaze at me over her book, letting her expression speak for her so I just blurted it out, "Mama, who's my daddy?"

She sighed and set her book down. This wasn't the first time I'd asked her this, but it was the first time in a long time.

"It doesn't matter, Ridley."

"Yes it does, Mama."

"No," her eyes went hard, "it doesn't."

"It matters to me!"

Mama squeezed her forehead as if she had a headache coming on, seemed to be thinking and weighing while her palm covered her eyes, then she dropped that hand and sighed again.

"He was just a boy I liked. A sweet boy."

I took a gasp of hope. These were more words than she'd ever told any of us about our fathers, and with my heart pounding, I prayed that she would say more. She didn't want to, that was obvious by the way her eyes were flitting left and right in indecision, but then she said as if from a distance:

"He went in the Army."

"What was his name?" I asked breathlessly.

"It doesn't matter," she said, shutting it all down with the finality of set cement. "A lot of boys went in the Army."

I stood and waited and nothing more came.

"C'mon, Mama, tell me," I whined.

"Why do you even care about that, Ridley?" She was getting her color up now, which provoked the same in me.

"Because I want to know!" I half hollered, stamping my foot. Mama gave me that look.

"You're my baby and nobody else's," she said hotly. "So forget about it."

I was now trembling, the red coming down, and I fought against it but I couldn't. "I can find out!" I threw at her.

"Oh you can, huh? You think you're that smart?" She said this so sarcastically that I wanted to scream.

"Yeah, I'm that smart," I said instead.

"Well," she said with a little laugh, "if you're so smart, go teach Time how to roll his tongue."

That snapped me back. Mama, Tommy, and I could roll our tongues. Robbie, Timewall, and Priscilla couldn't, and the mystery of that had set off jealousies when we were younger, and maybe even now for all I knew. Mama had returned to her book, the signal that our talk was over, leaving me stranded there trembling. It was futile, and I knew it, so I left.

But I was smarter than Mama gave me credit for, and there was a motto I liked that I learned in history class. A Tennessee frontiersman named David Crockett said it, and I took it to heart: *Be always sure you're right, then go ahead.*

So yeah, I was right, and I went ahead. The heck with Mama.

......

BACK IN MY SHELTER, the rain drumming the plastic, the ground beneath me so mushy that I was afraid I'd accidentally poke a hole and let the water in, those thoughts piled one onto the other until I was desperate to get away, swearing that I couldn't last another day cooped up like this, trying to visualize how much money I had in that jar, knowing that it wasn't nearly enough; and how long would this have to go on? How could I possibly endure another day like this? And there would be more. It didn't just rain sometimes, it rained a lot of the time, and here I would be sitting, with nothing to do but think about things I didn't want to think about while bus after bus pulled out of that station bound for California and I wouldn't be on any of them because I'd let a stupid scrawny guy steal all of my things, and then Sherri left, and that hurt even worse, not like when Tommy left but close enough to think about.

"You mean ya got yur feelin's hurt?" Mama told me in the aftermath of Tommy's departure. "Well boo-hoo. What if ya got real hurt? What if we held ya down in the dirt an' beat on ya? How would ya feel then?"

It infuriated me when Mama talked that way, as if she had any idea what it felt like to lose someone the way I'd lost Tommy. But that didn't mean she wasn't right. Remembering what she said convinced me that I had to do something. The solution was there, I just had to act on it, even if I didn't want to.

Sometimes you just had to do what you had to do.

I stepped out onto Music Row the next morning with the Martin Junior on my back and my daypack over my shoulder. It was clear and sunny, the street already dry from yesterday's rain, and I was a little apprehensive. It was a nice day, no rain in the forecast, so I could be down busking on Broadway and bringing myself closer to my goal without having to do any of this. But yesterday had been bad, and close enough to today that I could still feel the boredom and despair as solidly as if I were holding a rock in my hand. I had showered at the rescue mission, and was wearing my denim skirt, boots, T-shirt and black jacket, and of course my hat. It was getting warm out. I pushed my jacket sleeves up to my elbows and took off down the sidewalk, holding Preston Cole's business card out as if it were a map to California.

The Dardanelle Agency wasn't on Music Row, but off in a neighborhood that wasn't too far from where Sherri lived. I thought about going by there afterward to see if Sherri was home, but shook that off. If she wanted to see me then she would have found me downtown, so that meant she didn't want to see me so I didn't want to see her either.

The agency was in a simple but well-maintained house that sat between other houses that were probably real homes. The only thing distinctive about it was the faux granite sign perched low in the small front yard. I went up to the door with a fluttering stomach and pushed the doorbell.

I heard the doorbell chime, like something in a store, not in a house. I waited as if under a thousand eyes for the door to whoosh open. When it didn't, I had to swallow hard and reach out a hesitant finger to stab the doorbell again, my finger just hovering there as indecision got a grip; and I'd convinced myself to just forget it and was about to turn away when the door opened and there stood Preston Cole with his perfect jaw and perfect hair and dressed identically to the other day.

He seemed to stumble for recognition, but then it came and he smiled broadly with teeth too perfect for any human being.

"Well," he said. "Are you ready for the whirlwind?"

"I'm ready to get a thousand bucks," I answered.

chapter nine

......

PRESTON WAVED ME INSIDE and shut the door behind me. I was standing in what was once a living room. There was a fine-grained desk sitting on durable gray carpet, some barrister bookcases filling a far wall. The walls were also gray, decorated with framed certificates, album covers, and autographed 8x10s of famous people. Tall slender vases held plastic plants. Chairs with chrome arms and legs were aligned under the big front window, while musical instruments were propped in one corner, acoustic and electric guitars, a fiddle, and a steel guitar on its stand. Everything was professional and tasteless at the same time.

"Is this your office?" I asked him.

"No, this is reception. My office is down this way."

He tipped his shoulder in that direction so I followed him, passing a kitchen nook that smelled like Starbucks, with a fancy coffee machine and glass canisters of whole beans. There didn't seem to be anyone else in the place at the moment, no dirty coffee cups on the counter, no sound other than us.

His office was a clone of reception, with no hint that it had once been someone's bedroom. The door in the opposite gray wall probably opened on a bathroom, while the former sliding closet held shelves of books. Bright aluminum micro blinds were closed on the lone window. The lighting came from the ceiling, fluorescent, like one of my classrooms at school.

He could have bought Mama's trailer for what his desk must have cost, which was wasted money because there were no photos on it, no items of a personal nature, just a laptop crowded by stacks of papers and manila folders. He gestured me into the chair in front of his desk, then took a seat and laced his fingers. He smiled thinly, looked away and then looked back.

"So, can I get your name now?" he asked uncertainly, as if I might explode on him for the question.

"Yeah, sure," I said. I had my hands in my lap. I was nervous. I wanted to run out of there as fast as I could but I would have felt stupid if I did.

"And...?" he asked with lifted brows.

"Oh, yeah. It's Ridley. Ridley Speaks."

"Ridley Speaks?"

The way he made that into a question bothered me.

"Yeah, that's right," I said with just a little heat.

"Hmm—well that won't do. We'll need something better." Propped on his elbow, a finger on his temple, he started shuffling through some papers.

"Why won't it do?" I asked with an extra measure of heat. He didn't answer right away, just sat there thinking, his finger on his temple.

"Riley—uh—Skye," he finally said to his desktop. "Yeah, that'll work." He looked up at me and smiled. "Riley Skye sounds much better."

"What's wrong with my name?" I asked, hotter still.

He gave me that thin smile, as if there were no question I could ask for which he didn't already have an answer, or else that he'd heard the same question asked so many times that there was no novelty left to it.

"You seem annoyed," he said, his smile giving way to a professional sternness. "You came to me, okay? I didn't drag you here. I have a job to do, which is to make you into a music personality—and you have a job to do, which is to let me do my job. This isn't going to work if I'm worried that everything I say is going to set you off. So before we go any further, tell me if you really want to be here. If you don't, then you can leave and neither of us has lost anything."

His voice was cool and even, but I felt as if I'd been slapped. And I felt foolish for having allowed my Blaize to peek out. I swallowed hard. A thousand dollars. None of this made a difference to anything as long as I had my thousand dollars and I was on that bus by the end of the week.

"Yeah, okay," I said weakly.

"Okay what?"

"I want to be here."

"Good." His smile returned. "So it's like this: A catchy name is important. It's like branding. Your name is okay but it doesn't have that punch. Understand?"

I worked to keep my tone calm this time. "Yeah, but you said this was only like three days. So who cares?"

"I care, my agency cares, you might change your mind about only doing a short-term gig later on, and this is the name that will be in the credits for this record. So, can we move on now, Riley Skye?"

I was having a hard time fitting that name into who I was, but what he said made sense so I nodded.

"Okay, good," he said. "So this next part is a standard contract." He slid some papers to the middle of his desk. "It says things like we own your voice on the record, that you can't perform for anybody else under the name Riley Skye, and that you won't be paid unless you fulfill this contract."

He slid the papers toward me, so I picked them up and looked them over. The print was small and there was a lot of it, with legal terms that could have further tangled a tangled ball of yarn. My instinct was to say forget it. I wasn't foolish enough to sign something I didn't understand, but at the same time, what did it really matter? All I wanted was my thousand dollars. Once I was on that bus, they could do whatever they wanted, I didn't care.

"Yeah, okay," I said. "You got a pen?"

He looked as if he'd anticipated that very response, which caused me to throw my judgment into doubt, but when he slid a pen over I took it and signed.

"Good," he said while making some notations on the contract. I saw him write *Riley Skye* on a line at the top, then flip through and sign his own name next to mine.

"Okay next," he said. "I need to see your I.D."

I sat up straighter to conceal that I hadn't actually jumped in my seat. "I don't have any I.D.," I said with a swallow.

His brows dipped. "Then how do I know that you are who you say you are?"

"Because I told you."

He sighed, sat back and asked, "Well, how old are you, then?"

I was ready for this question. I'd thought a lot about it. Because of my voice, and that I was a little tall, I was sure I could get away with it.

"I'm twenty-one," I said, a small lie that I could live with.

"So why don't you have any I.D.?"

"Because I was born in the wilderness." This wasn't really a lie if that's all anyone had ever told me. "I don't have a birth certificate and I've never driven a car."

His brows went up, not in humor but intrigued.

"You know, I actually believe you. No one would make up something like that. So you were really born in the woods?"

"Yeah, under a tree during a howling storm."

"That is...vivid. Fascinating, too, but we'll get into that later. And you say you've never driven a car?"

"No."

"Why not?"

"Because I didn't need to."

That seemed to surprise him more than anything I'd said yet.

"Well, okay...we'll work on getting you a state I.D. card, but we can do that later."

He took more notes, scrawling while I watched nonplussed, then he tapped all the papers straight and slid them into a folder. When he looked up again he said, "So now we need to get a photograph. Come with me."

He led me into another former bedroom that had camera equipment set up, along with an aluminum-looking umbrella and some bright lights.

"Stand just there," he said. "I like what you have on. It works perfectly."

I stood in the bright light, the camera clicked a few times, then he said, "Take your guitar out of the bag and hold it, okay?"

I did, and the camera clicked a few more times. He paused there, finger on lip, then said, "Sling it over your back, then look at me kind of over your shoulder. And give me a little attitude, like you did when I met you."

Giving him the attitude wasn't that difficult. He seemed to like what he'd captured, so we returned to his office where he poked at his laptop, tapped a button, and his printer took off. What came out was a color photograph of that pose he liked, and I have to say, I liked it too. We didn't have photos in the trailer. Mama didn't do photos. I don't know why. I suspect that she'd never had a photo made in her life, so the only photos I'd ever seen of myself were either at arm's length with my phone or what they put in the high school yearbooks, and those yearbook photos were always small and black and white and taken in a hurry so that the next student could sit. This one showed me in a way that I'd never seen myself. I looked stronger than Mama, and that thought just flowed warmly into my stomach.

He printed off some more photos, slid them into the folder, dropped the folder into a drawer, then stood.

"All right. That's everything," he said. "Are you ready to go?"

"Go where?"

"To the studio."

To the studio? So it was real, not just wishful thinking, not a grasp at brittle straw.

"Yeah, okay," I said, a little dizzy but the good kind of dizzy, the hard cider kind. We walked to the front door.

"You won't need that," he said, nodding at my guitar and then to the corner where the other instruments were parked. That yanked me out of my dizziness and back into myself.

"Then I won't play it," I said. "But I'm not leaving it."

He shrugged and we went outside to his car, which was an Escalade, huge and black and as shiny as polished garnet. I'd never been in anything like it, and had to practically climb steps to reach my seat. The thing was cavernous, with the sweet smell of leather. My seat was wider than me and the Martin Junior together, and seemed to place me yards away from Preston there across the console. There was no creaking as we pulled out, no rough and stumbling engine, no sound at all from the outside, as if we were in a high-tech cocoon insulated with money.

We proceeded through the neighborhood and beyond, making lefts and rights that soon left me confused. I looked for that odd Batman building and couldn't see it anywhere. At last, we pulled into some corrugated buildings that reminded me of the Blue Place but these were gray.

"Is this it?" I asked, even more confused, a little disappointed as well. I'd thought that we would be somewhere on Music Row, with tourists watching as I got out, snapping photographs and clamoring for autographs. Instead I held my own door and stepped out onto a dusty parking lot littered with cigarette butts.

"This is it," he said.

"I thought we'd be on Music Row or something."

"Not every studio is on Music Row. Okay, let's go in and see what you've got."

I followed him through a dingy door streaked with rust, thinking that this place was more like a tobacco shed back home. The inside looked equally depressing, a tobacco shed without the tobacco. Then we went through a door into a tight room packed with equipment. It was chilly in there, uncomfortably so. I tugged my sleeves down. A man sat behind a board that had more switches and knobs than the Space Shuttle. He looked at me and nodded with a smile. In a corner was a booth with a big window.

"So Deke, this is Riley," Preston said. "And Riley, this is Deke. He's the sound engineer."

Deke looked like a cowboy, with a leathery face, wild black goatee going gray, and short thinning hair. He wore jeans, weathered boots, and a black T-shirt that said *Brooks & Dunn* below the skull of a longhorn cow. I couldn't guess how old he was.

"Hi," I said.

"Hey," he said.

"So where's Albert?" Preston asked Deke.

"Running late. He said to just go ahead."

"Hmm...there's not much to go ahead with if he's not here," Preston said.

"Who's Albert?" I asked.

"He's the producer."

"Oh." That meant nothing to me.

"I guess we'll just have to kill time," Preston grumbled.

"We could do a sound check," Deke suggested, which didn't seem to mollify Preston but he nodded anyway.

"Yeah, sure," Preston said; then to me, "Just go in the booth. Deke will talk you through it."

I went somewhat bewildered into the booth, pulling the door behind me. If Preston's Escalade had been a cocoon of quiet on the roads, this was a cocoon of quiet in outer space. The walls were thick with soundproofing panels. There was a single chair with earphones clamped over the backrest, a microphone on a stand, and another microphone hanging from the ceiling. Beyond the thick window, Preston and Deke looked as if they were actors in a silent movie that was playing on the wall.

"Okay, so Riley," Deke drawled, his voice coming from speakers in the ceiling, "you can hear me, right?"

"Yeah," I practically hollered, trying to project my voice through the glass.

"You don't have to shout," Deke said. "We can hear you fine. Just talk normally."

"Okay," I said, feeling naive and ignorant and uncomfortably out of my element.

"Okay, so show us what you've got."

"You mean you want me to sing?" My heart pounded at that prospect. I couldn't sing *a cappella* the way Mose could, not without something else to hide behind.

"Yes, Riley," Preston said impatiently. "That's why we're here."

I could see my reflection in the glass. I had a wavering look verging on panic.

"Uh, can I play my guitar, too?" I asked. Pleaded, really.

"Sure. Go ahead."

Relieved, I unsheathed the Martin Junior, slung the strap over my shoulder, strummed a few cords, but then pulled up short.

"What song do you want me to do?" I asked.

"Anything you want, Riley. This is just a sound check." That was Deke speaking.

"Okay," I said, my thoughts flying through all the songs I knew and not knowing where to land. If I were out on the sidewalk this would be easy, but in here I felt as if I were under a microscope, observed too carefully and closely, any mistake magnifying into incompetence and maybe they'd kick me out and I wouldn't get my thousand dollars after all.

I just stood there nervously thinking, growing more nervous as I watched Preston shake his head and glance at his watch; and I searched for a place that was safe and I saw Mose there on the bridge, his reassuring smile and warm confidence, and I grinned and my shoulders started bouncing and I positioned my fingers for B flat and I sang *Mack the Knife*.

I saw nothing beyond the window, it was a blurred screen, and I sang as if Mose were with me, the sound so pure in that little booth, and the song flowed and I bounced to it, grinning like a carefree little girl and swinging my guitar, and when the final verse came I punched that last word, strummed that last chord, and sent my hand aloft in a high arc of triumph.

Preston was looking at me with widened eyes, while I could clearly see Deke mouth *Wow!* He pressed a button on his console and his voice came in over the speakers.

"That was *great*, Riley. Man, I've never heard that song live before."

"Thanks," I blushed.

The speakers went silent. Beyond the window, I could see Deke speaking earnestly with Preston, then Preston nodded. Deke fiddled with his board, pushing buttons and turning knobs as if he were actually *flying* the Space Shuttle, then he came back on the speakers.

"So hey, Riley, you feel like doing another one?" he asked.

I was still feeling so rarified that I was up for practically anything. "Sure," I said in a breath. "What do you want to hear?"

Preston leaned to Deke's microphone. "Play that one you were doing when I first met you."

My rarified spirits followed gravity to the ground.

"But that's just a poem," I said uneasily. "It's not a real song."

"That doesn't matter. Just do what you can. Let's hear what it sounds like in a studio."

I had to work up the courage to strum the first chord, repeated that a few times while I organized the poem in my mind. It didn't have a title, I hadn't given that any thought yet, I just strummed and hummed until I found it, inside where no one else could see, and then I sang:

Mama told me not to cross the street without looking both ways...

I was completely in my head, while at the same time I could feel the music all around me, as if I were being born from it. I got the tempo just right at the second verse, that urgent 3/4 beat, and I hollered out the lyrics as if I were standing toe to toe with Mama and with my Blaize unleashed:

*And Mama told me
Not to come around
When her door was shut
The towels on the ground...*

And I could feel it in me, as if I were back there again, standing outside of myself and watching it all from a distance.

Mama found out she was pregnant just before Halloween after we'd come down from the mountain, after I'd started the first grade and when we were still living in public housing; and then, as if the Earth had tipped over, we found out that Aunt Joss was pregnant, too.

Mama was her usual self, shrugging it off and not even beginning to bulge yet. Aunt Joss cried a lot, so slender and beautiful then that it seemed she couldn't be the person she came to be. They left us with a neighbor one night and went out, not too long after they'd given us the news, and when they returned in the early hours of the next morning, banging up the stairs and making enough racket to wake the entire place, Aunt Joss was hysterical.

Tommy and I watched wide-eyed from our neighbor's cracked door as Mama angrily fought the lock on our own door across the hallway. Aunt Joss was sobbing, her shoulders heaving, and Mama finally kicked the door open and pulled Aunt Joss inside, closing it with a slam behind them. Tommy and I had both noticed the same thing under the single bare light bulb in the hall ceiling, that Mama's face was badly bruised.

When Mama came to retrieve us later that morning, she was different, harder, short-tempered. She pushed us through the door into our apartment, Tommy holding Robbie because Robbie's squirming and flailing was too much for me to handle. We stood inside our doorway waiting for Mama to tell us what to do, to tell us what happened, but she left us there and went off to her room instead, where we could hear Aunt Joss sobbing out, "*I think he killed him, Blaize. I think he killed him! Oh my God! What are we gonna do now?*"

Mama's door slammed shut after that. Tommy made breakfast for us in a silence so heavy that it was hard to breathe. What followed from then were changes that often left Tommy and me huddling together for comfort, while Robbie began sucking his thumb. Always a fussy baby, I think it was Robbie who got the worst of it, so accustomed to being held and cuddled by Mama that it was too much of a loss for him when she stopped, or perhaps a shock.

I woke up coughing one night and ran to Mama's room so I could sleep with her and feel safe, to find her and Aunt Joss, with almost identical swelling bellies, lying fully clothed on top of the bed, too lethargic to respond to my pleading and stamping, and amid a smell that made my coughing even worse, so I fled back to my bed and coughed alone under the covers. It was around that time that I started finding towels stuffed under Mama's door when I got up at night, and then eventually during the day as well.

Timewall was born while I was still in the first grade. When Mama told me my new little brother's name, with a detached expression that had become normal by then, I bent my brows and went to ask Tommy what kind of name that was but he only shrugged. Lainey came right after that, Aunt Joss seeming not to know what to do, the sore on her lip getting worse, her figure bloated as it would remain from then on.

We moved to the trailer. Tommy and I were both excited at first, as if this big change meant that things would go back to the way they were. Aunt Joss stayed in bed most of the time, while Mama busied herself with taping newspapers in all the windows. We were now clear across town from public housing, so I was surprised to spot Uncle Bates from the school bus window one morning, sitting on a bench just across the railroad tracks next to the help center. He was there one weekend when I went out to breathe better air, mumbling to his feet. He noticed me and waved me over, and I shinnied onto the bench. He didn't smell bad that morning.

"So how are you today, pretty girl?" he asked. His smile seemed to hurt.

"I'm okay."

"And how's your new brother doing?"

I shrugged. "Okay, I guess."

"Hmf." He looked away, clenching his teeth, his jaw muscles throbbing, then asked, "So what does he look like?"

I shrugged again. "He looks like a baby, what else?"

"Does he have dark skin?"

"He has baby skin, Uncle Bates," I said matter-of-factly, as if this should have been self-evident. What a strange thing to ask.

He looked at me pointedly. "And how's your mama?"

"Okay, I guess."

"Hmf. I was there, you know."

"Where?"

"At the Mar—" He seemed to have startled himself, biting his tongue midword. He shook his head. "Nowhere." he said. "Don't listen to an old man."

We sat in silence for a while. I kicked my legs in boredom. Uncle Bates was looking out as if he were seeing something, but there was nothing there except the Sharpe Mart across the street. He shook out of that and said, "You know, I knew your mama when she was about your age."

I jumped in place excitedly.

"You did!"

"Yeah. She was the sweetest little thing, just like you."

I beamed at that praise, and at the comparison.

"If you ever need anything," he said, "you just come find me. Okay?"

"Okay," I said, basking in the warm light of his words.

And I did go to him when I was older, after I found out that Mama was pregnant yet again, but I didn't want to think about this anymore so I changed key to E minor and went into the third verse:

> *Then those better days when Mama shined*
> *With boots and jeans dancing in time*
> *Motors and men and braids so fine*
> *A tooth-missed smile returned in kind...*

I had to work to shake off those darker memories, and some of that surely showed up in my little performance because when I finished the reprise in E minor, with the lines—

But my mama
My mama
She never told me how to love

—both Preston and Deke were standing and giving me silent claps and I had to dab at an eye.

I came out of the booth as if I'd run a mile in the heat, sweat on my brow despite the cool, to a Preston who seemed legitimately impressed and a Deke who made no attempt to withhold his enthusiasm.

"That was amazing, Riley," Deke said with a healthy grin. Preston gave him a look and Deke nodded in return, something unsaid between them.

I set the Martin Junior down and wiped my forehead, wondering what came next, and in barged a man with a graying comb-over who was rounder than he was tall, wearing khakis that strained at his waist, a blue button-down shirt, and brown loafers.

"Hey everybody," he said. "Sorry to hold you up. So where are we at with this?"

"Just finished a sound check, Mr. Albert," Deke said.

"And...?" The man, Mr. Albert, had yet to look at me.

"And it went pretty well," Preston said.

"Good."

Mr. Albert turned to me then, scrutinizing me as if I were a plastic-wrapped package of ground beef in the meat department. I thought he might reach out and poke me to see if I was fresh. Fortunately for him he didn't.

"So you're the girl," he said, not as a question.

"Yeah, I guess I am," I answered, bristling a little at his manner.

"Hmm." He looked me up and down once more. "I detect a little mountain-hollow hillbilly in your voice."

"Yeah, so what?" I bit back, the red creeping into my vision.

"So you're no Loretta Lynn," he said haughtily, "so lose the hick accent."

And the red exploded in a Blaize of heat.

chapter ten

......

THE ONLY THING MAMA would have done that I didn't do was curse and punch the man in the face; but while I didn't use curse words, I did use some close approximations.

When I came down from all that, my vision clearing and a little rationality trickling back into my brain, I realized that I'd just Blaized it all away. There would be no thousand dollars now, no bus ticket by the end of the week. I would have crumpled on the spot if I weren't preparing myself for the inevitable counterattack. Deke was laughing hysterically, not at me but at Mr. Albert, while Preston looked as if he'd just walked in front of a hurtling manure wagon.

I got myself under control in a hurry and readied myself for the next round, focusing on Mr. Albert, my nostrils flaring, but he only stood there chuckling smugly, which about lit me up again all by itself.

"You found a feisty one, Preston," Mr. Albert said, his eyes locked on me with an infuriating glint that I almost reached out and knocked into next week. "I like that in a girl. We have a signed contract, yes?"

That question wasn't meant for me.

"Yeah, Albert, we do," Preston said.

"Then go get her dressed up and let's see what else she can do." Mr. Albert threw me a parting chuckle and left the room.

"Jesus Christ, Riley!" Preston blurted, either awed or horrified.

"My name's Ridley!" I hurled back at him.

"Not if you want a thousand dollars it's not. So c'mon, then." He started for the door.

"Where are we going?"

"To get you in costume."

"*Costume?*"

"Yeah, that's right."

"Why do I need to wear a costume?"

"Because I know you're right for this but you still have to audition."

"You mean I have to audition for that fat man?"

"Yes, Riley," he answered in exasperation, "you have to audition for that fat man."

He led me back out into the tobacco shed, and then through chalky corridors that triggered unsettling memories. My throat tickled and I stifled a cough.

We stopped at a gray steel door that opened on a room crowded with clothing of all kinds, seeming to occupy every chink, rod, and lip that a clothes hanger could hang from. There were makeup stations and mirrors on one wall, everything else a crowded cavern of colorful clothing.

"Yours are there on the middle station," Preston pointed. "So get changed and I'll be waiting outside."

I walked to my station, lifted what was to be my costume, and exclaimed in disbelief, "These aren't clothes! These aren't even a swimsuit!"

Preston slumped and turned back. "That's the costume for the video, Riley," he said wearily.

"*Video?*"

"Yeah, of course. You've seen a music video before, haven't you?"

"Well yeah, but—"

"So now you're in the music business and videos are part of it. It's in your contract. That's just the way it is."

Preston left the room while I gaped after him. My costume comprised red-sequined short shorts that showed more cheek than I could have seen if I'd stood naked looking over my shoulder into a mirror; bikini bottoms would have covered more. The satiny pearl, tissue-thin top would have been less than a bra if not for the long sleeves, like something people put on their poor dogs. The top did have some strategic extra stitching around the bust, otherwise I might have been better off just walking into the audition naked.

The worst were the platform shoes, which were also pearl and were held on by straps, more like clunky sandals than actual shoes, with a heel that sort of thrust me forward and off balance. I'd never worn heels—ever—and didn't know how I could possibly cross the room in them let alone stand without turning an ankle and falling in a heap.

A thousand dollars. A thousand dollars.

How much indignity was worth a thousand dollars? How much indignity was California worth? What would Mama have done? Mama would have told me, "There ain't nothin' worth givin' yurself over to like that, 'cause if ya git in ya might cain't be able ta git back out."

But Mama wasn't here, I wasn't Mama, and I wanted that thousand dollars. Mere days from now, when I was on a bus bound for California, soaking in all that Arizona canyon country you see in Westerns, I wouldn't look back at this and laugh because I probably wouldn't be giving it a second thought.

I came out awkwardly in those platform shoes, afraid of tripping and falling, my legs seeming to be pushing up into my behind. I couldn't imagine how any woman would like dressing in something like this, but apparently *all* men liked it, a good enough reason not to do it. Mama told me right before I left, her expression brittle although she would never have admitted it, in words that made me cringe and beg her to stop, that men would do anything we asked to get what they wanted. I wanted to fling those words off my fingers like mud, but I now knew they were absolutely true by the way Preston was looking at me. I could see it in his face, in his eyes—in that moment, I could have made him do anything.

"You look amazing, Riley," he said with a certain airy desire that proved the point.

"Why didn't you all just ask me to sing naked?" I groused.

"Because that would give the show away," he said. "So let's get on back so you can clinch this deal."

I handed him the Martin Junior.

"You carry this," I said. "I'm afraid I'll fall and break it."

Deke was fiddling with a video camera when we returned to the sound room. Mr. Albert was sitting in a chair, a knee crossed, looking me up and down as if I were modeling lingerie, pausing at those places he had no business even thinking about.

"So what we're going to do, Riley," Deke explained while adjusting a last something, "is tape you while you sing. This isn't for the video, but so that Mr. Albert can see what you look like on the playback. Okay?"

"Okay," I said with some trepidation. "Do I get to play my guitar again?"

"No, not this time."

An icy streak rushed from my temples all the way down to my barely-covered—well, you know. Deke noticed my discomfort and gave me a supportive smile.

"Don't worry," he said. "You'll have headphones on so you can hear the music. Here are the lyrics." He handed me a sheet of paper. "The parts we need you to sing are highlighted. Easy, right?"

"Yeah, okay," I answered dully. He winked.

"You'll be okay. I promise."

I went clumsily into the booth, put the headphones on and took my position, trying to concentrate on the lyrics I was supposed to sing, the chill air raising goose bumps on my bare legs. Deke's voice came over the headphones.

"So listen, Riley," he said in what seemed a disembodied whisper. I found myself leaning forward as if to hear him through the window. "The song is three twelve. I'm going to run it through for you so you can hear what it's doing, and then on the next pass we'll add your voice. Okay?"

"Yeah, okay."

"So here it goes."

It was a slow to medium tempo Country song, three chords and the truth. All I had to do was sing *drinkin all night, drinkin' all day* at just the right times while the male vocalist (who sounded like Tim McGraw but wasn't him) spilled out his sappy love woes, then I joined the chorus at the end and that was it. Considering the lyrics, I couldn't imagine how my ridiculous costume would make any sense in the video, but then music videos seldom did what I thought they should, especially for songs that I liked.

I nodded to Deke that I had it, so he started the song again. It really wasn't a bad song, kind of sad in a way, steady guitar work, a lot of emotion. I was swaying to it, no bouncing around, just a soft, silky sway, like sea grass in a gentle current. There wasn't much else to do. I was still swaying when the song ended and Deke's voice came through the headphones.

"Okay, that's it, Riley. We're good. You can come on out now."

Mr. Albert was studying a screen closely when I came shivering out, hugging my arms, and only then did I realize that if he didn't like my performance I wouldn't be getting my thousand dollars. I loathed the man, but it was all up to him. Just like that, I'd given him power over me, with nothing I could do to get it back.

Preston was looking down over Mr. Albert's shoulder. "I think it works," Preston said.

"Yeah, it does..." Mr. Albert trailed off; and then he snapped to and stood. "Yeah, it works." He directed that to Preston. "Get her back here in the morning and we'll start laying tracks."

And just like that he busied himself out the door.

"Good work," Deke said to me. "I knew you had it."

That was a compliment and I took it that way, but the whole thing seemed such overkill.

"But I didn't really do anything," I protested. "Anybody could have done that."

"That's where you're wrong," Preston said with a relieved smile. "So go get dressed and I'll drive you home."

We didn't broach the home topic again until I was back in real clothes and sitting in the Escalade.

"So where to?" Preston asked.

"Oh, just drop me on Broadway," I answered casually, or what I hoped sounded casual.

He looked at me skeptically. "Riley, you're not homeless are you?"

"No!" I sputtered as if flabbergasted. "I have a home."

And that wasn't a lie. I did have a home, one that was mostly okay except on rainy days.

"Then tell me where it is so I can take you there. And I have to pick you up in the morning, too. Remember?"

"Well, uh..."

"Jesus—you *are* homeless, aren't you."

He was shaking his head now, as if he should have guessed or even assumed. I thought about having him drop me at Sherri's house, to tell him that's where I lived, but that would have made it hard to be on time in the morning. I wasn't ashamed of anything, I just didn't want him thinking of me as a charity case.

"Only kind of," I said, the only thing I could think to say.

"So look." He was tapping the steering wheel, focused ahead. "This isn't my first rodeo. I get it. And you're too proud for your own good, so I'm going to drive you to a hotel where we have an account, and if you want to stay there you can, and if you don't you can walk to Broadway yourself. Just be back when I come to get you in the morning. That sound okay?"

"Yeah, that's okay," I said, relieved to be done with it.

"Okay, then."

The hotel was tall, and just up from Printers Alley. I looked over nostalgically as we drove past my little alcove, as if it had been years since I'd sat there to play. Preston pulled up to the curb in front of the broad lobby doors, threw it in park and killed the engine. It was still pretty early in the day, bright beyond the canopy, plenty of time to perhaps busk a few dollars and find something to eat. The popular pancake place would be closed—too bad—but the other one would be open, the pancakes dripping with butter and syrup. I could already feel that buttery syrup sliding down my throat, sighing at the anticipation of it.

Preston cracked his door. "I'll help you get checked in," he said, which startled me back to the present.

"Uh," I mumbled stupidly.

Preston just smiled. "We have an account here, Riley. It won't cost you anything."

"But—"

"And I'd rather have you here in the morning where I know you'll be instead of wherever else, because if something happens, how am I supposed to find you?"

There was too much logic in that to object, and he said it wouldn't cost me anything, so why not?

"Okay," I said.

Preston took care of everything at the front desk, handing me a card key and pointing to the elevators. A porter wanted to carry my daypack and the Martin Junior, but I rebuffed him clumsily. Why would he want to carry my daypack and guitar when I could obviously do it myself?

"Eight o'clock," Preston said. "Right here, okay? Tomorrow's going to be a long day for you, so get some rest."

"Okay," I said a bit sheepishly.

"I'll see you in the morning, then. Bye."

And he left, taking with him my worry that he'd want to go up to the room with me.

The porter pressed the elevator button for my floor, good thing because I'd never been in an elevator. And I'd never stayed in a hotel, not even a motel. All I knew about any of this was what I'd seen on TV, which is the only reason I knew to slide my card into the door lock at my room. Honestly, I wouldn't have figured it out otherwise.

The room was bright and plush, with a view toward that Batman building. The bed would have filled my room back home, and I couldn't figure out how to turn the TV on. The bathroom was as big as half of Mama's trailer, with towels so thick and soft that I could have sewn them into winter clothes. The water came out hot enough to make steam, and there were soaps, shampoos, and a hair dryer. It was a fantasy world that I'd never experienced, never imagined, so lush that I giggled inwardly.

I went to the window, pulled the gauzy drapes and stood staring way down, where I could see some of the places I'd set up to play, but I was too high to make out whether anyone was down there playing right now. The towels smelled so good. I was hugging one to my chest, breathing it in, and I felt like a princess in a high castle, that I could just wave my hand and the whole world would see me.

And Mama would be invisible.

······

I FOUND OUT LATER that evening, after some awkward questioning and with my stomach growling anxiously, that the food was free as well, so when I came down the next morning I made straight for the restaurant. I felt fully confident now, having explored every floor of that hotel last night, and with skin so fresh and clean that it squeaked. I sat to breakfast and ate all I could, assuming that this would be my last opportunity to eat this well for a while.

I had my daypack and the Martin Junior with me, ready to go do what I had to do then get my thousand dollars and board that bus. I was wearing my jeans and black jacket, freshly laundered by the hotel and smelling as nice as the towels upstairs. Preston frowned when I met him out front.

"You going somewhere?" he asked, eyes darting to my daypack, my guitar, my jeans.

"Yeah, to sing that song and get my thousand dollars."

"Oh, okay, I understand," he nodded. "So look, it won't all be done after today. You still have the video to do and some publicity stuff."

"*What?*"

"It's exactly what I told you when I met you." He turned and pointed up a street. "Right over there as a matter of fact. A few days. That's what you signed up for."

"You said a few days in the studio, not all this other stuff. I'm supposed to sing that song while you all do your video, then you pay me and I get to go."

Preston chuckled as if to a naive child. I had to work hard to keep the red out of my eyes, but then he came back in a placating voice and said, "This is all new to you, Riley. I know. Today you're going to lay those tracks. Then you'll come back here, and tomorrow they'll start shooting the video. A few days, right? That means three, maybe four, but that should do it."

"You're going to bring me back here?"

"Yeah—well, not me but a driver will."

"Why not you?"

"Because I'm working with other people, too. And because, well, after I take you to the studio this morning, my part of this is over."

"What does that mean?"

"It means that I found you, got you through your audition, and now it's all up to you. Albert's the producer. He'll give you your schedule and arrange for transportation. There's nothing else for me to do."

Something about this bothered me as we drove to the studio, the route still so confusing that I didn't know where we were. He'd told me the truth—that much I accepted—but the future that would roll out after he left seemed a maze of uncertainty. He dropped me at the Gray Place but didn't get out.

"Go get 'em, Riley," he said through his window. "And good luck."

And then he sped away.

I stood outside the rust-streaked door, uncertainty now gnawing at me. It was going to be another nice day, I had all my things, and I could just turn around and walk away. But why? What was I afraid of? I could take care of myself with that misogynist Mr. Albert. It was the unknown that stirred in my stomach, an unknown world that I didn't know how to navigate. Preston knew, and I'd grown to trust him, even as I could see Mama wagging her finger in my mind.

You trust people too much, Ridley.

Yeah, Mama, but you had to trust someone, even if only the guy who sets the traffic lights, otherwise you'd never be able to get across the street.

I went inside.

Deke and Mr. Albert were there, no one else. And I didn't have to wear that skimpy costume this time, I just had to drop my things, go in the booth, and sing my parts of the song.

I thought it went great after the first take but Mr. Albert said otherwise—and then through take after take until my throat was sore and I could tell that Mr. Albert was losing patience out there. I tried not to concentrate on him but on the microphone in front of me, singing when I was supposed to, instinctively inflecting my voice from one take to the next in hope of stumbling into whatever it was he wanted.

We broke for lunch—sandwiches from a machine—then came back and went at it again; and then late enough in the afternoon that my feet were aching and my voice was barely a hoarse whisper, Mr. Albert proclaimed that he'd found what he was after and I dropped into a chair and fought to stay awake. He had a driver take me back to the hotel, where I was too weary to even go to the restaurant. I went straight up to my room, drew a hot bath, and got in bed after that, the day waning beyond those gauzy curtains.

·······

I WAS IN THE RESTAURANT the next morning when a different driver came in and hollered, "*Riley Skye?*"

I was eating pancakes and not paying enough attention to recognize a name that wasn't my own.

"*Riley Skye?*" he hollered a second time, loud enough to draw every eye in the place, including mine.

"Oh yeah, that's me," I said, hurrying a last bite. "Sorry."

He led me out to a European sedan, gunmetal gray, had me sit in the back seat, and did not help me angle the Martin Junior in.

We took the interstate south, past shopping malls that occupied more acreage than Bilbo, and on into rolling hills, exiting onto a back highway that wound between groomed pastures and stands of trees. He eventually turned into a long gravel drive that ran Only Street-straight between columns of mature maples, ending at a circle drive in front of a modern mansion, where he let me out. There was no one in sight.

"Do I go in that house?" I asked him dubiously.

"No," he answered, pulling the shifter into drive. "The shoot's around back."

He pulled out, crunching through gravel that sounded a lot smoother than our Bilbo gravel, leaving me standing there with my guitar and daypack as if I'd been dropped at a dusty four-way intersection in the middle of nowhere.

I wandered dazed around that huge house, seeming to encounter another extension of it after every turn, wondering if I'd wander my way into Mississippi before I found the back of the place; but at last I made a final turn and saw spreading out before me what looked like nothing less than a disturbed ant hill.

The mansion didn't have a backyard, it had back *acreage*, as smooth and green as a golf course, and flowing around a pond that was more of a small lake, finally catching up against dense woods in the distance; and between me and that pond were men in black T-shirts, dozens of them, hauling equipment cases, laying cable, hanging truss, setting up lights, and rolling out enough gaffer tape to entomb the state capitol.

I looked for anyone even remotely familiar, but couldn't seem to separate individuals from that dizzying confusion of stagehands. I spotted some trailers off to my right. The people near them weren't wearing black T-shirts, so I went that way. I thought I'd at least spot Mr. Albert, but I didn't see him, just knots of people talking as if all this were somehow under control. Over at the pond, a smooth-faced guy in boots and a white cowboy hat was walking eyes down along the water's edge as if deep in thought. He looked no older than me, just a kid, really. I didn't recognize him, but assumed he was the male vocalist I'd sung along with the day before.

"Riley Skye?" a man with a clipboard asked.

"Yeah, that's me."

He was eyeing my guitar and daypack, seeming displeased for some reason. "Why'd you bring that?" he asked.

"Because I wanted to," I answered, trying to keep my voice level but a little Blaize did slip out.

He rolled his eyes. "Whatever," he said. "You're in that trailer over there. Go get in costume and meet me under that tent right over there. Can you do that for me, honey?"

He was a slim man, craggy face and he needed a shave, and I could have put him on his behind with one flying kick. He laughed when he saw what was in my eyes, then quickly went off to bother someone else.

There were five girls in the trailer, all of us with the same kind of hair and looks, and in various stages of undress, although our ridiculous costumes did little to remedy that. My costume was lying there with my name on it, or rather Riley's name. I sighed, found a place to park the Martin Junior, discretely drew the knife from my boot and slipped it into the zippered pouch on the gig bag, then got to it.

A woman came in to mess with our hair and makeup, then led us outside to the tent, where we stood like a hapless cheerleading squad waiting for someone to tell us what to do. None of the girls was talkative, each as sullen as a midnight store clerk. I found myself edging away from them just to add a little distance, just a foot or two back so that I wouldn't catch whatever they had.

The man with the clipboard came bounding over. "Okay, you're up," he said. "Follow me."

He arranged us in a tight group at one end of the pond, where we were instructed to smile and look virginal and sing our lines when we were cued, the smooth-faced boy ambling slowly along the water's edge, kicking at rocks and singing his song.

"drinkin' all night, drinkin' all day," we sang together in take after take until we were all grouchy and snarking at each other, and then we broke for lunch. Thank goodness.

There was a buffet set up under one tent. I nibbled and kept my distance, and suddenly recognized one of the girls.

"Hey, I saw you singing on Broadway," I said excitedly, thinking that maybe this would break the ice and then things wouldn't be so tense.

She turned to me with a dismissive look. "No you didn't," she said, and that was that.

I don't know how to describe how bizarre all of this was, or how desperate I was to get it over with. I felt like a fox in a leg trap, prepared to chew off my own limb to get away from those people.

We resumed after lunch, the same thing over and over, take after take, while I was certain that our first take was surely good enough. None of us knew what they wanted. Maybe more teeth, more energy, more jiggle—and jiggle is probably what it was, so we had to find some way to all jiggle at just the right time if we were ever going to be done with it.

"Okay, that's got it," someone hollered, and we all slumped in relief.

It was mid-afternoon by then. A man in jeans and a blue windbreaker gestured toward a van. He had heavy brows, and dark eyes that seemed bored with it all.

"Go get in," he said. "We're leaving soon."

"Aren't we going to change first?" one of the girls asked.

"Not now. Later."

"That's bullsh—," the girl mouthed back.

"Just do what he says," another girl muttered in resignation.

The other girls were all in the van now, and I hadn't made up my mind yet.

"Get in, get in," the heavy-browed man ordered me in a tone that had me grinding my teeth.

"Are you taking us back now?" I asked.

"No, I'm taking you to the after party," he said with annoyed impatience.

"I don't want to go to a party," I came back defiantly.

"Too bad. Check your contract. No party, no pay."

"*What?*"

"It's in your contract, girl, so let's go."

I couldn't think quickly enough to make sense of this. "Where's my guitar?"

"In the back of the van. Just get in."

"I want to see it."

"We don't have all day, girl."

"I want to see it now!"

"Just get in, would you?" He pushed me in the small of my back, his sweaty hand on my bare skin, and I spun around, a single breath from hammering his nose into his skull. He saw me clearly, knew exactly what I was about to do. He stepped back.

"Okay, girl, it's your call," he said as if he were reasoning with a rebellious teen. "Get in and get paid, or walk home broke. What's it going to be?"

"C'mon, let's just go," one of the girls whined from inside.

Something was wrong. Every instinct was screaming at me to grab my guitar and bolt for the woods right now.

"Where is this party?" I asked, feeling the heat of my breath.

"It's downtown, and we're going to hit traffic if we don't get moving—or you can walk if that's what you prefer, but we're going."

He went around and climbed in behind the wheel, started the engine and pulled it into drive. The van crunched forward a few inches while I stood there with one hand on the door trying to decide what to do; and then, still undecided, deriding myself but with no clear alternative, I jumped inside

chapter eleven

......

THERE WAS A TENSE SILENCE in the van as we made our way back to Nashville, as if everyone knew something that I didn't. I kept rising from my seat, trying to get a look over the two girls in the back to see if the Martin Junior was really there, grasping for any handhold as I was bounced around, sometimes banging my head on the ceiling. There was so much stuff crammed in the back that I couldn't tell. I was too anxious to sit still. My chest felt hollow.

"Hey, could one of you all look back there and tell me if you see a guitar?" I asked those girls. "It'll be in a black gig bag."

One of the girls made a half-hearted attempt to look over her shoulder, then turned back and shrugged. The other was gazing through the window as if she'd tuned out the world.

"Why don't you just sit the f—down?" the girl next to me muttered. It was the girl I'd recognized but who'd claimed otherwise.

I set my teeth. "Why don't you just mind your own business?"

She glowered at me. The guy with the Neanderthal brows flicked a sharp glance in the rear view.

"You think you're special, don't you," the girl said mockingly, "making a scene like you're better than us or something?" She laughed and looked away, then said over her shoulder, "You'll find out soon enough."

"What are you talking about?" a girl behind us asked. She had an apprehensive look on her face, eyes that couldn't quite settle on anything.

"Nothing," the girl beside me mumbled. "Just nothing."

We continued on, howling up the interstate then creeping through traffic, the strong odor of car exhaust coming into the van. I coughed and swallowed and cupped a hand over my nose. Finally, the low sun burnishing us from the left, then behind us as we rounded an exit ramp, we pulled up to a hotel that wasn't in downtown proper but on the other side of a loop of freeways.

The moment brow man opened our door, I leapt out and ran around back for the Martin Junior. The relief I felt when I found it there was like nothing I'd ever experienced, as if I'd been weighted underwater and had just managed to free myself and come up for air. I had it over my back and my daypack on my shoulder before the last girl was even out of the van.

"You can't take those inside," brow man said in a disparaging tone that ground like glass in my ears.

"Why not?" I barked back, and I could feel the red rising. I glanced at his knees, figured I could side-step and take out the left knee easily.

And then what, though?

"It's a security thing," he answered, a little less smug, stepping back perhaps unconsciously. "Nobody can take bags in, and especially not anything as big as that gig bag."

"I'm not leaving my guitar," I half growled, fed up with insolent attitudes and people telling me what I could and could not do.

"So we're back to that again." he said dismissively. "Look, girl—it's the same as before. If you don't go in, you don't get paid. And you can't take your guitar in with you, so you either leave it here in the van or you start walking, your call. And I need to get in there so I'm going to lock this door, and once it's locked I'm not unlocking it again until we leave. So what's it gonna be?"

I stood hovering in indecision again, simply unable to reconcile my roiling instincts with my vision of being free and on that bus, all of this behind me and forgotten.

"Okay, darn it," I said in a huff. Brow man wisely did not chuckle or even smile.

"Okay," he said. "It's locked up right here. It's safe. So let's get inside."

This hotel was as fancy as the one Preston had put me in, but a different kind of fancy, less about personal accommodation than commercial accommodation. We strode quickly across the lobby, then down a carpeted ramp to some doors that said *Ballroom*. The other girls were already out of sight.

"This is it," brow man said. "Just go through those doors."

"What about you?" I asked.

"I'm not dressed for it. And anyway, I'm not on the guest list."

He spun on his heel and left, while I looked at that door in doubt. A gray-suited man with a square jaw and the heavy build of a football player opened the door and waved me in—and inside was another of those rarified worlds I knew only from movies. Men in tuxedos, women in evening gowns, crystal lighting, and crisp waiters carrying drinks on silver trays. I became acutely conscious that amid this opulence, I was dressed in what wouldn't pass for underwear.

I walked stiffly through this, covering myself down there with my cupped hands. The men looked and leered, some appreciatively, most lewdly. The women seemed unamused. A waiter appeared at my side carrying a tray with a single glass.

"Your drink, ma'am," he said.

I looked at him as if I were in a stupor, too dazed by everything to interact with anyone.

"Uh-uh," I shook my head.

His fake smile fell, but then he nodded and took off. I spotted the other girls across the way, each with a drink in her hand and flashing teeth at the well-dressed men who'd gathered around them. I wanted nothing to do with those girls but couldn't think of anything else, so I weaved their way.

"Ah, here she is," one of the men said. "Number six."

I looked for Mr. Albert but didn't see him. I did recognize the faces of a few male Country stars, some wearing black cowboy hats, and boots that shined like patent leather, their wives or girlfriends in glittering gowns.

"You need a drink," the man said gaily, raising his hand for a waiter.

The same waiter who'd offered me the drink earlier materialized at my side, and again dropped his smile when I declined. The man who'd signaled actually frowned, but then seemed to shake that off, turning his attention elsewhere.

I stood there stupidly as furtive eyes probed every part of me. I just stood there, conversation flooding all around me, the other girls downing their drinks and looking for more, flirting with the men, some hanging on the men's arms. Someone squeezed my behind and I flicked my hand back like a horse's tail, spun around but couldn't make out the culprit. No one was talking to me or even trying to. I felt naked and dizzy, beyond dazed, and wished to the core of my being that I had the Martin Junior on my back, at least some armor between me and them.

There was a low stage across the way, backed by gold filigree curtains. The smooth-faced boy from the video was there, adjusting a microphone. Someone handed him an acoustic guitar, which he hung over his shoulder like an ornament.

"Okay, girls," a man said over the din, taking the glass from one of the girls. "Get on up there."

He meant the stage, which apparently meant that we were expected to go up there and sing background for the smooth-faced boy, which would in turn expose our nearly naked bodies to the scrutiny of every eye in the place.

We were herded up there as if we were farm animals meant to be milked or bred or slaughtered for supper, clumsy in our platform shoes, each of us skipping and stumbling to keep up. They arranged us as they had for the video, well off to the side, where we stood being visually molested while our microphone was set up.

The lights dimmed and I exhaled in relief, just that little bit of cover for my waning dignity. Some of the girls seemed woozy now, tottering in their ridiculous shoes. One of them put a hand on my shoulder for support. And then a spotlight snapped on, blinding in my eyes, and the smooth-faced boy started his croon; and when our time came we sang our lines as if by rote—*drinkin' all day, drinkin' all night*—some of the girls just barely mouthing along but the rest of us carried them and I guess it sounded all right.

The applause was deafening when it was done, the smooth-faced boy taking a bow and then shaking hands as he left the stage. The lights came up and there we still stood, a practically naked ensemble left on display while glasses clinked and conversation flowed again, with no one telling us where to go or what to do now.

The red caught up with my humiliation. I began to see busted lips and broken noses out there among those pretty, entitled people. I could feel the raw savagery and righteous retribution of it, my blood warming, my nostrils flaring. I wanted my money and I wanted my guitar, and I was perfectly able, willing, and ready to beat them out of the next man I caught probing my crotch with his eyes. And it was enough, I tell you. Enough! I made fists and was about to leap off the stage and wade through them like so many drunken rednecks when a portly man—not Mr. Albert—hurried apologetically on stage.

"Sorry, girls," he said. "There's so much to keep up with tonight." He caught the look in my eyes and flinched. "Okay—so." He quickly looked away. "We have a smaller gathering for you upstairs. Just come with me."

The girls filed after him while I stood my ground. He looked back at me and seemed confounded.

"I want my guitar and my money," I said with my fists still bunching.

"Oh, for God's sake," the girl from next to me on the bus complained, rolling her eyes.

"Soon," the man said, seeming harried. "You've just got this one last thing to do."

"Don't tell me," I said sarcastically. "It's in the contract, right?"

"Yeah, it is. But this is it. Really. So c'mon. Please?"

My teeth ached, I'd ground them so hard, but I fought back against the red and followed along, having come this far. Just get it over with, get my money, and get gone. Those were the thoughts that sustained me.

We entered an elevator, just us and the portly man, which carried us past floor after floor into the heights of the hotel, dispensing us in a dimly lit, semi-circular room with a bank of curving windows that looked out on the city lights of Nashville.

It was well after dark now. I had no idea the time or how long we'd actually been at this. I had to pause to let my eyes adjust. Gradually I began to make out small round tables, each with a low flickering light on it, and plush two-person booths arranged around a small, spotlighted half-moon stage in front of the windows.

The man waved us toward the stage so we went. Now I could make out people at those tables and in those booths, couples mainly, men and women dressed as richly as those downstairs; then we were on the stage, that spotlight in my eyes, and I felt dizzy at that height, as if I might fall backward out those windows. We just stood there under the spotlight.

Low mood music was playing over speakers. I didn't see any microphones, any sound equipment. Perhaps we were meant to sing, but sing what, *drinkin' all day, drinkin' all night*? That made no sense.

One of the girls stumbled and had to be held up by another, who herself seemed woozy enough to topple. This was like a lounge, then, I guessed, unobtrusive waiters quietly serving drinks. I tried to make out faces. There were no more than twenty people out there, mostly couples, but I could make out men sitting singly at some of the tables.

The girls were swaying on their feet, making me dizzier still, what with those windows and the heights beyond, visible out the corner of my eye. My mind reeled, dizzy, displaced from my body, and I began to make out details in a spinning confusion, as if I were twirling and seeing something new each time I came around. Over there, a man and a woman kissing deeply, and there, a man with his hand between a woman's legs, and there—

A man with a dark complexion and severe eyes came forward and waved one of the girls to him, and she went, drunkenly it seemed, and he sat in his booth and she dropped to her knees and her head bobbed; and then another man came up and took another girl, who yanked back weakly but was drug off anyway. Soon I was alone on that stage, overwhelmed, thinking none of this could be real.

The girl who'd sat beside me on the bus was straddling a man while he fondled her breasts. And a man over there had a girl cupped in his hand, working his fingers as if on a fretboard while her back arched and her naked breasts rose and fell, and I felt sick to my stomach now that I understood, and a man reached out and took me by my left wrist.

"Come on, baby," he said in a voice that sounded foreign.

I looked down at him as if detached from myself, disbelieving that anyone would dare touch me, let alone grab me that way.

"Come on!" he ordered this time, giving my wrist a jerk.

And a dam burst, releasing a red tide that gushed forth in a furious instant. I yanked back, grabbed his wrist, twisted hard, then rammed my palm in and broke his arm at the elbow. The cracking joint was loud enough to startle everyone to attention.

He howled as if he'd just been castrated. I kicked him in the chest, sending him backward into the girl with the bobbing head, who stood and screamed. All around me there was activity, the spotlight still bright in my eyes, and I kicked out of those sorry shoes and sprinted for the elevator, pounding the button, all kinds of commotion at my back, tables and chairs screeching, women screaming, men cursing.

The elevator door opened and I dove in, frantically stabbing at buttons, a man coming at me as the doors closed, making them slide open again, and I hopped on my left leg and kicked him in the face with my bare right foot, maybe breaking a nose but not skin, then the doors closed and the elevator dropped.

The doors slid open at some unknown floor. I didn't wait or even think. I bolted out into a carpeted hallway, passing the richly-varnished doors of ornate suites, and then around a corner, where something slammed into the side of my head and I can remember hitting the floor but nothing else.

······

I AWOKE ON A COLD hard floor in the dark, with a painful knot above my left temple, as if a nail had been hammered into my skull. I lifted myself onto hands and knees, hissing at a sharp ache that seemed to project from behind my left eye. I blinked in the darkness, breathed evenly until the pain slid further back and wasn't as obvious, then sat up on folded legs, grasping for any clue, any scrap of understanding about where I was, why it was dark, and why my head ached so badly.

It came to me gradually, in snippets of memory, just a flash here and there that I eventually weaved into a clearer picture. We had been on that stage. They were making the girls do things. A man grabbed me. I ran. Something hit me in the head...

The ache wasn't as sharp now, more of a throb. I reached out tentatively and felt close walls all around me. I lifted my hands above my head and stood, my hands jangling into something while I was still half stooped over. I felt carefully, traced forms with my fingers. They were empty clothes hangers on a rod, no question. I was in a closet, then. I reached blindly forward, colorful pricks of color sparking in my vision, found a doorknob and tried to turn it. The door was locked. I pushed against it, a metal door cold on my shoulder and too solid to budge. I ran my fingers down to the floor, to the narrow gap beneath the door, wide enough only for the tips of my fingers. No light was coming through, so whatever was on the other side was dark as well.

I explored the interior with greater care, running my fingers over every inch of surface, and found nothing but flat walls. I tried to dislodge the rod that held the clothes hangers, but it was anchored solidly. The clothes hangers had metal loops around the rod, so they were of no use to me. There was nothing else I could do. I sat and waited for whatever might come next.

It's eerie the way time passes in the dark. You have no sense of it. Hours perhaps, or maybe only minutes. Or maybe even days. I needed to pee, that's all I knew. My eyes found light as if they were desperate for it, those pricks of color, like a winking starry sky wherever I turned my head; and with concentration I could make them move, form patterns and images, and this whiled away whatever time there was.

I peed in a corner then scuttled away, too humiliated to bear it, waiting in dread for the pool to spread out and find me but it didn't. I stayed pressed in the opposite corner, hugging my knees, waiting, the pricks of light the same whether my eyes were opened or closed; and then I couldn't tell whether my eyes *were* opened or closed without reaching up to touch them.

A band of blinding light shot through from beneath the door, jerking my attention to it as if to water in a burning desert. It was as if I could feel the light, feel its warmth. I could see my toes now, found them oddly surreal, as if not attached to the rest of me. I held my hands down and saw my fingers, and I smiled at the marvel of it, then the door opened and it was as if the sun had exploded in my face.

I was handled roughly, trying to shield my eyes while being jerked along, the floor beneath my feet bare cement, through doors one after another that clunked solidly when they closed, finally into a room with cheap wood paneling and a single curtained window and I was pushed into a chair.

Someone was behind me, pressing down on my shoulders, the grip strong, like iron. I could see better now. The room was nondescript, a tired wooden desk and chair, a standing lamp, nothing else.

I found my voice.

"Let me go," I said in a growl. I didn't struggle against that grip, I didn't have the strength for it, but every muscle in my body was tensing like a spring, preparing to uncoil at the first opportunity.

"Oh, I don't think so, girl," a man's throaty voice said. "We've seen what you can do. Was that some kind of kung fu sh— or what?"

I didn't answer, I seethed. I felt my blood heating from my teeth to my toes, that dull room taking on a red patina. The door clunked open behind us, then clunked closed, footsteps coming around, a chair scraping across the floor, then parked in front of me. A man sat—and it was him! Brow man from the van! I bit down hard to control myself, my breaths coming hard and hot.

"Where's my guitar?" I growled.

"You should be more worried about yourself," he said with an air of disregard.

"You should be more worried that I'm not worried."

He laughed as if he couldn't believe what he'd just heard. "You talk big for a chick in a chair, you know that?"

"And you talk big for a guy who's about to get his butt kicked by a girl."

He laughed again, shaking his head. "Man, where are you even *from*?"

"I'm from the mountains."

"Which mountains?"

"The *only* mountains."

He didn't know what to make of that. I craned my head left and right, trying to take more in, and there I saw it, the Martin Junior in the gig bag, parked against a wall beyond my left shoulder, my daypack right beside it. My knife was in that bag, the knife Mama gave me when I was thirteen. She told me that she carried it when I was born, and that I should have it now. There was nothing special about it, just a hunting knife with a green paracord handle, but I'd held on to it all these years as if it contained a secret history, as if it might be etched with my true origins. If I could reach it somehow, these men would learn how a deer felt when it was hung and gutted. But I couldn't reach it, so whatever happened next was up to me. Blaize wouldn't be a part of it.

"You caused us a lot of trouble, Riley," brow man said, dropping the mirth and getting serious.

"My name's Ridley," I spat at him.

"I don't give a sh— what your name is!" he came back hard. "There are some pissed off people out there who want a piece of you, so here's what we're going to do."

He stood and came toward me, forcing my legs apart with his knees, standing there between my bare spread-eagled legs, those shorts doing nothing to conceal my private parts, and he grinned down on me and I glared back.

Sex wasn't what he wanted or he would have already taken it. He wanted power over me—but that wasn't going to happen. I thought quickly. I could lock my legs around his knees, maybe get him on the ground, but those hands on my shoulders were too firm and unyielding. Maybe I could kick back from his body, knock the chair over and get free that way. I pushed back against that grip on my shoulders, felt as if I were pushing against concrete. I relaxed my shoulders, perhaps I could slip out that way, roll fast and make it to my knife, but those hands came down even harder, compressing me in place.

Brow man was wearing the kind of smile that leaves cuts and bruises. He went to the desk. "This will get you in line," he said. "It always does."

He came back with that smile, and he revealed a syringe in his hand.

"I'm going to shoot you up," he grinned. "And I'm going to shoot you up again tomorrow, and I'm going to keep shooting you up until you're on your knees begging for it. And then I'm going to give you to that guy whose arm you broke and—well—what happens then is up to him."

I won't deny that I was apprehensive—no, I was terrified, but I wouldn't let him see that. I wasn't going to give him anything. The man behind me took a steel grip on my left arm, while brow man approached with the needle, squeezing it lightly until a few drops spilled out. He was lowering it to my arm when he paused. "You know," he said, looking up at the man behind me, his expression puzzled, "they're usually crying like hell by now. Hmf."

He shrugged that off and pushed the needle in, and I felt a warmth rise in my arm then flow into my chest, like buttery pancake syrup oozing into every part of me, rising up both sides of my neck to my head; and I swam in a dreamy euphoria that eased away every doubt and fear and troubled memory, setting the world off in a place where it couldn't touch me, and I said to the stars that seemed to be falling into my eyes, I said, "Oh Mama, now I understand. Now I understand why it was so hard."

chapter twelve

......

THAT WOMAN TARA put Aunt Joss in the kind of rehab that only rich people could afford. Mama did it cold turkey.

We stood numbly outside for the longest time after Tara drove away with Aunt Joss and Lainey. By we I mean Tommy, Timewall, and me. Priscilla was too young to know any different, Robbie had run off somewhere, and Mama had stalked back into the trailer. We just stood there, looking toward the tracks, expecting that big black car to turn around and come right back. Tommy was the first to accept the finality of it. He steered us inside with the firm authority of his thirteen, almost fourteen years, with Timewall looking over a shoulder after every step, expecting Lainey to come running back alone if nothing else. Those two had always been close that way.

Mama was in her room with the door closed, no towels on the floor, and not a sound coming from inside. I made dinner for us that night, mac and cheese and frozen peas and chocolate milk to drink, and not a peep from Mama's room. I got Priscilla bathed and ready for bed while Tommy took care of Robbie and Timewall, then we all went to our rooms and turned out the lights.

I couldn't sleep that night. Priscilla was tangled up in her sheets over there, as sound asleep as a snake in the snow, but I lay awake not even tossing and turning, just pondering how impermanent everything in life seemed to be, and how tenuous the bonds between people were. Did this mean that Aunt Joss wasn't our aunt anymore? Now that Lainey had a grammaw and we didn't, did that mean she wasn't one of us? Or worse, that she'd never been one of us in the first place? I suspected that Timewall was thinking the same things on the other side of the thin wall that separated us. I felt sorriest for him.

Mama's door was still closed and locked the next morning. Tommy stood in front of it scowling, then shook his head and came to breakfast, which was cornflakes with the last of our milk, and tangerine-colored orange drink. Robbie bolted out the door as soon as we were done, off to begin his apprenticeship tormenting hikers. Tommy and I got everything cleaned up while Timewall kept an eye on Priscilla in the other room. Now that Lainey was gone, and with Robbie a breed apart from the rest of us, Priscilla was now the closest in age to Timewall. Priscilla's relationship with Timewall as she grew older was always better than with any of the rest of us.

There was nothing to do for the remainder of that day. Giving me an inside look of his intentions, Tommy left me with the kids while he went out to scrounge us up some food. He hadn't been gone long when the screaming started in Mama's room.

Well, not screaming, really, because I don't think Mama was capable of that, but there was moaning and cursing, which grew more manic with each passing hour, to the point that Priscilla was curled up in a corner with her hands over her ears and Timewall had gone ghostly white. I took each cry, or outburst, or however it might be described, as a stab in my heart, feeling actual pain. Timewall went to Mama's door with a look of such devastating heartbreak that I actually almost teared up. Almost, but not quite, and having been brought that close just made me angry, nostrils-flaring, seeing-red angry that Mama would do this to us.

Timewall tried to get in but Mama shouted him away from the door, in a wild, wailing voice that set a terror loose in me, as if demons were erupting from within her. And then as suddenly as it began, it stopped, all quiet behind her door, and I wondered if Mama had died, but then disregarded that because nothing could kill Blaize.

It was still quiet when Tommy came home, carrying a gallon of milk that was expired and some bread that was a little moldy. When I told him what had happened, his jaw muscles bunched and he pressed his lips hard, and then I made us a dinner of instant potatoes and powdered cheese and we all went to bed.

This time the cries and commotion started in the middle of the night, sending us leaping from our beds as if the trailer were on fire. Tommy was at Mama's door, banging on it and angry enough to kick it in.

"*Stay out!*" Mama shrieked through the door, and as much as Tommy looked ready to kick it in anyway, that was still Blaize's voice, a voice you didn't mess with. We spent the rest of that terrifying night huddled together, even Robbie, Timewall holding Priscilla, Tommy holding me, and me holding Robbie. It was a night I thought would never end.

It was quiet the next morning. We had all fallen asleep in a pile. Robbie was sucking his thumb, but the moment his eyes popped open he snatched it out and looked around in a panic. I quickly closed my eyes to spare him. Considering the kind of boy Robbie was, I wonder to this day why I even cared.

Mama came out weakly that morning, dark pools around her eyes, her hair a damp tangle. She went to the kitchen, going by us as if we were the neighbor's kids, drank a glass of water, then went back and fell on her bed, leaving her door open and letting out a smell that reeked of vomit and sick sweat. Tommy closed her door with a look of revulsion, then herded the kids to the table for our breakfast of toast and margarine.

Mama gradually began to improve after that, coming out of her room two, sometimes three times a day, even talking to us once in a while. Was there food? Did she need to get us some money? Tommy stiffly reassured her that we were good, even though we weren't, but she accepted his assurances and went back to bed. She slept long hours through the days, coming out for a drink of water or to use the bathroom, always lethargically, returning to her fetid bedroom immediately afterward, often lashing out at nothing, which sent us into our corners to wait it out; and then after a couple of weeks it seemed as if we had her back. She was her old self again, abrupt and no-nonsense, clean, not bad-looking for an older woman, but if she smoked a lot before, she smoked even more now. I would cough hacking coughs and tell her that I couldn't breathe.

"Then go outside," she'd say irritably.

It had been hard, and now, with my head off in a distant place of such cottony contentment, I understood why; and with that understanding came a peculiar kind of pride, that my mama, that Blaize, had beaten addiction all on her own, without rehab or other drugs to make her feel better or people in circles to talk with. I now understood how tough Mama really was.

I awoke with those thoughts in my mind, back in that dark closet, feeling groggy, a little dizzy, my head seeming too heavy for my neck, and I remembered it all. I remembered everything, and I saw red even in the darkness.

Mama was tough, but so was I, and no needle was going in my arm ever again. I'd kill someone before I'd let that happen, a thought that filled me with the firmness of cold steel.

What day was it? I didn't know. Was it morning, afternoon, or night? I didn't know. How long had I been out? I didn't know. But I did know that at some point someone was going to open that door, and when they did I was going to be ready.

I would have traded the Martin Junior just to have my knife. I was barefoot, all but naked, outweighed by probably a hundred pounds or more, but somehow I had to take those men down. I'm not even sure Tommy could have done it. My mind wasn't working as quickly as it needed to, maybe because of whatever they'd shot me with. I shook my head and kept shaking it, trying to jar something loose. I pounded my head and almost cried out at the pain. The knot above my temple—I remembered that now, too. The pain seemed to help, though. I began to think with a simmering clarity, to visualize the human body, the knees, elbows, solar plexus, where best to strike. The man who'd held me was strong. Maybe he was the man who'd been watching the door to the ballroom, the football player-looking man. Could I bring down someone that size with my bare hands? I didn't think so. And then, as if a light had clicked on above me, I looked up and smiled.

The clothes hangers were made of wood. I'd been able to tell because I could feel the grain. I reached for one, twisted and twisted until the loop over the rod broke and I could bring the hanger down. I flexed it against my knee and felt it give; then I pulled it hard against my knee until it snapped, the wood coming away from a metal frame; and now I had two wooden stakes in my hands, with ends sharp enough to prick my finger. I smiled again.

Then it was all about waiting, in that timeless darkness in which entire birthdays might have passed. I could be an old woman now for all I knew, old like Mama but still as tough as Mama, tougher even. After all, she'd never had to deal with anything like this. What did she know?

I was ready when the light blazed through from beneath the door. I crouched low right at the door jamb—and when the door cracked open I struck like a cornered copperhead, half-lidded against the glare, stabbing the man in his thigh, ignoring his howl as I jumped up and drove the other end into his neck. I didn't wait, gloat, or anything—I ran. I ran hard and fast, through one door and then another, through a maze of corrugated walls and dusty cement, automatic fluorescent lights flickering on as I went, and with a memory of this kind of place that drove me onward, as if a map of each door and corridor were there behind my eyes; and I flew through a large echoing room where women were sleeping on pallets, rousing in alarm as I barged in, mostly young women, even girls, with dark skin, light skin, frightened almond eyes blinking in the flickering light; and I gave them just that moment of pause before I hurried on, leaving bare footprints in the dust, banging through doors until a final door opened into humid night and an empty parking lot with a border of bushes; and I hurled myself across that parking lot, jumped the bushes, tumbled into some kind of ditch, leapt out in one bound, and kept on going.

I might not have breathed the entire time. If I did, I don't remember. All I knew was that my heart was pounding out of my chest, I was dripping sweat, my feet were raw, and I'd bolted around building after building, across street after street, until I was running down the middle of a wide, well-lit street and ahead was a crowd of people who packed that street from one side to the other. I plunged into them like a wolf into a herd of buffalo, daring to look over my shoulder for the first time and seeing no one coming from behind.

I was packed so tightly now that I couldn't move, still desperate to run but that was impossible. I threw out elbows. People hollered at me, indignant curses and worse. And then the sky exploded in light, followed by a distant thunder. I fell to my knees and covered my head, as if the very sky were about to crush us, being kicked and knocked around as people shouted and cheered, their eyes fixed above as starbursts lit the sky and my shadow trembled beneath me.

I couldn't breathe. I pushed and shoved my way to the side, throwing out punches and taking some punches in return. I growled, low, guttural, and shoved even more violently. I wasn't a person anymore, I was an animal, and I'd maim if I had to. Fortunately, I guess, it didn't come to that.

I worked my way into a dark alley, the pavement grimy beneath my feet, lights exploding in the sliver of sky above me, my shadow flashing ghoulishly on the walls; and then I came to stacks of wooden pallets beneath a metal awning, and only then did I turn to look back. The alley was empty, just trash cans and a smell that bothered my throat; and beyond this a crowded snapshot of people in the distance, as if through a long, dark tunnel, their heads turned skyward, streaks of light arcing above them; and my chest was heaving, my legs trembling, and I backed into a space between those pallets, plopped onto my behind, and worked to breathe, my heart thumping so hard that my breasts were bouncing in time with it.

It was the Fourth of July. I realized this when my breathing finally slowed and my heart found a safer rhythm. *The Fourth of July!* So those were fireworks up there, not the sky crashing down.

Just fireworks.

······

THE NEXT SUMMER after Mama got clean, she drove us to Johnson City to see the fireworks. We rattled up the interstate, all of us crammed in, even Aunt Joss and Lainey because Aunt Joss's new car was too small. Aunt Joss was better now, smiling even, while Lainey was pretty in her nice clothes, and her hair looked so soft. Tommy sat up front with Mama and Aunt Joss. The rest of us were in the back. Timewall and Lainey sat side by side against the door. I was stuck between Robbie and Priscilla.

We arrived at a big, open park, with expanses of mowed grass and running tracks and ball fields. Mama spread out a blanket and got us settled while Aunt Joss brought popcorn and cokes from the car. The night was soft and warm, with only a few lights on at the ball field over there, but those were too far away to wash out the sky, leaving us in semi-darkness but not pitch black. There were other people out as well, populating the green spaces with their own blankets or lawn chairs. Tommy said he thought he recognized a girl, and he loped off, with Robbie loping after him, not to follow Tommy, I'm sure, but just to get away. Priscilla was curled up asleep next to Mama. Timewall and Lainey were sitting off by themselves, so that left me alone behind Mama and Aunt Joss, and when they started smoking in tandem I had to back away into the grass.

The night seemed to hold its breath in the seconds before midnight, and then *boom—boom, boom, boom*. We'd seen fireworks before, shot from the mountains beyond Bilbo, but these were a marvel of light, bigger and louder, with crashes of color across the sky that seemed to have substance, as if I might gather them in my hands and watch them sparkle between my fingers. I lay back beneath the spangled sky, the colors seeming to be right before my eyes, as if they were meant only for me, and I felt...I'm not sure, but I felt okay, no dark, gnawing thoughts or even darker memories. I silently thanked Mama for bringing us.

I could have lain there and gazed all night, in the cool grass and caressing breeze, but soon enough it was over. Too soon. Cars were beginning to pull out, their exhaust wafting my way, tickling my throat. Mama stood and helped Aunt Joss up.

"Ridley," she said, "go find Tommy and Robbie. It's time to go."

I got up grudgingly and plodded off in the direction the boys had gone. The park was really large, with islands of trees interspersed with the various activity fields. I went around one of those islands of trees, then followed a path that went alongside a rusty chain-link fence. The night was suddenly quiet and still, the lighting dim, casting long ephemeral shadows that rose up the trees to my left. There were no people anywhere, but this was the way that Tommy had gone. I was completely alone in the night, feeling as if I'd wandered into a far, desolate place even though Mama was really only just beyond those trees. I was about to give it up and turn back when I sighted a man walking the same path not too far ahead.

I kicked up a step to catch him, to ask him if he'd seen anyone, but before I got close enough, two men slipped out of the woods and cornered him against the fence. The men were laughing. The man I was following looked scared, although I don't know how I could know that since I couldn't make out his face. Then the men knocked the poor man to the ground and started kicking him, just kicking and kicking and laughing, and I froze mid-step and gasped. That's when the men noticed me.

"Well, whadda we got here?" one of them said in a voice that sent a chill through my belly. The poor man on the ground was writhing and moaning. "Well, c'mon, girl. Come on over here."

I stood frozen in place, my last breath caught in my throat. Their faces were in shadow, but I could make out a malevolent grin with a dark gap in it, as if the man had fangs, as if the man were a four-legged predator stalking me in the night. All of that raced through me in an instant, and then I turned and ran. I ran as fast as I could, panic sweat in my eyes, and I could hear them behind me, coming closer, their footfalls hard and heavy and all too near; and they were spitting curses, hollering out what they were going to do to me; and then ahead a big man coming my way, his face darkened by the night, and I was trapped and I couldn't breathe, and I just stopped, nowhere to go, fence on one side, woods on the other, thick woods that would tangle and trip and they would have me; and I was terrified and didn't know what to do.

And then a thought shot through me: What would Mama do? She wouldn't be scared. She wouldn't run. She would stare them down, raise her chin and dare them to do their worst.

I turned and faced the men, my hands bunched on my hips, my nostrils flaring, and now I could see the men and they weren't pretty, and what was on their faces was just...meanness. My knees trembled but I held my stance. That's what Mama would have done.

They were almost on me when they pulled up short and hard, looking past me. A big warm hand rested on my shoulder and I jumped in fright.

"It's okay, baby girl. Run on back to your mama now."

"Well, Bo Bates," one of the men sneered. "Decided to get up off your bench, did you?"

"Uncle Bates!" I exclaimed with an exhilarated breath. "You're here!"

"Yeah, honey," he said, his eyes locked on the men. "Run on now."

He gave me a little push so I took off, but then stopped after some steps and looked back.

"Grady," Uncle Bates spat as if the name were filth in his mouth. "So you're picking on little girls now?"

"She isn't so little. Just about right, I'd say." He must have thought he'd said the cleverest thing, smiling as hard as he was.

"Who's that piece of sh— with you?" Uncle Bates asked with complete disinterest. "What? Did Skeeter throw you out when he met that girl, so you got you a new partner now? What's their boy's name? Billy isn't it? Not named after you, his best friend? Man, that must of stuck in your craw."

The man—Grady—turned his smug smile into a frown then threw himself at Uncle Bates, who reared back with one meaty fist and drove it straight into Grady's face. Grady's knees kind of sagged and he went down, while the other man took on a look of quavering doubt and fled into the woods. Uncle Bates kicked Grady in the head, then knelt down with cracking knees and a rasping breath to pick up something from the path.

"Looks like you lost another tooth, Grady." Uncle Bates stood with effort and disgustedly flung the tooth away as if it were a turd. "So you understand me—I'm looking after that girl and all her kin, and if I ever see you again, I *am* going to kill you. Do you believe me?"

Grady lay prone. Uncle Bates kicked him in the belly.

"Do you believe me?"

Grady could only nod urgently, no breath for anything else.

"Good," Uncle Bates said, and then he turned and saw me there. "I told you to run to your mama," he said angrily. "Now go!"

I had never heard Uncle Bates raise his voice. It scared me and I ran to Mama and told her what happened. She went as stiff as steel and her nostrils flared, but then she breathed that out and hustled me into the car. Tommy and Robbie had shown up on their own, and Tommy's look was only a little less stiff than Mama's. It was a few days later that Mama gave me the knife. Tommy started teaching me how to fight the very next day.

A week or so later, the episode behind but still haunting the back of my mind, I spotted Uncle Bates on his bench and went to sit beside him. He didn't look well, purplish and veiny in the cheeks, and he reeked of whiskey.

We sat quietly, Uncle Bates watching something I couldn't see, but I finally got bored and just blurted, "What did you mean that night, Uncle Bates?"

He looked down at me and there was a sadness in his cloudy blue eyes, a sadness that I could feel like a knot in my chest.

"It's nothing, girl." He turned his gaze back to whatever, belched and just sat there.

"It's something," I said. "What did you mean?"

"You didn't need to see that," he said, still looking off. "You've got enough to worry about."

"I'm not worried about anything, I just wanna know why you were there."

He sighed. "Because I've gone and gotten old."

"So?"

Now he looked at me, the sadness replaced with something I couldn't read.

"I told you a long time ago that I knew your mama when she was little. Do you remember?"

"Yeah."

"Well, I wanted to help her, too, but I couldn't."

"Why not?"

"Because things don't always go the way we want them to. Nothing can be done about it, it's just the way things are. But here you are now, and there we were and this time there *was* something I could do. So I did it and I'm going to keep on doing it."

"Doing what, Uncle Bates?"

"Keeping watch, honey. Just keeping watch."

"Keeping watch on what?"

"On all you kids."

"So why don't you ever come to our house and watch us there?"

"Because your mama's mad at me."

That made no sense to me at all. Why would Mama care anything about a drunken old man?

"Why's she mad at you?"

He tightened up, purple cheeks trembling. "That's enough of that," he said sharply. "Talk about something else."

And so now I had another mystery to ponder.

••••••

I WAS STILL IN that dark alley, practically naked, no money, my guitar gone. I had nothing—*nothing*. I was worse off than even before. Sure, in the morning I could make my way to camp, dig up my jar, buy some clothes, have some left for pancakes, but every dime I spent would be irreplaceable. Without the Martin Junior, there would be no more busking, no way to start again.

It seems that for everything you try to do, there's always someone else trying to keep you from it. And there's so much ugliness in the world, those men all those years ago, the scrawny guy, what those music people expected us to do for our thousand dollars. It was a sooty world, a sooty life. Everything that touched me seemed to leave smears and prints, and the only thing I could think to do was run home to Mama.

That thought made me physically ill. I was trying to hold my stomach down when a door opened across the alley from me and a man in a long apron stepped out into the rectangle of light from the doorway. I tensed and pushed myself farther back into shadow. He was a stocky man, older, with a thin wispy beard and a curl of lip that made him seem to be smiling at some inner joke. He lit a cigar and blew out a thick cloud of smoke. The cloud drifted toward me and I pinched my nose in a panic, covered my mouth, and pushed my head down between my knees.

My breaths were catching, the way it is when you're underwater for too long. I could taste that harsh cigar smoke, felt it picking at the inside of my throat in little spasms that were coming up like stifled sneezes, and I fought it but I couldn't and I coughed.

"Holy sh—!" The man jumped back in a kind of stocky bounce. He saw me then, clearly in view once he knew where to look. "Damn, girl, you scared the hell out of me!"

There was no reason to hide any longer, so I stood, fists bunched, ready.

"*What—the—?*" he mouthed, stupefied. He turned to the empty alley as if a dozen people were standing there as witnesses. "You all seeing this?" he said, raising his hand from the top of his head to roughly even with the top of mine. I towered over the man by a full head and part of the shoulders. "Good Lord, girl, how tall are you?"

I didn't answer, just watched him for his next move, which was to look me up and down but without a drip of lewdness, as if he saw stranger things than a tall, practically naked girl every day.

"Well, I seen weirder," he said as if he'd read my mind. "Heck, I come out one night and seen a guy giving a prostitute the high hard one right there where you was sitting; and he was doing a pretty good job so I pulled up a chair to watch the show, and when the prostitute got up I saw that she was a he, and I said, 'Oh, sh—' and got my butt back inside." He went distant, shook his head, then added, "Couldn't sleep for a week."

"I'm not a prostitute," I said, clenching my teeth.

"Heck, I didn't say you was, but whatever you are, this isn't where you want to be doing it."

There was no indignation in his voice, just an inner mirth, as if everything had a joke in it somewhere. I relaxed my fists. This man was harmless, even funny in a clumsy way.

"Why?" I asked him. "Why shouldn't I be here?"

"Because this is where they bring the bodies in. Some people are squeamish about that. Are you squeamish?"

That question went over my head. "*Bodies?*"

"Yeah. This is a funeral home. They bring the bodies in the back way, because, well, there's a coffee shop out front and we wouldn't want those folks to see all these bodies coming in, now would we. It might upset their cappuccinos or their lattes or whatever the heck. Right?"

"Yeah, right," I said, nodding and coming closer. I found that I liked this man for some reason.

"So are you squeamish around bodies?" he asked.

The closest I'd ever come to a dead person was at Taylor's funeral, but his casket had been closed.

"I don't know," I said. "I've never seen any."

"Well heck, come on in and I'll show you one."

I backed up a step at that. "No, I don't think so."

"Suit yourself."

He took a puff on his cigar and was kind enough to blow the smoke away from me, then he looked me up and down again and said, "You don't have much, do you."

"No," I shook my head dismally. "I lost everything."

"Well, that's easy to see. You look kinda strong, though." He lit up with a thought. "Say—you want a job?"

chapter thirteen

······

I WOULD HAVE BEEN STARTLED out of my shoes if I'd been wearing any shoes to be startled out of.

"A job?" I asked with my jaw unhinged.

"Yeah. I could use a hand around here. It's nights, though." He shrugged. "You get used to it after a while."

"What would I have to do?"

"Lotta things. Wanna take a look at a body now?"

"Not really." I made a face. "But—"

"Yeah, first time you're never sure. You either spew bits or you go, *eh*, no big deal."

"O—okay," I said carefully, clutching my stomach just in case.

He grinned. "That's my girl. C'mon in."

He flicked his cigar into the alley and went in. I padded in behind him, apprehension in my every breath, my toes curling when they touched that cold floor. And it was cold, not just the floor but everything. I hugged my arms. The place was gray, and quite literally lifeless, with a smell that wasn't unpleasant but still caught ticklishly in my throat. The lighting was fluorescent, as cold as everything else. There were what I guessed you would call gurneys parked along a wall and with the unmistakable points of foreheads and toes tenting up through the sheets or shrouds that covered them.

I wasn't queasy. Morbidly curious, perhaps, and with an anxious edge, but not queasy.

"So those there have already been embalmed," he said, pointing toward the gurneys parked against the wall. "Did them just tonight.

There'll be more in the morning after they fish the drunk fireworks folks out of the river and such, but that's day shift and not my problem."

I just stood there hugging my arms, flexing my cold toes, unconsciously stooping over to match his height.

"So you ready?" he asked, and that curl of lip just curled even more. The glint in his eyes said he was getting a kick out of this, but all in such innocent humor that my Blaize stayed well out of the way.

"Yeah, okay," I said, unsure if I really was.

He pulled a drape back to expose a waxen face. "I do good work, huh," he said cheerily, grinning and bouncing on his toes.

"Yeah, I guess" I whispered as I bent down for a closer look.

This was a gray-haired old man, but he looked as if he should be modeling old-folks clothes in a dusty store window.

"This guy went down a flight of stairs. He was a real mess, but I fixed him up. A little cotton to fill out the cheeks, some super glue and airbrushing—you can't tell at all, can you."

He was still grinning and bouncing, an expectant look on his face, as if he were a night artist who'd never been appreciated, who'd never seen his own work in the light of day.

"He looks, uhm..."

"Go ahead and touch him if you want."

I recoiled from that and he laughed.

"Really," he said. "Go ahead and touch him. You won't catch anything."

I reached out with my A string index finger, timidly, but then swallowed and gave that waxen face a poke—and then I snatched my finger right back, rubbing it with my thumb, feeling nothing on my fingertip but a cold spot. I had expected my finger to sink in sickeningly, but that old man's face felt as taut as canned ham.

"See what I mean?" he said. "Nothing to it. Now for the real show. I just took this one out of the cooler. She's still fresh."

The way he said that made my stomach lurch down deep.

"So those over there by the wall are on dressing tables," he went on. "I have to move them myself and that's getting hard on me these days." He looked at me pointedly, but then smiled that away. "That's why you're here—that is, if you want to be. Anyway, these over here are on embalming tables, that's why they've got the gutters running around, to catch the fluids and such."

"Fluids?" My stomach did a slow roll.

"Yeah, blood and stuff. No big deal. We wear rubber gloves."

I swallowed hard and he pulled the drape back. This was a middle-aged woman with dark hair. She was gaunt, but looked as if she might come-to and hop off the table with a hangover. There was a rusty smear of blood on her forehead.

"So she was in a car crash and isn't all put together down lower," he said. "That on her forehead is airbag rash. Airbags can really do a number on you. She's gonna take some work, but not by me. I'll get the washing and embalming done, but they'll have to pretty her up in the morning."

"Washing?" I asked distantly. I couldn't help but stare at the woman, who might have still been alive while I was lying unconscious in that closet, if not the second time then the first time for sure, just not that long ago. It seemed sad. Terribly sad. And a waste.

"Yeah. That'll be your job, too. Sponge them down and clean them up before I put the tubes in."

My stomach was okay, I guess, just a little unsettled, like after a bite of pink chicken.

"So," he said, flicking the drape back over the woman's face, "what's your name, anyway?"

"I'm Ridley," I mumbled, my eyes still on the draped woman.

"Well, Ridley," he smiled, "whadda you think? You held up pretty good. I've seen grown men run for the toilet long before now."

I stood up straight, still hugging my arms. "What's your name?"

"I'm Willie. Willie Tailor. My mama said I might of come out a Turner but she could tell that I would be a Tailor for sure." He smiled wide, as if there were some joke there that I should have gotten. I gave him a dubious smile in return.

"So you only need to say yes or no," Willie went on. "We got rooms upstairs to stay in. That's part of the deal because we're on call all night. We gotta share a bathroom but I don't mind if you don't."

My stomach was fine now. Roadkill looked worse than any of this. My fingertips were turning blue, though, and I probably had deep blue lips like a Goth girl or something.

"So how does it work?" I asked, opening my arms to prove a point. "I don't have anything."

"How old are you?"

"I'm eighteen." I couldn't see any reason to lie about it this time. He gawped in incredulity.

"The heck you are! Well I'll be damned. But at least you're old enough so I don't have to be worrying about contributing to the delinquency, you know?"

"I guess," I said. "But I don't have I.D. or anything."

"Didn't figure you did since you don't have pockets to put it in. It don't matter. Your pay comes out of mine, and I'm not telling if you're not. So are you with me?" He was smiling as if the answer were too obvious already.

"Okay, yeah," I nodded. He held out his hand, which was as cold as a lake trout in January, and I shook it, giving my hand a discreet sniff afterward.

"Good," he beamed. "So let's go get you set up."

He led me up some tight wooden stairs to a pair of small dark rooms that had windows looking out on the alley. He flipped a light switch. Twin bed, beat up dresser, old-fashioned TV with the little round antenna on the back. The bathroom was a small cubby across the landing from the rooms, a narrow shower stall, toilet and basin. Clean, thank goodness.

"So you take the room on the right," he said. "I'm on the left. And don't go in the bathroom without knocking first because the door lock's broke and I'm kinda shy when my pants are down around my ankles. Don't want no girls to see."

I snorted. It was dark on the landing but I could still see the mischievous gleam in his eyes.

"So I guess you've had a rough day," he went on. "So get cleaned up, get some sleep, and maybe I can find you some clothes around here. I'd loan you some of mine but you'd poke out of them like a scarecrow. There'll be something down there, I'm sure."

"Thanks," I said, now so weary that he had to reach out a hand to prop me up.

"See you later, then," he said, parking me against the door jamb, and then he thumped down the stairs.

......

THE SLAM OF A DUMPSTER lid out in the alley jarred me awake the next day, with what looked to be afternoon light coming through the window. My view through that window was of a red-brick wall, with just the barest slice of cloudy sky above. I was clean, feeling drowsily wonderful, and I was completely naked because there was no way I'd put that costume on again, not with all it had been through and what it represented.

There was a knock at the door, so I wrapped a sheet around my shoulders and went to answer it. It was Willie, and the moment he saw me he jerked his eyes down, squeezed them tightly, and sputtered to the floor, "Good Lord, girl, don't come to the door looking like that!"

"Well, how am I supposed to look?" I snapped back, caught off guard.

"You should at least put some clothes on."

I gaped at him in disbelief. "I'm more covered up than I was when you saw me last night!"

"Yeah, but now you set my imagination a-going, and I got enough imagination to loan some out with interest. Oh, Lordy, you make a man wish he was a year and a month younger."

I don't know what it was about Willie that he could say something like that and it didn't sound bad. I couldn't help but laugh at the way he blindly held out some clothes to me, as if a stray glimpse might turn him to stone.

"I found these for you," he said, eyes still tightly squeezed. "I think they'll fit."

I took the clothes, and then his other hand came up holding a pair of high-top sneakers that looked as antique as an old iron stove. I took those into my arms as well.

"Thanks," I said with a smile.

"Yeah, okay." He turned for the stairs, still averting his eyes. "Our shift starts at eight, but come on down at about seven so I can show you a few things. I expect this will be a busy night."

He paused at the top of the stairs, then backed toward me in afterthought, a hand held out behind him.

"Oh yeah, take this money as an advance so you can get you something to eat." I took the bills from his fingers, two twenties, and if that wasn't ironic I don't know what would be. I thanked him again.

"Okay, okay," and he retraced his steps stiffly to the stairs and went on down.

That encounter kept me chuckling for minutes afterward. Mama would have called Willie a rare bird. I thought of him as that fun uncle we'd never had, and felt a pang at that, the what-might-have-beens if we'd had someone else for a mama besides Blaize.

Willie had found me some denim overalls and a blue flannel shirt, as well as socks and underwear and things like that. Everything fit pretty well. It occurred to me that these might have come from a dead person, maybe a farmer who'd fallen off his tractor, trading his farm clothes for the Sunday black suit he would wear during the viewing—and for eternity, too, I guessed. But these were clean and smelled like fabric softener, and I put them on without feeling creepy about it.

I went downstairs and through the morgue (that's what Willie said it was called), thinking I'd see Willie along the way but he wasn't there, just a young guy with a dark complexion and long, fine brown hair that hung low enough to interfere with his work. If he hadn't been attending to a body, I would have made him for a busker. Who knows? Maybe he did both.

"Hi," I said, going by.

"Hey," he said in return. "You're Willie's new girl, right?"

"I'm not anybody's girl!" I snapped at him, my Blaize boiling up just like that.

"Sorry," he said with a wince.

He had clear blue eyes that seemed to just leap out at me. I felt bad.

"No, I'm sorry," I said. "My name's Ridley."

"I'm Chris."

"Good to meet you, Chris."

"You too."

He reached back with a rubber band and tied his hair into a pony tail that was more like a horse's tail. His hair was longer than mine, and it looked so soft.

"You don't play guitar do you?" I asked.

He smiled faintly and shook his head. "Naw."

That disappointed me for some reason. "Well, you looked like maybe you did."

He shrugged and returned his attention to the body he was working on.

"Well, see ya later," I said.

"Yeah, see ya."

The day was closer to evening than noon. I walked around the area to situate myself and found that I wasn't far from Broadway—which meant pancakes—so I hurried over, passing buskers along the way that set my lip trembling. The Martin Junior was gone. I'd never be able to find it again, like armor stripped in battle. I examined the streets. They looked different in the light of day, less sinister, less confused, but the route I'd run remained a mystery of panicked flight. I doubted I'd ever be able to retrace my steps. I felt as if something had been torn from my body. How could I live without my guitar?

The pancakes filled my stomach but did nothing for the rest of me. The syrup was tasteless. This was what they meant by having the blues, and I found myself playing Cockadoodle's Blues shuffle to the air, my fingers moving from fret to fret as if the Martin Junior were as close to me as the souls of those people at the funeral home were to their loved ones, close but not touching, never to be touched again. What was there to do but feel sorry for myself, which I swallowed back in anger the moment the thought entered my mind. That's something Mama wouldn't stand for, and neither would I. I wouldn't make myself miserable, or anyone around me either. Instead I was angry that they'd taken the Martin Junior from me, and if that's what it took to cope then I would use it.

Back at the funeral home in the lowering light, a rancid smell in that alley that I hadn't noticed last night, I found Willie outside the door smoking a cigar.

"Well," he grinned, the cigar clamped in his teeth. "Don't you look just like the farmer's daughter."

He didn't give me a chance to agree, disagree, get indignant or laugh, he just took the cigar out of his teeth and launched into a story.

"I knew a farmer's daughter once," he said. "I couldn't of been fifteen or so, helping out this fella on his farm. He went off to the barn to do something or other, and out onto the porch comes his daughter carrying a pitcher of sweet tea, and she kind of smiles at me in a way that says I need to go get me a glass of that sweet tea, so I go up on the porch and sit beside her on the step.

"And we're drinking sweet tea and I'm flirting to set a record, and whadda you know she takes my hand and hauls me off to her room, and I'm yanking and tripping to get out of my pants, and I never seen a girl get out of overalls that fast, and then I fall back on my butt because that girl is hairy all over, I mean gorilla hairy and I think I might go throw up somewhere, but then I think, heck, horses have hair too, right?"

This was the first breath he'd taken in all of this.

"Right," I said doubtfully.

He couldn't suppress a grin. "Right. So I hop in the saddle and put the spurs to her, and just as I'm galloping full out and about to jump the fence her daddy comes barging in and I figure I'm a goner for sure, went about as limp as a wet lasso right on the spot, but he only rears back, grinning like a country fool, and says, 'Thank God. Finally!' and goes on out, and I'm thinking 'What the heck?' and feeling that something's awful strange about all of this, so I grab my pants and go out the window, showing my white behind to every cow from there to Sunday."

He stopped then, put that cigar back between his teeth and puffed clouds of smoke that seemed to have smiles in them.

"Willie, you are a dirty old man," I said, smiling myself but in an embarrassed way.

"Well," his brown eyes sparkled, "I never said I wasn't old."

We got down to business after that. Chris was gone, so it was just Willie and me alone in the morgue, which didn't creep me out the way I was afraid it might now that all the adrenaline was out of my system. Willie fixed me up with an apron, rubber gloves, and a plastic visor, which I wore like a bumbling novice as I followed him from one supply cabinet to another, learning where everything was, then to the sinks, the towels and sponges. He opened the cooler doors, rolling out the trays to show me the bodies we'd be working on, watching me closely for a bad reaction, not with a serious squint but with that same humorous glint. He seemed satisfied with what he saw.

And then he put me to work.

We hauled out the body of an old man and placed it on an embalming table.

"This guy had a heart attack or something at home," Willie said. "His people cleaned him up, so we don't need to do it again. I can just start the embalming. But this guy over here—" he opened another cooler and pulled out the tray, "—he fell in the tub and cracked his head. That happens a lot to old folks, so keep that in mind in fifty or sixty years."

He said that accompanied with his mirthful look. I expected him to bite his tongue at any moment.

"So you'll need to clean him up a little," Willie went on. The man's face was a mask of dried blood. "Help me get him on a table and you can get started, and I'll be over there working on the other guy."

We did that, and now it was my moment, to lay hands on a dead person and not lose my pancakes in the process. I was fine, I really was, sponging the man's face until his grandfatherly aspect came out and he seemed as if he'd been a nice man in life, his wrinkles and folds lifting up from the corners of his mouth, as if he'd never let a frown intrude on his day. His privates were kept private under a white cloth, which gave me some reassurance because I supposed I would be laid out like this someday.

I got the job done and wheeled the table over to Willie, who was ready with his tubes and pumps.

"So what I do," he said, "is cut here above the collarbone and put in the tube. This is where the embalming fluid goes in. And then I cut down here and put in a tube. This is where the blood and stuff comes out; and when I'm done, if he's not in too bad a shape, I'll pack his cheeks and airbrush him some, then we'll put him on a dressing table, cover him up, and roll him over there by the wall. He won't have to go back in the cooler after the fluid's in. They'll dress him in the morning, and if somebody needs a lot of work, I'll leave that for the morning, too. So let's find another one for you to work on, and when I'm done here you can help me move him to a dressing table."

And we worked through the night hours. I didn't feel so much uneasy around the bodies as I felt that I was invading their privacy. They were mostly old, none my age and thankfully no kids. I found myself wondering if any of them could be my unknown grandfather or grandmother, and how I would feel if one of them were and I was in the family soon to be presented with their loved one for a final visitation. I wondered how Jayson and his father felt when Taylor lay like this, and why I felt so empty of anything at his funeral. Mama put us through a lot, but we'd never seen death. This was a different perspective, making all our trials seem insignificant in comparison, not worth the tears that might have been.

We broke for what Willie called "lunch" and went out into the alley, where he lit a cigar and puffed lazily. I stood at a distance and noticed a faint smell on myself, that embalming fluid, and prayed it would wash off. Willie turned to me with that glint of his, took a deep breath as if to launch into a story, but was interrupted just then when an ambulance pulled in. "Hey fellas, whadda you got?" he asked the men in the ambulance.

"Murder vic from the coroner."

"Well, wheel it on in."

The ambulance drivers handled everything with cool detachment then left us, as two words echoed in my head and my morbid curiosity bubbled like baking soda in a bottle of coke.

Murder vic?

"Yeah, so we get these from time to time," Willie said with a sigh.

He pulled the drape back to reveal the waxy chocolate face of a young hispanic man who couldn't have been but a year or two older than me. He had a smooth face, hair like coal, and the so-sparse mustache of a boy only now becoming a man. Willie pulled the drape back farther and I gasped. The boy had been cut open from each collar bone, joining below his throat to form a single line down past his navel, then stapled back together. He looked as if he had zippers in his skin, as if he could be unzipped like a sleeping bag and spilled into the night.

"So that's called a Y incision," Willie commented. "The coroner did that to get evidence."

"Evidence of what?" I asked as I peered closer.

"Bullet fragments and such. Signs of drug use. Things like that." Willie examined some paperwork. "Looks like we can leave this one for the morning, so help me get him in the cooler."

We resumed our work, one body after another, moving them from table to table, a growing collection of them parked against the far wall.

We took our last break out in the alley as dirty light began to come down through the sliver of sky above us.

"Well, that's it, "Willie said, chewing on his cigar. "You got through it. How do you feel?"

"I feel tired," I said, and I did, so dragging worn out that I wasn't sure I could make it up the stairs to my room.

"I can see that. But you did good, real good. And I'll tell you something else: Don't just go on up to bed. That gets you in a state where you just sleep from shift to shift and never do anything else. I'm going for breakfast. You wanna come?"

"Yeah, sure," I said, not sure at all.

"Okay. Let's clean up shop and we'll get going."

Chris came in and gave us a wave as we were on our way out.

"He works alone?" I asked Willie.

"Only till eleven, then his help comes in. He'll work on that Spanish boy, then they'll spend most of the day dressing and such."

We walked to the popular pancake place, which brought me so close to the pedestrian bridge that my heart ached. There were no buskers out, too early for that. I felt that I had been cast out of a world that was now across an ocean, a stranger on familiar streets, my home a half-hour walk away but I was too tired to even consider going there. I thought about Mose, thought I could feel his grin on me, and how that by itself would be my bridge back into that world but it all seemed so long ago now.

I ordered pancakes. Willie ordered eggs, bacon, and biscuits with gravy. We ate in silence, Willie glancing at me from time to time as if there was some question he was afraid to ask.

"Well, it isn't my business," he finally said, all seriousness in his eyes, none of that mirth, "but would I be out of line if I asked you how you got in this spot?"

"It's a long story," I said wearily.

"I get it. It's not my business anyway."

"No, that's not it," I said quickly, afraid that I'd hurt his feelings and not wanting that on my conscience along with everything else. "It's just... well, it's a lot."

"I hear you," he said, that glint returning. "So did I tell you about my wife?"

That actually woke me up a little. *"You're married?"*

"Yeah." He seemed glum though he wasn't. "It is the fate of many men."

"You say that like you're in jail or something."

"Not so much a jail, but, well, for instance: just the other night I was in bed with her, sucking her toes."

"Sucking her toes? Gross!"

"Hey," he acted offended. "I saw it on TV. It puts spice back in the marriage."

"That's just gross, Willie."

"Not as gross as doing it was. I mean, those toes are so ugly—I gotta tell you—it was all I could do not to upchuck right there in our bed."

I was laughing so hard by then that I was dribbling syrup down my chin, suddenly worried about nothing.

Nothing at all.

chapter fourteen

······

OUR NIGHTS BECAME tragically routine. I say tragic because nothing about death should ever become routine. But it *was* routine and I felt bad about it, cooler to embalming tables to dressing tables, park them along the wall, a steady progression of people whose lives and memories had just vanished from one instant to the next. Willie warned me not to let myself feel so much for people I'd never known, but I couldn't help it. I would still see their faces days later, not like ghosts, but memories to be kept.

I started making up poems as I worked, reciting them in my head as a kind of distraction from everything:

> *White hair and white lace*
> *Lying with such grace*
> *Her smile warm and kind*
> *For those left behind*
> *Will she be remembered*
> *For years and years gone by*
> *Or will she be now*
> *Only in my mind*

Not all our nights were busy. Sometimes there would only be one body to work on, and we would go to our rooms to sleep and wait, and maybe be awakened in the small hours by an arrival or else sleep till dawn only to drag through the day in a listless state.

I liked Willie a lot. He had a heedless, humorous way about him that couldn't help but make you chuckle, even during his bawdier stories. I was grateful that he'd helped me. I wanted to demonstrate that gratitude with loyalty, but I knew that this could only go on until I had enough for that bus. Now I worried that I'd break his heart when that day came.

We had breakfast together most mornings.

"You sure like pancakes, don't you," he said, more curious than amused.

"Yeah," I answered without elaborating, which he took as his cue to talk about something else.

Mama always made sure that we had a special something for our birthdays. It was like some kind of mission she was on, to prove to us that she was a good mother. When my eighth birthday came around, though, she was fast in her room, towels under the door, and I waited in seeping despair as the hours spun around till dark and it was time for bed; and I climbed into bed more crushed than I would ever let on, and Tommy brought me a cupcake, all he could scavenge, and we sat together quietly so we wouldn't wake Lainey and set her to fussing, and he whispered, "Happy birthday, princess," which was nice but I didn't feel like a princess.

It was later that night, I can't say when but I was sound asleep, cupcake icing on my lips, when Mama came in and rustled me from bed.

"C'mon, baby girl," she said hoarsely, gathering me up and walking me outside. She couldn't carry me because I was too big for her by then, and she was fat with a new baby anyway, so I just went along sleepily, rubbing my eyes, and she put me in her car and we bounced over the tracks.

I fell back asleep in the front seat, the warmth coming up from the heater and I felt so secure, so safe and warm with Mama there. When she woke me, we were at a place with bright lights. She took me by the hand and walked me in. I was in my nightie, and she was fat and not steady on her feet, so people were staring as we went by, Mama glaring them back even though her eyes looked glazed and her head seemed to be floating. She put me in a booth then sat across from me, folded her arms above her belly and smiled weakly, her missing teeth making her seem pained.

"You get whatever you want, baby," she said. "Something special for your birthday."

I perked up then because this meant that she remembered after all, and I gave her a happy smile that made her eyes go even redder, and a waiter came and showed me pictures of pancakes, some with strawberries, some with blueberries, others with bananas and walnuts. They looked prettier than a cake and I couldn't decide, and I finally just said I wanted cherries and he said sure, they had cherries.

"Whip cream, too," Mama added to that. "And syrup. And ice cream—two scoops."

She lit a cigarette but they made her put it out before I started coughing too badly, and the syrup made my throat feel so good that I wanted some to take home as a present.

There was always syrup in the kitchen from then on, and I'd put it on everything, toast, mac and cheese, and especially frozen corn. Aunt Joss would laugh at that when she was sober enough. Mama wouldn't laugh, she'd just look off somewhere, the same way Uncle Bates did, and I'd squeeze out more syrup and get it all over my hands, and Tommy would scold me but Mama would shush him and tell him to let me be, and he would, and I felt special.

So yeah, Willie, I do love pancakes.

······

I COULD HAVE SLIPPED out on Sunday to see Mose, and the following Sunday, too, but I didn't. I wanted to, but without the Martin Junior I felt that I'd be showing up as just me and that wouldn't be enough. I could get by with my voice as long as I had a guitar to smooth it out, but by itself my voice would be too ugly. It would ruin his songs, people wouldn't drop money on his velvet cloth, and he'd be too polite to say it but he'd have to be thinking that he wished I would just go somewhere else.

So I stayed away, loitering aimlessly through Sunday afternoons, Willie off with his wife and my world a morgue. It had been a slow weekend. Chris was sitting on a stool, staring at nothing, tuning out while waiting for a body to come in.

"Hey," I said, coming down the stairs. He looked up, his gorgeous hair spilling over his shoulders.

"Hey."

"Not much to do, is there."

"Nope."

"So why don't you go home?"

"Because they'd just call me back. Weekends aren't usually this slow. Something's gonna come in. Always does."

"Hmm." I toed on over to him. "You look like a guitar player, you know?"

"Yeah, you said that before."

"But you really do." I wanted to reach out and touch his hair so badly that I was blushing. "How do you get your hair to look so nice?"

His eyes darted to mine then away. "Nothing special."

I was close enough now that I could just raise my hand a little and I'd be able take his hair in my fingers.

He looked at me, way up in his personal space, and a brow lifted.

"You've got something on your mind," he said.

"I do not."

"Yeah, I think you do."

"Then tell me what you think it is." This is shameless, I know, but I did say that I liked sex as much as the next girl; and if Chris didn't get the hint real soon I was going to knock him off that stool.

"I think maybe..." His eyes followed the stairs up to the landing.

"I think maybe, too."

He grinned and we went up.

Afterward, feeling luxuriously lethargic, the lazy afternoon sun filtering through the window, Chris's smooth chest under my fingers, I was thinking of going again when he said huskily, "You're amazing."

"Stop."

"No, really."

"You don't have to say that."

"But I want to say it."

"Why?"

"Because it's true."

I sighed and pulled my hand away. "It's only true when you're in bed with a girl. Later on it's just all the same."

"Is that really what you think?"

"It's what I know."

"Man, somebody really did you wrong, huh."

I pulled back, my Blaize leaking out. "Nobody does anything to me that I don't let them."

"Are you getting mad?"

"Yeah, I'm getting mad."

"Sorry."

"Sorry for what?"

"For just trying to get to know you."

"I don't want you to get to know me."

"What do you want then?"

"You already gave it to me."

"Is that all you're about?"

"It is right now."

He got up in a huff and pulled on his pants. I draped the wrinkled sheet over my shoulders and went to let him out, and when I opened the door with a jerk there sat Willie in a lawn chair.

"Willie?" I screeched. "What are you doing?"

"Heck," he said unabashed, "I was just listening to the show. And it was a good one, too. Damn, girl."

Chris pushed past Willie without a word and clomped down the stairs. Willie got up creakily and folded his chair.

"You know, girl," he said, opening the door to his room. "Not everybody's out to get you."

"Why don't you mind your own business?"

"That sounds like something I'd better take up. See you tonight."

And he closed his door and that was that.

......

OUR NIGHT IN THE MORGUE started out at a good pace but tapered off after midnight. Willie sat through those long hours reading a magazine, while I worked on my poems. I was writing them down now because they'd become too many to keep up with otherwise. I was using a notepad from the funeral home, flipping pages like a journalist consulting her notes.

"You know," Willie said as an aside through the cold stillness of the morgue, his eyes fixed on his magazine, "the front office likes your poems. You must of left one on a dressing table, and somebody found it and passed it along to the bereaved family. They told me that the family was touched—I mean not physically touched because a funeral home is not the place for that kind of thing, but they appreciated it. There might be some side money in it for you if you go up front tomorrow and ask about it. You could put them in with the obits and whatnot."

"I'll think about it," I said.

But there was nothing to think about. Writing the poems was for me the same as playing guitar, something I did for myself. But I did chuckle at the irony that I might one day find myself busking poems for spare change. I pictured myself in a Dickensian scene, ratty wool clothes on a wet wintry day, my fingers poking white through my fraying gloves, standing in the slush under a Victorian streetlight reciting poems to the passersby, catching the odd coin tossed from passing carriages, and mouthing mournfully, "Please sir, I want some more."

I shook that out of my head. Boredom generates the strangest mental pictures, doesn't it?

Chris signaled the end of our shift when he came in, throwing a look at me that wasn't necessarily hostile but didn't invite conversation. He took in the morgue and saw how empty it was, so Willie only had to shrug to communicate what kind of night it had been before turning stiffly for the stairs.

"I'm too tired for breakfast this morning, Ridley," he said wearily.

"Me too," I said with the same weariness, falling in step behind him. Chris said nothing, just parked himself on his stool to wait.

We weren't half way up the stairs when someone banged on the back door. We paused to savor the first stimulus we'd experienced in hours. Chris hopped up and went to the door, and then we heard him blurt, "Holy sh—!"

That was enough exclamation to turn Willie around.

"Whadda you got?" he hollered across the morgue.

"Hamburger," Chris hollered back.

That was all it took to put pep back in Willie's step. I had to practically leap aside as he hustled back down the stairs. The attendants rolled in a body under a sheet splotched with blood that was still wet, Chris going white as he flipped the sheet back over the body's head.

"What is it?" Willie asked an attendant.

"Motorcycle Boomer versus concrete," the attendant said as Chris signed for the body.

"What?" I asked, more of a whisper.

"Late-life crisis," Willie explained. "Or end-life crisis now, I guess."

"What does that mean?"

The attendants were now helping Chris get the body on an embalming table.

"It means an old man who thought he could be young again," Willie said as he hurried over.

The attendants snapped off their gloves and went out the door as Chris wheeled the body into his work area, Willie shouldering up right beside him as if the two were the co-discoverers of DNA. I came forward hesitantly. Willie pulled the sheet away. Chris blanched. I gulped.

"So this," Willie said, showing no discomfort whatsoever, "is what happens when your grasp exceeds your reach."

I never knew what to expect when Willie got philosophical like this.

"So what this fella did when he turned sixty," Willie continued, "was go out and buy himself a big motorcycle." He winked at me. "He should of just done the toes, you know?" My stomach gave a little twerk. "So he's not wearing a helmet, of course, so when he came off that bike he just slid on his face and cue-balled into the curb." Willie lifted the matted head. "Look back here. There's brains coming out where it cracked his skull."

The body was dressed in jeans, which had been cut as high as his crotch by the paramedics and now looked like denim chaps, and a black T-shirt that was so torn and tattered that it wouldn't even make a serviceable rag. They'd cut his boots off somewhere, so his feet were bare and starkly white. The rest of him was road rash on an oozing scale, forehead, cheek—the tip of his nose had been ground off—shoulders, elbows, knees... In a word, hamburger.

"I can't fix this," Chris said in a weak voice.

"I'm not sure I can either," Willie said, "but I got nothing better to do. I'll stay and help if you want."

"Yeah, I want."

If Willie was going to stay, then so was I. "I'll get him washed up," I said, going for my apron and gloves.

"Good," Willie said. "Chris? Let's you and me go to the storeroom. We're going to need a lot of stuff."

I'd made hamburgers for the kids, and this was a lot like that. The gutters around the table were running as red as a Civil War battlefield before I got that body clean enough to do anything with, flecks of blood on my visor, and it only looked worse afterward, all that road rash a warm-water scarlet now, like third degree burns over most of his body. My stomach was holding up, though, and I wondered what that meant about me.

Willie and Chris returned with a cartload of supplies, epoxies and sprays, as if they were preparing to work on a car in a body shop.

"That looks good, Ridley," Willie said. "Fine job."

Then it was my turn to step back while they got to work, embalming first, then using pastes and glues as if they really were repairing a dented fender. They worked well together, each focusing on a specific area, Willie giving me a running commentary. Chris remained tight-lipped throughout, and not because of the condition of the body. Willie kept looking at him, then looking at me, then back to Chris. Willie seemed to sigh, then he launched into a story.

"So did I ever tell you about ole Tuck Dixon?" he asked to the air, his hands busy on the body. "Those Dixon boys were hillbillies through and through, but Tuck took it even further than that." He chuckled. "Good ole Tuck. We was working in a barn, hauling tobacco in to hang, and that tobacco farmer had the prettiest heifer that stayed in that barn when the tobacco wasn't in, and ole Tuck just up and decided he was going to have that heifer."

He paused to give us a prurient look.

"Now everybody knows you can't do that. A heifer's too tall. Things just don't line up right, and you're liable to get kicked in the crotch anyway. You gotta stick to sheep and goats and such, but Tuck had his eye on that heifer and he was by God gonna figure something out, so after we was all finished and gone for the day he climbs up in the loft with a rope and figures he'll just lower himself down until he does get it lined up right, but something happens and he gets himself tangled up buck naked in that rope, dangling there with his johnson right at eye level, and he can't get loose, and we're all long gone, and he coulda hollered to eternity and nobody woulda heard, and you know them cows, they got a tongue that's rougher than sandpaper, and well..."

Chris was now giving Willie the most awed look of revulsion, while I, with a face of disgust, only just then realized where this story was going.

Willie chuckled and went on, his hands still busy on the body, "So I guess that heifer liked what she saw because she ambled on into that barn and went to work on poor Tuck, and when we showed up next morning ole Tuck was just hanging there, licked raw from bellybutton to bee-hind, his johnson looking like a peeled sausage, kinda how this fella looks."

He gave a satisfied smile and waved that smile around, while I put a hand to my mouth to hold back what might be coming up, and Chris was laughing so hard he had tears in his eyes; and then I started laughing (but without the tears), and Willie just looked around too pleased with himself and said, "Good."

They did a passable job on that body. Anyone with imagination would be able to see through their work, but that body would hold up during a normal visitation unless someone bent close for a parting kiss. I wrote a poem and placed it with the body.

> *Motorcycle*
> *Breast and bone*
> *A calling missed*
> *A journey home*
> *Feel the wind*
> *Feel the air*
> *Feel the tears*
> *Through silver hair*

"I like your poems," Chris said, coming up behind me unannounced. I looked around for Willie but he was gone off somewhere.

"You do?"

"Yeah. I think there's money in it if you wanted."

"Naw. I just write them for myself."

"I get that."

"You do?"

"Yeah. Some things are personal, right?"

"Yeah."

We went silent until it became awkward. I couldn't think of anything to say, and Chris was biting his lip.

"So anyway—" I finally got out.

"So look," he said at the same time.

This happened in movies, not in real life. I gave him a flustered expression and he went on:

"I think you're okay," he said.

"You're okay, too."

"I'm glad you think so. I didn't mean to get personal with you."

"And I didn't mean to be such a you know what."

He laughed. "So this is probably not a good time to bring it up, but I have a motorcycle. Wanna go for a ride sometime?"

That body had been road-rashed to a meat market visual, but let's be honest, we all think we know better than other people, that what happens to them will never happen to us.

"Sure," I said.

"Great."

Chris was off the next day so we went for that ride. Chris had rules, though: I had to wear jeans, no skirts or shorts. I had to wear leather gloves. And I had to wear a helmet.

His bike was an older Honda with a classic look and a lot of chrome. He powered us out onto a parkway that ran south of town, across a decorative bridge that spanned a wide valley far below, the hills rolling by like a movie background behind actors on a stage, the air warm, the sky blue enough to reveal a pale moon. I had my arms firmly around his stomach, and found myself begrudging those gloves because I couldn't feel anything. The hair coming out of his helmet whipped and clung to my lips and I didn't mind.

This went on lazily. I rested my head against his back and could smell him, a manly smell of leather and sweat that made me tingle. He didn't try to talk while we rode. The rush of the air was enough.

We eventually pulled into a wayside and got off the bike, then sat in the grass, the bright sun a splendid dream of contentment. I was combing his hair with my fingers.

"I wish I had your hair," I said softly.

"Your hair's pretty nice."

"But it's not like yours. It's not this soft."

"I have my mother's hair. My dad's is curly."

"I have my mother's hair, too," I said

"What's your dad's hair like?" he asked.

"I don't know."

"Oh." He rebounded from that quickly. "I've got two brothers. How about you?"

"I've got three brothers...and a sister."

"Wow. Big family."

"Kind of."

"Can I ask where you're from?"

"I'm from the mountains. How about you?"

"I'm from here," he said with a sigh, as if disappointed. "I bet the mountains are nice, though."

"They are, mostly. Some days they make you feel small."

"I think I know what you mean. I rode my bike to the Smokies once. It was a great day and I could see everything. I even saw a bear. You ever seen a bear?"

"I've seen lots of bears."

"Do they scare you?"

"Naw. They're just like people. Sometimes they're in a good mood and sometimes they're in a bad mood. You can tell by looking, just like people."

"I think bears are kind of scary."

"Well, people can be scary, too."

"Yeah."

Chris was a fast learner. This was the kind of conversation that worked for me, enough to keep busy but not enough to be too revealing. I was winding his hair around my fingers, drawing him closer, that tingle racing up my stomach and my chest going hollow, and I knew what this meant but darn it, I couldn't stop.

"Are you sure?" he asked me.

"Positive."

It didn't remind me of Taylor—well, outside in the sun but Chris wasn't like Taylor at all. He was gentler, more patient, and he would laugh if something was funny, not just put on a tight face and count the seconds. I could have lain with him all day and night, my legs locked around him so he couldn't get away, and if he tried I'd eat him like a black widow. But the sun was getting lower and I had to get back for my shift, and in another week or two, tops, I'd have enough for the bus, and that meant leaving Chris behind as well, and I knew how to battle that emotionally but I didn't want to.

We stopped for pancakes on the way back, which got me in a little late. Willie didn't seem put out, instead he kind of gleamed in an infuriating way, making me blush and Chris go awkward.

"You didn't miss much," Willie said to me. "Just this body here and another in the cooler. They didn't need any washing. You might need some washing, though."

"Willie!" I exclaimed.

"Hey, birds and bees, girl. Did you try the toes?"

I thought about that as I blushed, and I thought maybe I'd just give it a go if there was a next time.

"I'd better get going," Chris said so clumsily that I laughed.

"Yeah, you'd better," I said with a look.

He smiled back at me.

"See ya in the morning."

"Yeah, see ya."

I did not go upstairs to wash up. I wasn't irresponsible like Mama, we did it safe.

Willie was inserting the tubes into the body he had out. There wasn't anything for me to do at the moment, so I took my notepad off the counter, sat, and started working on a poem:

> *Sun and sky*
> *The rush of wind*
> *Soft grass beneath me*
> *Soft grass beneath him—*

A bang on the door brought me out of that.

"I'll get it," I said to Willie.

The attendants had the body at the door when I opened it.

"Whadda you got?" I asked.

"O.D. from the coroner," one of them said.

They wheeled the body in and I pulled back the sheet, covered my mouth and choked back a sob.

It was Sherri.

chapter fifteen

......

I BACKED AWAY in horror.

"That can't be her," I uttered in shock.

The attendant checked his papers. "Says right here, Sherri Adeline Bowman, O.D. The coroner signed off on it."

Willie bustled over, all but rubbing his hands at something new coming in. "Got a good one, Ridley?"

I couldn't speak. I was backing farther away, as if some distance might make it all unreal.

Willie took in the look on my face, and in one perceptive breath dropped all humor and went serious and professional.

"I'll take that," he said to the attendant, reaching for the papers. He studied them, flicked a glance at me, too stunned to even meet his eyes, then asked the attendant, "Would you help me move her, please?"

The attendant flicked his own curious glance at me but then lent a hand. They moved Sherri onto an embalming table, Willie seeming to be taking the utmost care, as if he were laying a child to bed. He lowered her head gently onto the cold metal, taking a moment to brush the hair from her eyes. The attendant gathered his things and left.

"You knew her?" Willie asked quietly.

I could only nod.

"Was she your friend?"

I nodded again, half nods, disbelief.

"I'll take care of her, Ridley," he said in such an uncharacteristically earnest voice that I darted a look into his eyes, and what I saw in those eyes was not the bawdy, eccentric man he made himself out to be, but a sober, compassionate man instead. "You go on over there and sit down for a while. I'll take care of everything."

I parked myself on Chris's stool, looking on as if it were all playing out in the unreality of black and white.

Willie pulled the tubes out of the body he'd been starting on, then slid it onto a cooler tray and closed the door. He handled Sherri with a tender touch, drawing the drape back reverently, as if it were the flag on a soldier's coffin, folding it neatly and setting it aside. Sherri was naked underneath, too gaunt to have been the girl I knew. Where was her voice, her beautiful voice? Where was it now? Willie solemnly covered Sherri's privates with a fresh white cloth. Even from where I sat I could see the Y incision, an obscene violation of her dignity.

I bit my lip and edged closer, hugging my arms and feeling as if the air carried an extra chill. I took a sharp breath when I noticed the tracks on the insides of Sherri's arms, like the pricks of filthy chickens' feet. I couldn't accept the implications, refused to accept them. Sherri wasn't like that. She'd never defile herself with drugs.

Willie was so deliberate in his work. He did everything, even moving Sherri to a dressing table without as much as a grimace. He made Sherri look like a sweet girl sound asleep, and when he was done he gestured me over. She looked so pretty, so lifelike now, as if she were feeling the music with her eyes closed, pausing for breath between verses.

I owed her a song. I owed her at least that, but I was helpless without my guitar, hopeless and alone. I missed the Martin Junior with a throbbing ache in every part of me, as if it was another lost friend. I must have said something aloud because it seemed only minutes later that Chris hurried in with a guitar. It was something cheap you could buy online for fifty dollars, but I plucked the strings and it was in tune and that was all I needed. Chris and Willie stood back at a respectful distance while I found the chords I wanted, and I sang a tragic tune by Montgomery Gentry, the lyrics burrowing into my chest as they never had before:

> *Weatherman says it might hit ninety-five*
> *September's gonna feel more like July*
> *He's callin' for a night that's warm and mild*
> *I think he missed it by a mile*

He just don't know that you're gone
I feel a cold one comin' on...

When I finished the song, I just lowered my head and stood there, not knowing what to do next or what I was supposed to be feeling.

Chris came up and looked at me in concern mixed with awe. "I didn't know you were so good," he said in a hushed voice.

"I wasn't that good," I said dully. "She was."

"Who is she, Ridley?"

"She's a girl I sang with. She went away. I thought maybe she was making records right now."

Willie came over.

"Why don't you take the night off, Ridley," he said with a paternal hand on my shoulder. "You two go off somewhere and I'll take care of everything else that needs doing. Says here that the visitation is tomorrow, up front in the chapel. You probably want to go to that."

"Yeah," I nodded distantly.

"Okay. Chris, you'll look after her, right?"

"I don't need looking after," I grumbled.

"Yeah, well, Chris can look the other way, then. Okay, Chris?"

"Yeah, Willie."

We went outside, the muggy night air scratchy in my throat. Chris had his motorcycle there.

"You wanna ride?" he asked.

"Naw, I just wanna walk."

"Okay, that's cool."

We walked out of the alley, then onward aimlessly through the night, turning onto Broadway without specifically meaning to, just flowing with the tourists. The Nashville Visitor center was across the street. I could make out the place I was sitting that day.

"What do you see?" Chris asked.

"Over there," I said, pointing limply. "That's where we met. No, we actually met before that but that's where we really met."

It seemed so long ago. Lifetimes.

"Were you singing?"

"Not really—well, kinda. Then we got together later. I thought she was weird at first, but...her voice was so beautiful."

We continued on mostly in silence, until finally we were at the foot of the pedestrian bridge, brilliantly lit and with couples walking hand in hand. Our fingers brushed and then intertwined, as if they had their own will, and I surprised myself by not pulling away. We went up together to the center where Mose liked to sing, and I leaned on the rail and looked out on the river, inky black between smears of reflected light. The football stadium was dark and hulking to our right, the towers of downtown glittering to our left.

"I used to sing here with Mose," I said, another memory that seemed a lifetime ago.

"Who's Mose?"

"Just an old man who likes to sing Louis Armstrong. His voice is so amazing."

"Your voice is—" he stopped himself.

"It's okay," I said. "But my voice isn't amazing. Sherri's voice was amazing. Mose's voice was amazing. I can't compare to them. It's not right to even try."

"I don't really understand," he said. "But if that's what you believe then I'll go along. Still, I wouldn't mind hearing you sing some more."

I wanted to wrest that out of my head with anger, but my Blaize was gone off somewhere, sleeping or hibernating or maybe lying in a casket.

"Where'd you get that guitar, anyway?" I asked him.

"It's my little brother's."

"Won't he mind?"

"Naw, I doubt it. As good as you play, you must have your own somewhere."

"I did. It's gone now."

"What happened to it?"

I felt a throb in my temple. "I don't want to talk about it."

"Okay. I won't push it. Maybe you'll want to talk about it some other time."

"Thanks. I might...maybe...I don't know. We'll see."

I looked back behind me, following the river toward the park where my camp was hidden. I wanted to go there, urgently, as if between those plastic walls I could conjure the time before all this, when it was just me and my armor and no one else could get in. But I'd never be able to find the place now. It was too late, too dark.

"Let's go back," I said. "Willie might need help."

"Are you sure?"

"Yeah, I'm sure."

And sure enough, Willie was slammed with work. I wondered what had gone on to set off such a procession of dead people. Chris pitched in too, and by early morning we had everything under control. The work was good and distracting, but I felt bad for Chris. He would be dead to the world for his shift, which would begin in just a few hours.

"You should go upstairs and try to sleep a little," I said. His eyes were bloodshot. He probably hadn't slept in twenty-four hours, would be sleeping right now if not for me.

"Yeah, I think I'll do that."

He pulled himself up the stairs.

Willie came on over.

"You should go up too," he said. "The visitation's at eleven. The family dropped off some clothes, so I got her dressed. She's up front in her casket. She looks nice."

"I'd like to go see her. Will they let me?"

"Yeah. Nobody's here anyway. But are you sure? Maybe you should wait till tomorrow."

"This *is* tomorrow, Willie."

"Yeah, but it still feels like yesterday."

"I know."

"Okay. Just lift the lid. There's a light right there on a table."

I went up front and switched on the light. They'd put Sherri in a polished walnut casket. I lifted the lid and found her dressed in white, like an angel. I would have only needed to hear her sing to complete the image. I sat and pondered, and then I wrote a poem:

> *She was a princess*
> *As pure as light*

And when she sang out
I saw angels fly
I'll remember her always
And I'll sing by her side
Because her voice was mine
A voice in the light

I tucked that poem into the casket where it wouldn't be seen, and then I went upstairs to bed.

······

I AWOKE IN THE LIGHT of morning, spooning Chris and feeling flustered about it. I still had last night's clothes on, jeans and the flannel shirt. I drew away silently and went to the bathroom. The morgue was quiet but I could hear voices coming from up front; and in a panic I leapt down the stairs to look at the clock on the wall. It was only nine. I had time.

I hurried out into a sultry morning, sprinted to the thrift store and found a black dress that would do. The only black shoes that fit me had heels and I groaned; but they would have to do as well, so I bought them and sprinted back.

Chris was up when I came banging in. His eyes went wide as I shinnied out of my jeans and yanked off my shirt.

"What's the rush?" he asked.

"The visitation's about to start and I'm a mess. I need a shower, bad."

I went naked across the landing, showered, and when I came out, Willie was just leaving his room.

"Good Lord, girl!" he blathered, clenching his eyes and looking away. "Now I don't just need imagination anymore."

"C'mon, Willie," I complained. "I'm in a hurry."

"Yeah, in a hurry to give me a heart attack."

"You'll live."

I darted into my room and began to work myself into that dress. Chris was propped up on pillows, watching the show, and I wanted to smack that look off his face...well, playfully anyway.

"I've never seen you in a dress before," he said, his eyes roving.

"And you probably won't again," I said back.

"Aw."

I didn't have stockings to wear with those shoes, and I needed to shave my legs, but the hem was low enough to hide all of that unless someone was down there poking around on hands and knees. I ran fingers through my hair and tied it back, took a look in the mirror and figured this was good enough. I didn't dare take the stairs in those shoes, so I padded down barefoot, slipped into the shoes at the bottom then staggered across the morgue on ankles that threatened to roll with each step.

People were already gathering when I made it up front. Now I felt intrusive, as if I had no business being there while Sherri's family grieved. Sherri's casket was open and adorned with white drapes and a delicate spray of white flowers. Willie had done a great job. In the light of day, Sherri really did look as if she were only sleeping.

"Did you know my daughter?" a woman asked from behind me.

I turned, startled, and saw the woman that Sherri would have become. She was fiftyish, slim. Brassy hair, though. Her nose was red and her eyes were swollen.

"Yeah, I knew Sherri. Her voice was so beautiful."

"She always loved to sing. Even when she was a little girl." Her shoulders heaved once but she checked that stoically. "But this was no life for her. I warned her—"

This time her shoulders heaved and didn't stop. I wanted to reach out a hand but it didn't seem my place. She covered her eyes and sobbed, while I stood feeling like a bystander and with no words to make it better.

"And drugs," she sobbed. "I didn't think Sherri would ever do that."

"Sherri didn't take drugs," I said firmly.

The woman looked at me, her eyes red and full of hurt. "That's what she died of," the woman said wetly. "The coroner told us."

"Well, he was wrong," I came back with a bit of Blaize, which had no business showing up now and I felt awful. She only looked at me sorrowfully and shook her head. A man came up and escorted her to a pew, where they sat and he held her with an arm around her shoulders.

I went and sat in the back after that. There were maybe a dozen people in total, most of them older, a couple of kids, perhaps Sherri's brothers, perhaps nephews. A preacher came in and said some words that rang disingenuous to me. I don't think he really knew her; and then the visitation ended and the people filed out. The front-office people came trotting in then, closing the casket and gathering things with stolid efficiency. They rolled Sherri's casket to a side door where a hearse was waiting.

I didn't go to the graveside service. I had gone to Taylor's graveside, and had stood there emotionless while tears spilled around me and long, anguished hugs were exchanged, making me feel as if some fundamental something set me freakishly apart from normal people. I couldn't endure that feeling again. I wouldn't.

And then there was what her mother had said. Sherri didn't take drugs. I was sure of it—but then how sure could I really be? How well had I really known her? Not well, in truth, and now it was beginning to seem as if we'd never known each other at all, just passing acquaintances on the street. How could I stand at her graveside with those thoughts? How could I show only counterfeit emotions while other people were truly grieving?

I went up and changed back into jeans. Chris was on shift in the morgue. Willie was either gone home or gone to bed. When I came back down, Chris asked, "So how'd it go?"

"Okay, I guess. I've only ever been to one funeral before. This went pretty much the same."

"I've never been to a funeral. Can you believe that? Working in a place like this and I've never been to a funeral."

"Well I hope you never have to."

"Me too. So what are you going to do for the rest of the day?"

"I don't know. Go get pancakes, I guess."

"Wish I could go with you but there's too much going on here."

"That's cool."

I went to the popular pancake place, but felt too awful to really enjoy anything. No amount of syrup could soothe the knot in my throat. How could I have doubted Sherri? We hadn't simply been acquaintances passing on the street, we'd made music together. We'd entertained people. They'd clapped and cheered for us. And Sherri was no frail girl. I remembered with a dark chuckle how she'd kicked that guy back while she was singing *Cherry Bomb*, how fearless she'd been, as if she'd had her own inner Blaize.

And Sherri was no drug addict.

I knew this with certainty now that I could think it through. Users have a way about them, a kind of flighty look, as if a tremulous panic lies right below their skin, the terror that they won't find their next fix. I saw it in Mama and I saw it in Aunt Joss, and they still carried that residual look even after they got clean, as if it were haunting them from behind their eyes. Sherri never had that look, never, from the first day we met until that night we sang together, and yet her arms had been tracked up as badly as the most derelict user in a grimy back alley. I simply couldn't account for it.

At least using a needle was something Mama wouldn't do. How she found the presence to avoid it I don't know, especially during those even leaner times when she started cooking it herself, shake and bake style down at the old depot; and that stuff she made wasn't nearly as potent as the stuff that the man at the Blue Place made. I remembered Aunt Joss complaining about it, that flighty look in her eyes. But Mama somehow made do with her little glass pipe. It was Aunt Joss who tried to shoot it.

Priscilla was born by then, still a baby, and she was crying one night so I got out of bed to see. It was dark in the trailer, and Mama's door was open to her own dank and darkened room, Priscilla bawling in a crib in the corner. I stood in the doorway, catching the light from Mama's alarm clock, and I saw Aunt Joss in a deathly hue, angling the needle at her arm.

I didn't understand, of course. I would have turned around and padded back to bed if Mama hadn't suddenly exploded in the night.

"No! No, no, no...!" she shrieked, jumping up from her rank pillows and slapping the needle from Aunt Joss's hand. They didn't see me standing there petrified in the dark, and I *was* petrified, because Mama had never physically lashed out at anything except men who couldn't keep their hands to themselves. And certainly not at Aunt Joss, poor tormented Aunt Joss.

The needle landed at my feet and I picked it up because curiosity will override just about anything. I was about to test the sharp end with my finger when Mama came rabid out of the dark and snatched the needle from my hand.

"No, baby! Never!" she wailed, and then she jammed that needle into the floor, bending the needle flat, and Aunt Joss just sobbed pathetically and I ran back to my bed to hide.

I left the pancake place and walked with no destination in mind. It was still fairly early in the day, already hot, traffic belching up and down the street, irritating my throat.

Poor tormented Priscilla, too. It wasn't her fault that she was such a bitter girl, her personality had been imprinted long before she could talk. She drew the bad luck of being one child too many. Even Mama, the indomitable Blaize, had limits to what she could keep up with. Her grasp had exceeded her reach. With Aunt Joss and everything else, Priscilla was simply more than Mama could take on.

Priscilla hungry, out of formula, so Tommy gave her powdered milk. Mama never nursed Priscilla as far as I knew. Priscilla on the floor with her little arms out and her fists balled, crying to be held, which meant Tommy or me so we took turns. Priscilla with dirty diapers and nothing left for us to use except old T-shirts. You wanted to think that she'd eventually find her own inner Blaize and get over it, but she never did. She found her inner Priscilla instead. I don't blame her. I can't stand her but I don't blame her. She was about four years old when Mama got clean, but by then the emotional damage was done.

Maybe Mama was right in a way. Ugly times *can* be worse in the remembering of them because too many memories of those ugly times just pile one on top of the other until they crowd out everything else.

I tried to focus on Sherri. Just on Sherri. I had gone a mile or more, and now Music Row was coming up on my left. It occurred to me that no one from Sherri's house had been at the visitation, or at least no one who had the unkempt look of a struggling musician. I wondered if her friends even knew!

So I hustled on, now with a mission, those dark memories back where they belonged. I found the house eventually, after searching back and forth along streets that all looked the same. I went right up to it and banged on the door. This time a guy answered quickly, not the same guy as before but he looked just as ratty, as if there were no way to make it in the music business without paying your dues in body odor and a slovenly appearance.

"Yeah, wha's up?" he asked apathetically.
"Do you know Sherri?" I asked him.
"Who?"
"Sherri. The girl that lived here."
"Oh, the chick, yeah. Hey, you seen her? She needs to kick in for the rent."

My stomach went cold. He didn't know and I had to tell him. "Listen, uh," I said with a swallow. "Sherri died."

"Naw, no way," he said, shaking it off, his greasy hair flinging like a fry-line mop.

"Yes way," I said testily. "I saw her."

"Really? F—! Man, what are we gonna do about rent?"

My Blaize shot up like a rocket. "Don't you even care?" I all but shouted.

"Man, I didn't even know her," he came back sharply. He seemed to be pondering, then: "Hey, you need a place to stay?"

I was grinding my teeth. How had Sherri fallen in with these losers? She would have outshined them even on her worst day.

"Look, does she have any stuff here?" I asked.

"How would I know?"

That was it. I pushed in past him.

"Show me her room," I ordered, and he was at least perceptive enough to catch the menace in my voice. Or perhaps fortunate enough.

He led me through a house that I could only describe in my mind as a flop house. I didn't know what that meant but it seemed to fit. Our route followed the narrowest track of empty floor, all the rest cluttered with clothes and mattresses and musical instruments. Sherri's room was a small back bedroom that contained a single mattress and a dresser that was worse off than the one I had back at the funeral home, along with a chair that was so crowded with clothes that it would have been impossible to sit on it. I recognized the bright yellow top she'd been wearing when we first met, draped over everything else. There were cowboy boots lined up against one wall, including a pricey pair of blue ones that she must have reserved for special gigs; and on the floor beside her mattress were some books and papers.

"So are you cool now?" the guy asked me.

"Yeah."

"Great, because I've got things to do. See ya around."

And he left me there, perusing Sherri's things. I didn't know what I was supposed to do. Try to carry the stuff out? Notify her family? There was a framed photo on the floor of Sherri and her mother, both much younger, Sherri maybe thirteen and looking as innocent as a colt. I bent to the books and papers and absently straightened them into a pile. The books were about the music industry, the papers mostly sheets of lyrics, others with scrawled names and phone numbers. A business card fell out of the papers as I was tapping them into a neat stack. I picked it up to slide it back into the pile, but then went stiff.

It was Preston Cole's card. From the Dardanelle Agency.

chapter sixteen

......

FINDING PRESTON'S BUSINESS CARD in Sherri's things was a stunning coincidence but still only a coincidence. I'd heard people say that there were no coincidences in life, that things only happened for a reason. I never bought in to that. Coincidences happen every day, like when I would think of a song then turn on the radio and it would be playing, or like when I would be going out and Tommy would be coming in and we'd both get to the door knob at the same time, twisting against each other and wondering why the darn thing wouldn't turn. Coincidences are just random things. They don't need to be explained.

And that's what I was thinking while I was flicking Preston's card with my fingernail, that it was only a coincidence, if not a serendipitous one, because it reminded me that I needed to have a word with him—and depending on how it went, he might truly regret bothering me that day in Printers Alley.

I left that house taking nothing except Sherri's blue boots, which was wrong of me but I felt that Sherri would have wanted me to have them. And they even fit me, which was a coincidence that did just possibly have some deeper meaning. As for the rest of her stuff, I would notify her family. There was nothing more I could do.

I headed straight to Preston's office, bent on yet another mission and working up a healthy head of Blaize as I went. By the time I got there I was snarling inside and prepared to hurt him in a way that would prevent any future generations of Prestons from coming along to make nuisances of themselves. I didn't ring the bell this time, I barged right in.

Everything looked the same as before, the plastic plants, the empty desk in reception, the musical instruments propped in the corner. Preston appeared in the hallway, and I have to hand it to him, he didn't bat an eye when he saw me.

"Riley! It's so good to see you."

"You didn't give me my thousand dollars, so it's Ridley," I growled back at him.

His brows arched in amusement. "As you like," he said. "Nice boots, by the way." He went around and took a seat behind the reception desk as if there were nothing unusual about anything, laced his fingers, smiled patronizingly, and said, "So what can I do for you?"

I was not quite trembling with rage. Mama would have already thrown a fist into the man's smug face.

"You didn't tell me what they wanted me to do," I said through clenched teeth.

"What did they want you to do?" he asked so blithely that I took a step forward and bunched a fist. He flicked a look at it. The smile stayed put.

"You know."

"No, I don't, except sing, make a video, and do some publicity. Did you do all of that?"

"*Publicity?* Right. That's a joke."

"Why is that?"

"Because they were making us have sex."

Now he leaned forward on his elbows and gave me an incredulous look.

"They were making you? They held you down and forced you?"

"Well...no, not exactly."

"Right." He leaned back, a little too glib for my liking. "So maybe they had some bigwigs there that needed a little flattering. That's the way the business works. It doesn't have to go too far if you don't want it to. Believe it or not, some girls actually get off on it."

"Well, I didn't."

"Your call."

He had me questioning myself now, replaying the dizzy confusion on that stage. If I hadn't let my Blaize out...if I hadn't broken that man's arm? If I'd just controlled myself and flirted a little, would they have given me my thousand dollars and I'd be in California right now instead of here?

"What about my money?" I asked, faltering.

He shook his head as if despairingly powerless.

"You weren't working for me, Riley. You were working for Albert. And if you didn't fulfill your contract then he's not going to pay you. I'm sorry, but that's the way it is. There's nothing I can do unless you'd like me to try to set you up with another gig."

"*Another gig?*" I gawped. "You can't be serious!"

"Still your call, Riley." Now he had on that professional face, the no-nonsense face he'd worn while he had me signing those papers. "It's a hard business to break in to. Some people are tough enough for it and some aren't."

"Was Sherri tough enough?"

"Who?"

"My friend Sherri. She had your card."

He shook his head and chuckled. "Riley, you will find my cards in every bar and restaurant in town. And I don't know who your friend is. Sorry." He stood. "So look, I've got work to do. If you'd like me to see if I can find you something, just let me know. Otherwise, I hope it all works out for you."

With that, he went down the hall to his office and closed the door, while I stood there dumbly questioning everything. It all seemed so reasonable now, so easy to misinterpret. I left without doing anything, feeling as if I'd just been bested once again by Mama.

Back at the funeral home, Chris wasn't around. I was vaguely disappointed, and vaguely disconcerted that I was disappointed. Willie already had a body out on an embalming table.

"Hey, girl," he said, aproned, gloved, and bent over the body. "You're a little late. Did you go to the graveside?"

"No."

"Why not?"

"Because I didn't feel like I belonged. I mean...I didn't really know her that well."

"Hmm." He set down a scalpel and turned to me. "Hey, nice boots."

"Thanks."

"Anyway, you knew her well enough to sing for her, didn't you? And to be shaken up by it. Right?"

"Yeah, maybe..."

"Want to talk about it?"

"No, it's nothing."

"I figured as much." If there was a note of disapproval in his voice, he covered that with the mirth in his expression. "But if you change your mind I'll be here all night."

He chuckled, back to the endearing Willie. I didn't chuckle with him, though. I didn't have the courage to tell him that I was a little late because I'd gone to the park and dug up my jar of money, and between it and the money I'd already earned from him, I had enough to leave. I should have been ecstatic, running for the bus station, but I wasn't.

"So, you ready to work?" he asked.

"Yeah," I answered with a sigh.

"Okay, good, because we've already got a few in the cooler."

I'd lost track of the days. I counted back silently while I worked, but no amount of muddled concentration could resolve it for me, as if days or even weeks had simply vanished, leaving behind untethered memories.

"What day of the week is it, Willie?" I asked across the body I was washing.

He glanced at his watch. "Well, it just turned into Thursday."

"Already?" I mouthed, wondering how the days had so easily slipped away. I could be in California by Sunday, just shake Willie's hand, say thanks, and go. He would be hurt, I could picture the look he'd have, another dark memory to store out of the way. I would be across the country and stepping off the bus at about the same time that Mose would be setting up on the pedestrian bridge to sing *What a Wonderful World*, yet another memory to misplace somehow. And then there was Chris. My head ached.

Chris came loping in right on time. There was an uncomfortable moment when I thought he was going to try to peck me on the cheek.

"How are you feeling?" I asked, holding out my palms just in case.

"A lot better. How about you?"

"A little better, maybe."

"You should go catch up on your sleep now."

"Yeah, I should."

"I was heading to breakfast," Willie cut in. "You wanna go with me?"

I really just wanted to sleep, or maybe run to the bus station, or maybe drag Chris upstairs with me. I couldn't make up my mind.

"Sure," I said tiredly.

Perhaps that's where I needed to start, drop the news on Willie at breakfast, see how he took it, maybe have him pass the news on to Chris and then I could be out of it, on my way. I couldn't understand why I was being such a coward about this.

We went to the popular pancake place, where I ordered what I always ordered and Willie ordered what he always ordered. We sat as if there were nothing left to say, nothing new between us that required comment. No more spice in our relationship.

They brought our food and Willie dug in, while I picked listlessly at my pancakes, each bite seeming to stick in my throat and the syrup didn't help at all.

"You think out loud sometimes," Willie said through a mouthful. "Did you know that?"

"What?" I felt a flush rising up my neck.

"Yeah. So what's in California?"

"What did I say?" I blurted, mortified.

"Couldn't make it all out. Something about a bus."

Your heart can palpitate sometimes and it hurts. That's what mine was doing.

"It's just something I've been thinking about," I said, with probably the same flighty look Mama had when she'd been using.

"Hmm. Well, it's nice out there, that's for sure. And I bet you've got enough for the bus now, too. Hate to lose you, of course, but I never figured you were here for the career."

"Willie, I—"

"It's okay, girl. I just paid you too much is all." He laughed in that way of his, luring a pained chuckle out of me. "Shoulda kept you on minimum wage."

"I don't want to leave."

"Yeah you do, so don't try to talk yourself out of it. We all have to move on sometimes, Ridley. It sounds like this is your time."

He mopped up the last of his gravy with a biscuit, plugged it in his mouth, and said, "You'll do good out there. You're very talented."

"No I'm not," I came back, a little shocked and heated at the same time.

"Why do you doubt yourself so much?" he asked with a penetrating look. "I've seen you do things most people couldn't, but you go on like you're some kind of barefoot farm girl who can't even milk a cow. I don't get it."

"It's not like that," I snapped.

"I think it is. And I also think you should figure it out so you can get on with what I know you're capable of."

I gave him a razor look. My nostrils were flaring by that point.

"You have a little temper, don't you," he stated with an infuriating chuckle, the mirth there in his eyes but I could only see red just then.

"No I don't," I ground out. He gave me the face of one of his bawdy stories, the comical face I had no defense against. "Well, maybe a little," I added weakly.

"Yeah. And usually I'd mind my own business, but you've grown on me a little. And good Lord, I've even seen you naked, so I think maybe I can tell you a few things without you blowing your top on me."

I snorted at that. It was impossible to be mad at Willie. "Yeah, I'm sorry," I said, coming down and shedding heat like a radiator.

"Don't be sorry," he said, "just listen. You need to go off and do what you need to do, but I think you've got some unfinished business here."

"What business is that?" I asked, working to keep my voice level.

"Well, for one there's Chris. The boy's smitten with you, you know."

"That's not my fault."

"Nope, it isn't. But it hurts people when you leave things hanging like that, and sure enough, down the road you find out that it hurts you a little, too."

"Then what am I supposed to do?"

"You talk to him, of course. Work his ego a little. He'll be mad at first but he'll get over it."

I didn't think I could face that, the necessary honesty of it, his emotions against my lack of them. How could he not be hurt even worse?

"And there's something else," he said, going deathly serious. That was unnerving coming from him.

"What?" I asked with foreboding.

"Your friend...I have to tell you, I've worked on hundreds over the years. Drug addicts, that is. It takes a lot of work to make them look good. I mean a lot of work. Their skin is bad and their eyes are dark and sunken, and no matter what you do with their lips they always seem like they're in pain. Even in death. It just kind of gets locked in. So we airbrush them and pack their cheeks and gums with cotton, and I might use a little glue to get their lips to look peaceful. But the eyes...that's the hardest. It takes a steady hand with the paint brushes, and my hands aren't that steady anymore."

He slid his plate aside and leaned closer.

"I guess what I'm trying to tell you, Ridley, is that fixing up your friend didn't take that much work."

The cold denial of it shot through me. "But the coroner said—"

"The coroner takes them apart looking for things to prove something. I'm the one who has to put them back together and make them look human again, and I'm telling you...she was easy to work on."

......

I DIDN'T SLEEP when we got back, I just lay through the day with my mind racing, reconstructing every word, every look, every gesture that Sherri had ever given me. It was all so brief, and that's what made it even more confounding. Sherri wasn't an addict. I repeated that to myself over and over as if that would make it so. Her poor mother had been convinced otherwise, and that seemed the greatest tragedy of all.

I came down at the start of my shift. If Willie was surprised to see me still there, he didn't show it at all. Chris was cleaning up his work area.

"Hey, Ridley," Chris said, giving me a puppy dog look that made my stomach knot. All I could think was, 'Boys...sleep with them one time and they fall in love with you.' Well, more than one time but still. Mama knew how to hold them off, but that was something else she never told me. Love was not only something I couldn't understand, it was a word I couldn't even say because it sounded so dishonest coming out of my mouth. So I couldn't be in love with Chris. I liked being around him, but love was something different. It had to be.

"Hey, Chris."

"Feeling better?"

"Lots."

"So, you ready to work?" Willie asked.

"Yeah."

"Good."

Willie's expression wasn't smug. It wasn't mirthful either. It just was.

That was a night that should have been called off a month in advance. Not a single body came in which, if you think about it, meant that no one had died so that was a good thing. Dealing with bodies, though, gives you grim expectations of what constitutes a good night's work.

"Why do you only work nights, Willie?" I asked him. "I mean, shouldn't it be the other way around, Chris on nights and you on days?"

We were both sitting on stools, staring blankly at gray walls. It wasn't even ten o'clock yet.

"I like the quiet," he said, his shoulders slumping and his belly pushing against his apron. Under the cold fluorescent lights, he looked eerily similar to Uncle Bates on that bench during a gray morning.

"But it's always quiet in the morgue."

"Nope, not during the day because the people up front are always coming in and out. And the phone rings off the hook sometimes. And every once in a while a bereaved family member will sneak past everybody and get a look at their loved one on the table, and they'll turn on you like you're a mad scientist doing experiments, or else—and this is the worst—they'll look at you like you can bring their loved one back to life. I mean, they look at you like you can really do it, all that hope and everything. Naw, I prefer nights."

He stood and pulled off his apron, his expression glum.

"So I'm gonna go on up to bed," he said. "You should too. If something comes in, they'll ring the bell."

He hung his apron on its hook then trudged up the stairs. I followed less than a minute later.

Chris came in for his shift and banged on my door to get me up. I'd been sleeping so hard that my eyelids were glued shut. I grudgingly crawled out of bed to answer the door. Willie was standing in his own doorway glowering at Chris.

"Slow night, I guess," Chris said with a wide-awake cheeriness that you wanted to mug and toss in the river. Willie just glowered some more then turned and slammed his door. I did the same but without the slam.

Later on, when the day's heat was up and my room was close and sticky because I'd shut my window against the alley noise, Chris pounded on my door again.

"What?" I hollered, burrowing deeper into my sheets.

"Someone up front wants to see you," Chris hollered back.

"Nooo," I whined. "I don't know anybody."

"C'mon, Ridley. It's that girl's mom."

That brought me up and partially awake. "What does she want?"

"She wants to talk to you."

"Ugh! Okay."

I pulled the door. Chris stood there in his apron, and now that I was awake I thought I might just yank him inside and at least make something exciting happen, but better sense fortunately found its way in.

"Where's Willie?" I asked.

"He went home a long time ago."

"What time is it?"

"It's like three or something."

I groaned. This was what Willie warned me about, getting your sleep cycles confused. I didn't know if I should shower and try to make a day of it, or go back to bed.

"Can you tell them I'll be down in a little bit?"

"Yeah, sure."

I didn't shower, although I needed to. I just wiped myself down, tied my hair up on top of my head, shinnied into jeans and T-shirt, slipped into Sherri's boots, and went on down.

I didn't know Sherri's mother's name and she didn't offer it. She knew my name, though.

"Ridley," she smiled falteringly. "I'm sorry to bother you."

"No bother," I lied. We were standing in one of the counseling rooms, as cold in there as the morgue itself, with an antiseptic smell that didn't quite mask the ever-present embalming fluid.

"I just wanted to say thank you," she said.

"Thanks for what?"

"For telling us about that place where Sherri was living. We didn't even know. Oh, it was so dirty! We took her things. I don't know what we'll do with them, maybe just keep them for a while. Just for a little while."

"I'm so sorry about everything," I said as sincerely as I was capable. I looked down at my feet and felt a stab of guilt. "Look, uh, these boots belonged to Sherri." I started to kick out of them. "I took them. I shouldn't have done that. You should have them."

She put out a hand to still me. "No, you keep them. I think she would have liked that."

"Are you sure?"

"Yes."

I still felt like a thief.

She sat down heavily, thoughts whirling behind her eyes. I took the chair across from her.

"I didn't know you worked here," she said. "You didn't have to...I mean with my daughter?" She looked so fragile that the wrong word might send her gushing a torrent.

"No," I said quickly. "A very nice man took care of everything."

"She looked so beautiful."

"She was beautiful."

She thought about that a moment. "So how did you know her?"

"We met on Broadway and sang together one time."

"That business is no good!" she spat, her cheeks trembling. "I told her. I just knew something like this would happen, that she'd get in with bad people and drugs."

"Sherri didn't take drugs," I stubbornly affirmed yet again.

"Then why did we lose her?"

That was the obvious question, the one I'd kept pushing against because there was no way to explain it.

It took me a while to get away from Sherri's mother, who seemed to need to sit quietly and pat my hand; and while I was probably the one who should have been patting her hand, nothing short of outright rudeness would have gotten her to let go. I finally lied and said I had to get back to work.

I went past Chris on my way up to my room. He had the body of a young woman on a dressing table, the stark Y incision blaring out even from a distance.

"Where's your helper?" I asked as I went by.

He was bent over the face, working on the eyes.

"Too slow today. I let him go home."

"Oh."

I went up, showered and shampooed, and when I came out of the bathroom I had an urge to just walk naked down those stairs, push Chris onto a table, and ride him like a rodeo; and I'd actually taken two steps down the stairs before I got ahold of myself. Now was not the time. Chris had work to do, and Willie would be along soon. If the old man saw me naked again, he probably would have that heart attack.

And then there was the decision I had to make, whether to show up for my shift, or say goodbye to Chris as if I might see him later and head for the bus station.

By the time I was dressed and back down to the morgue, that belly tingle was so amped and electrified that I couldn't focus on anything except Chris's hair, that beautiful hair, and I wanted to feel it on my breasts, on my stomach, and whatever else it might brush against. I went up to him with that feverish hollowness in my head, every breath in slow motion. He was still working closely on the eyes.

"Hey," I said in a sultry voice.

"Hey," he said without looking up.

"Whatcha got there?"

"O.D.," he said. "They're always hard."

"That's what Willie says."

I thought maybe I'd rub against him, stifle the tingle while he worked unawares, and something about that thought made me giggle.

"What's so funny?" he asked.

"Nothing," I said, biting my tongue.

I leaned in closer, maybe to brush my cheek against his hair, and then I went as sober as if I'd toppled into a freezing pond. The body he was working on—she was the girl from the van, the one I'd recognized from before!

This was no coincidence, no random event. Did I gasp? I don't remember. I certainly didn't scream or cry out, but somehow Chris knew that something was off because he looked up at me, still hunched over his work but with a note of something in his eyes.

"Are you okay?" he asked.

"I'm not sure."

"What does that mean?"

"I know this girl."

"What?" He set everything down and stood up straight. "How?"

"We did a gig together."

"A gig? With this girl?"

"Yeah."

"Well sh—, Ridley. What the f—?"

Chris seldom cursed, but right then it fit well enough that I barely noticed.

"You said she was an O.D.?"

"Yeah."

I leaned in to examine her arms, skin-toned now and with tiny metallic flecks from the paint.

"Why do you fix their arms if nobody can see?" I asked.

"Well...because it's the professional thing to do. And who knows what might happen when the body leaves us. I mean, maybe the casket gets dropped or something and people would see."

"How bad was it?"

"Her arms? Real bad."

"I think they killed her," I heard myself say.

"*Killed* her? Who killed her?"

"The money people."

"What are you talking about?"

In my mind I saw this girl as if she were in a daze, straddling a man whose pants were bunched around his ankles. I saw brow man, the needle, and I felt it, actually felt it going in; and it was all so clear now, so easy to see.

"They make you think they're doing you a favor," I said in my own daze of awareness. "They make promises and more promises. They say do this and do this, and then just this one last thing and that's all you have to do, but it's not."

"Who?" Chris blurted in exasperation.

"Those music people."

"Music people? Ohmygod! Did they do this to you?"

"They tried."

"You gotta tell somebody. You gotta tell the police."

"Tell them what?"

"Whatever you can."

"Why would they care? It's already done, right?"

"But...they have to care." He looked like such a boy now, so earnestly honest and believing in the world.

"I promise you, they won't. They'll just think I'm a dumb girl making up a story because I couldn't get a record deal."

"What are you going to do, then?"

"Whatever I can to make them pay."

"*Make them pay?* Ridley, if what you're saying is true, that sounds dangerous. I can't let you do it."

I fixed him with Mama's look. "It's not up to you to let me do anything."

"Damn, Ridley."

My nostrils were flaring, every muscle as hard as steel, and I Blaized out the door.

chapter seventeen

······

IT MUST HAVE BEEN over ninety degrees outside, diesel exhaust hanging in the air in a hoary haze, entitled SUVs blasting by as if they might jump the curb and run over a few pedestrians just to get there faster. I walked until my throat burned and sweat was drizzling down my back, and suddenly the morgue seemed like a cool escape from the chaos, something to run to, not away from.

Chris was gone when I got back. Willie was struggling to move a heavy body from the cooler to an embalming table. I darted in to help him.

"Thanks," he said. "That just gets harder and harder."

"I'm sorry I wasn't here. Where's Chris?"

"He left early. Said he had a thing to do."

"Oh."

We got the body situated, then Willie turned to me with the expression I'd hoped not to see. It wasn't that he was overtly sad, only that all the other expressions of his that I'd come to treasure were absent.

"You've decided, haven't you," he said glumly, as if anticipating my answer.

"Yeah."

"Well, that's okay. You can send me a postcard, right? Maybe a picture of you sunning on a beach? If your top's a little loose that'll be even better."

"Oh, Willie!" I blushed and grinned at the same time. "I can't do that. You'll have a heart attack."

"Yeah, I probably would," he chuckled.

That lightened the mood, but my feelings were still tender. Wistful is how I felt. That's the word.

"So Willie, can I work here one more night?"

"Sure, if you want to."

"And can we pretend that nothing's different, that everything's the same?"

"Can't promise you that, but we can try."

"Thanks. And when Chris gets here in the morning I need to see him in private."

He nodded thoughtfully. "So you're going to go ahead and tell him after all?"

"Yeah."

"You going to be naked when you do it? Can I pull up a chair?"

"Oh my gosh, Willie!" We both erupted in laughter.

"Hey," he shrugged innocently, "what do you expect from an old man who wasn't always so old?"

I was going to miss this. I really was.

I wanted my last night with Willie to be special in some way, something I could always keep in a fond place, and it was. The work was routine, enough bodies to keep us moving but not hard-pressed. When Willie slipped out into the alley for a cigar, I went with him.

The night was oppressively warm, the air carrying the stinging reek of car exhaust along with something chemical. Willie puffed his cigar in silence. I squatted in the space between the pallets and watched him.

"You can tell me now," I said after a time.

"Tell you what?"

"Why your mama said you could've come out a Turner but you were a Tailor for sure."

"Oh that," he chuckled. "You sure you want to know?"

"I'm pretty sure you want to tell me," I smiled.

"Okay, then here it goes: So Willie Tailor or Willie Turner? That's always the question, isn't it?"

"Huh?"

"Think about it, girl. You're sharp as a pin."

He grinned around his cigar. I pondered in bewilderment. Finally he gave up and said, "Okay, so I'll give you a hint: will...he...tail...?"

I was still lost, but then I got it and he let out a bellowing laugh that threatened to double him over.

"Oh, Willie, that's awful!" I exclaimed.

"No, girl, that's funny."

"That's sexist as heck."

"Sex is what makes everything work, isn't it?"

"Good grief, you're a dirty old man."

"Well, I never said I wasn't old."

How can you tell if you love someone? Is it the fullness in your chest? The way smiles feel so soft? The desire to hold someone close? I don't know. But I do know that if we'd had Willie back in those ugly days when Mama and Aunt Joss were using, no day would have ever seemed so ugly, and none of us would be the way we are now.

Chris came in on time as always. Willie gave me a look and a nod, so I took Chris by the hand and pulled him upstairs.

"Wait. What are you doing?" he blurted in incomprehension, stumbling to keep up.

"We need to talk," I said.

"What about? Are you still mad at me?"

"Just get in there."

I closed the door and pushed him onto my bed, where he bounced with a confounded look on his face. I stood with my back against the door and pulled off my top.

"Now?" he said, even further confounded.

"Yeah, now."

It was a necessity this time, something I just had to do. And I hated that. I didn't like having to use sex the way Mama did, but it was the only way I could think of to get Chris distracted enough to accept that I was leaving, and to accept it without throwing a fit. It wasn't fair to manipulate him that way, but things seldom are.

I shinnied out of my jeans, meeting his eyes, which were unnerved but expectant at the same time. At last I tugged off my socks, then I tiptoed over and ran my hands up under his shirt, digging in with my nails. He gasped and fell back, and I fulfilled every fantasy he might ever have, maybe a few of mine as well. When we were done, he was sufficiently languid for the next part.

My window was open, the air still sticky. A bird was chirping out there but I couldn't see it. City noises filtered in from the next block over. I propped myself up on pillows, my breasts rising and falling, trickles of sweat filling my belly button. Chris pushed up and lay back beside me, the sides of our damp bodies pressed together from shoulder to feet, our shared heat feeling as if it were burning our skin.

Now it was time, and no matter how much I'd practiced in my head, I couldn't find the right voice. My first words came out as a croak.

"So look, Chris," I said, coughing before I went on. "I need to tell you that I'm leaving."

"Leaving where?" he asked abstractly. He was tracing patterns in my stomach sweat.

"Leaving here."

That got his attention. He sat up straighter, leaned away a little. Now only our hips and thighs were touching.

"What? When?"

"Today."

"*Today?* Why? Where are you going?"

I'd decided that I had to be straightforward with him, no ambiguity. I learned in high school that boys will latch on to any word you misspeak, any tone that offers doubt. If you let that happen, they'll stubbornly cling to your ankles while you're trying to move on, convinced that you really didn't mean it, that there's hope, that you'll change your mind.

"I'm going to California."

"*California?* What's in California?"

"That's my personal business."

"And you'll never let anybody get close enough to know what that is, right?" he muttered bitterly, leaning farther away. Much more of that and he would have tumbled off that narrow bed.

"Look, don't be that way." I couldn't believe I actually said that. "It's where I was going when I got stuck here. None of this was supposed to happen. But since it did, I want us to always be friends."

"Yeah, that's what they always say," he grumbled, crossing his arms tightly on his chest and looking hard at his feet.

"Well, maybe they mean it."

"They don't mean it. They never mean it. They just do what they want and don't care who they hurt."

By "they" he meant me, of course. And this was tedious but I had to see it through.

"Why would you be hurt?"

"Because I like you."

"Chris, you don't even know me."

"Yes I do."

"Really?" I hopped around and sat back, facing him. "So where was I born, then? Where'd I go to school?"

"I don't know because you won't talk about it."

"Right. So what is it really that you like so much?"

He hesitated before answering, his eyes searching. "I like the way you sing."

"Is that it?" And while I'd practiced this in my head and had no reason to get riled myself, I was heating up a little anyway. "So you're getting all upset because I won't be here to sing for you?"

"No, not just that."

"So it's just about the sex, then. That's it, isn't it?"

"You make me sound like such an ass."

"I don't make you sound like anything. It's what you're thinking, not me." By now I had my hands on my bare hips and half formed into fists.

"That's not the way I feel."

"Then what do you feel? That we can't be friends unless you get laid?"

"No...no, that's not what I mean."

"So we *are* friends then. It's not just sex?"

"Yeah, we're friends," he conceded with a pout.

I relaxed my posture, felt the heat fading. "I'm glad, because I don't want to lose you as a friend."

"Me either."

"Good."

That was exhausting.

Now dressed and back downstairs, my clothes in a pillow case and Willie giving me a widened eye, I lingered to say goodbye. Willie came up and hugged me, a hearty hug that left me flustered but I still liked the way it felt.

"You be careful out there, girl. And keep your clothes on, will you?"

"I will," I laughed.

He sniffed and turned away. Chris walked me to the door, suddenly bashful. I wanted to stroke his hair one last time, but that would have undone everything.

"I'm sorry I said those things," he told me. "I didn't mean it."

"I know."

Affection then. Maybe not love but affection. I could understand affection. I could probably return it with practice.

"So one more thing," he said. "I went to the police last night and told them what you said."

"You did *what*?"

"Look, am I at least allowed to worry about you?"

"Yeah, I guess," I sighed.

"And you were right. They just blew it off and said they get accusations like that all the time."

"Hmm," I mused. "I wonder if those accusations are right all the time." I shook that off and pulled the door open. "Oh, well—anyway—"

"So you're just going to California, right? You're not going to try to do anything to those people like you said?"

"Right," I lied.

And I had to lie, because boys couldn't help but puff up their chests and charge in to save us, whether we needed saving or not, making things even worse. I'd seen enough of it in school, when boys would stand toe to toe growling at each other because someone said something about someone else's girlfriend, and in mortal embarrassment the girlfriend would be futilely trying to pull her boyfriend away, and sometimes things escalated and sometimes they didn't but it was always undignified.

So it was easy to project that when those boys became men, their behavior could have far-reaching consequences, and Uncle Bates confirmed it for me.

It was the morning I left home. I was crossing the gravel toward the trailhead when I spotted Uncle Bates sitting on the old depot dock and following my every step. Of course Uncle Bates would be there. It was as if, sober or not, he had some mystical ability to foretell every intention. I sighed and angled toward him.

"So you're heading out?" he asked as I came closer. He sounded cold sober.

"Yeah."

"This will hurt your mama."

"So what?"

"She loves you, you know."

"She's never said it. Not once."

"How do you know what's been said and what's been done?"

"I only know what I know, Uncle Bates. What else have I got?"

"You got a mama who'd fall in front of a train for you."

"Well she never did."

"You're getting a little hot, aren't you," he said with a hint of amusement. "Got your mama's temper, don't you."

"I got nothing of Mama's!"

I'd read the word *throttled* in a book once. I liked that word because it seemed to be a way that you could lash out without doing real damage, without seeing red, and I wanted to throttle Uncle Bates.

"Girl," Uncle Bates said in a mildly reprimanding voice, "you're so tall that you'd think you were the exact opposite of your mama, but if you were short you'd look just like her. And you've got her temper whether you think so or not. You've got her smarts too, I bet, and if it came down to it, you're probably just as tough."

"I'm not Mama!" I sputtered, and now I *was* seeing red and somehow he knew.

"Wipe that red out of your eyes, girl," he ground out, face gone hard and for a moment I thought he was about to throttle me himself. "No, you're not your mama. You're Ridley, a different person, but you came from your mama so you know a little of that got mixed in. Now sit down here for a minute." He patted the cement dock. "Just sit down and cool off a little."

I didn't want to but I did anyway because I'd only ever seen him this intense once before, and that was something I couldn't ignore.

We sat silently, Uncle Bates gazing at the trees and going distant the way he did. I calmed down. That cool morning air helped.

"I used to work here. Did you know that?" he said at last.

"You worked here? In this old depot?"

"Yep. Trains used to come through, and trucks would be coming and going over the tracks, and there wasn't a trailer court then, just some old cabins."

"So what happened?"

"Everything."

That was no answer to my question, just another mystery on top of all the others, mystery after frustrating mystery from there to the end of time. But then I remembered something, the biggest mystery of all, and he'd been there. He'd said so himself.

"Uncle Bates? A long time ago something happened with Mama and Aunt Joss, and you said you were there. Please tell me what it was."

The folds in his stubbly gray cheeks quivered.

"Baby girl, you don't want to know about that."

"Yes I do! That's when everything went bad, Uncle Bates. I had to live through it. How come I'm not allowed to know what for?"

"Because it could hurt people, Ridley. Is that what you want?"

"Why is it my fault? I didn't do anything, but I had to put up with everything."

He let out a deep bear of a sigh.

"Okay, dammit, I'm gonna tell you, but only because you're leaving and you're probably not coming back. I hate that, by the way. I'm gonna miss you like you were my own. But whatever happens, don't you ever tell your mama. Don't tell anybody. Do you hear me?"

"Yes, Uncle Bates," I said quickly, my heart thudding in anticipation.

"Okay, then." He seemed conflicted, clicking his teeth in thought before he went on. "So you were little," he said. "I can't remember how old, five or six or something like that." He kept his eyes fixed on the woods. "We were all over at the Mardi Gras Lounge to celebrate because they let Daryl out of prison." He looked at me. "You remember Daryl, right?" I shook my head. "Well, he was one of our people from up the mountain.

"Anyway, we were all there, your mama and Jocela and that Indian boy that Jocela ran with, and a bunch of other people. We were just drinking and dancing and having a good time. Your mama and Jocela were on the dance floor carrying on, and this guy—I don't know who he was, probably just a hill-billy down from one of the hollows. Anyway, this guy steps in and grabs Jocela by the arm and says, 'Hey, baby, let's dance,' and Jocela yanks her arm back and the guy gets a little wound up, and then your mama gets up in his face."

He paused to chuckle and shake his head.

"Well, as up in his face as she could get on her tiptoes, and she just stares him down the way she does, and the guy is blathering and can't keep the spit in his mouth, but he kind of starts to back away, like that's the end of it, but then that Indian boy comes running in with his fists flying, and he coldcocks that guy and puts him on the floor, and he keeps hammering away until the guy's face is a pulp, and your mama's trying to make him stop and she catches an elbow in her face by accident, and when that happens, well, Jocela jumps in screaming and hauls that Indian boy off and pushes him out the door."

He looked at me again, his eyes as gray as morning mist, then he turned back to the woods and continued:

"The whole thing didn't take but seconds, not even enough time for me to get in and do something. People were scattering, figuring the sheriffs were probably on the way, and your mama ran out after Jocela and the Indian boy, and after a second I ran out of there, too."

"So that's all it was?" I asked, disappointed down to my toes. The big bad mystery was just a bar fight?

"No, girl, that's not all it was, because that guy on the floor died before the sheriffs even got there."

My jaw dropped. Now it all made sense.

"So what happened to the Indian boy?" I asked queasily.

"He and his brother ran off to the reservation. They're still hiding out best I can tell."

So now I knew, and I could see it all clearly. The Indian boy was Nene, and he had to go into hiding or else he would have gone to prison. Aunt Joss had never been emotionally strong enough to cope with something like that, so Mama did what she had to do, and it was too much.

Back to Chris in the doorway, I gave him a smile and said, "Don't worry, I'll be on the bus in about an hour."

"I should be there, you know, to make sure you get on okay."

I gently pushed him back inside. "That's too many goodbyes for one morning." My eyes might have been misting, or maybe it was just something in the air.

"Bye, Chris," I said, and I stepped through the door and I didn't look back because I wasn't sure what I would do if I did.

······

It turns out that there's a benefit to having a brother like Robbie after all. Because of him, I knew exactly what to do and how to do it.

I hopped a bus and went to an Army-Navy store that was out past Music Row, where I walked the aisles and browsed for a long time, running an inventory through my mind, trying to anticipate everything I would need. I bought another camo daypack, then filled it with the other things I'd need: a pencil-thin LED flashlight, duct tape, a multitool, a small twist of heavy-gauge wire, a strong magnet, bear spray, a cheap BB pistol that still looked like something a soldier would strap on, and finally, a wicked-looking military knife that had a serrated back and a blood groove. I paid up, loaded my new daypack, then walked to a convenience store where I bought some bottled water, a few snack bars, and some of those little energy drinks; then I hopped the bus back to town and made my way to the thrift store.

Once there, I searched and found a denim skirt that looked a lot like the one I once had, a thin black jacket that was more gray than black, and a black Fedora that had a crease in the brim where someone might have sat on it. It was still fairly early in the day when all of that was done, so I went to the other pancake place (the popular pancake place was closed by then), ordered a stack, then sat back waiting for dusk to arrive.

I should have bought a notepad while I was out, but the thought hadn't occurred to me so I made do with a napkin and wrote a poem:

> *Journeys begin and never end*
> *So you follow and try to bend*
> *Your path toward a better day*
> *And find it where you couldn't see*
> *Better days that could never be*
> *It won't let you stop*
> *It won't set you free*
> *Oh where, then, will this journey lead*

The day fell beyond the windows, the shimmering pavement wilting toward night. I went out into the muggy air and walked toward the pedestrian bridge, being bumped and jostled on the sidewalks but I was too lost in thought to take much notice. I heard the twang of a guitar from across the street, buskers setting up for the night, and I wanted to be with them so badly that I had to squeeze my eyes and hurry on.

I topped the pedestrian bridge as the sun slipped gently behind the trees along the river, setting off an anticipation in the air. The bridge lights popped on in ones and twos, illuminating buskers here and there who smiled and laughed and strummed their instruments, in a world of their own that I was no longer a part of. I dropped some coins into a guitar case and received an exuberant thanks, then plodded on numbly toward the park.

My camp still stood, unfound and undisturbed. It smelled stale inside, but comforting at the same time. I lay back as the last ephemeral shadows of leaves melded into the black plastic, my fingers absently searching the dark for the Martin Junior. I fell into an exhausted sleep that was so deep I didn't even dream.

The morning rose sticky but clear, and for some moments I thought I was back in that earlier life, when things were simple and I went through my days untouched.

I wiped down with water from my bottle, then dressed in my new skirt, jacket, and hat. I slid the knife into my boot, adjusting it so it wouldn't rub my ankle. Then I shouldered my daypack, closed and sealed my camp, and said a silent goodbye.

At the top of the pedestrian bridge, I sat and waited, and it wasn't long before I spotted Mose coming up from the other side. I hopped up and stood with my hands behind my back, feeling a welling in my chest that almost burst when he saw me and gave me that brilliant grin of his.

"Well, Miss Ridley," he said with heartfelt warmth. "It's so good to see you again. I thought we'd lost you along the way."

"Nope. Still here," I said, beaming.

"Well don't you look pretty today. So where have you been, child?"

"Just doing some work. Making a little money. You know."

"Yes I do," he said with a gravelly laugh. He looked around, puzzled. "So where's that sweet Martin Junior?"

I frowned and looked at my feet.

"It got stolen."

"Oh, no—Miss Ridley, I'm so sorry."

"Yeah."

He set down his things and spread his black velvet cloth, then rested a hand on my shoulder and looked me right in the eyes, his gaze so sincere and caring that I felt my heart tighten.

"We can still sing though, can't we? Even without your guitar?"

"I'd like that."

"Well that's wonderful," he grinned, bending back with his hands on his hips. "So what song would you like to do?"

"How about *What a Wonderful World*?"

"Oh, I do love that one."

"But without my guitar, I don't know if I can," I said, studying the toes of my boots.

"Sure you can. We'll do it call and response, just like we did before."

"Okay. Yeah, I can do that."

"Good."

Mose started us off, standing tall, his hands clasped behind him, crooning to that gathering crowd as smoothly as if an orchestra were playing in his head; and I followed along, repeating those familiar lyrics as if they were warm syrup in my throat; and when that song ended we did another, and another, until that day felt like a dream resting on a cloud, and I was full and happy and wanted it never to end.

But it had to end, of course.

"I have to go now, Mose."

"So soon, Miss Ridley?"

It was past noon, getting hot. I had plenty of time, but if I didn't go now I might never.

"Yeah," I said sadly. "So look, Mose—I'm going to be leaving town pretty soon, so I don't think I'm going to get to see you again."

"Oh, Miss Ridley...I'll miss you, you know."

"I'll miss you too. I hate to go."

"No, no, that's not the way to think about it." He grinned so brightly that I had to smile myself. "You're young and you've got your whole life ahead out there. Who knows what you'll find? Something special, I bet."

"I hope so."

"Well, you just remember—if you're ever back in Music City, you'll find me right here and we'll sing some songs together. Okay?"

"Okay."

He bent to scoop up half his earnings to give me.

"No, Mose. Not this time," I said, holding out my palms.

"But Miss Ridley, half of this is for you."

"Uh-uh. I just wanted to sing with you again. That's all."

His brow wrinkled, but then the grin came back. "Well, it was a pleasure for me, too. You take care of yourself. Okay?"

"I will."

And then I turned for Broadway and didn't look back

chapter eighteen

......

I HUNG OUT AT Centennial Park until the Parthenon's columns began to cast long, angular shadows, and then I hefted my daypack and started walking, determined, resolute, but with a tremor inside just the same.

The route was confusing, and long on foot, but I still had an hour or so of daylight to kill. So I plodded on, using a tourist map as a guide, crossing the Vanderbilt campus, where I looked no different than the students who were out and about. I had changed into jeans and T-shirt, and as far as anyone knew, my daypack could have been full of books. I eventually reached Music Row, where I put away the map. From here on I could do it by memory.

There was still too much light when I got to the Dardanelle Agency, a diffuse gray. The sun had set but I would still be visible as a shadowy shape to anyone peering out a window. It was hard to be patient, but patience is essential when you're stalking someone. Or not really stalking, I guess, because I needed Preston to be gone when I went in. His Escalade wasn't out front, nor any other cars, so he probably wasn't there but it still wasn't dark enough yet. I circled the block to kill more time. Fireflies were strobing in errant flashes when I came back around, porch lights glowing under eaves. The Dardanelle Agency was dark and quiet. Finally I could get on with it.

I had to do this because I wasn't sure about Preston, whether he was involved or just a clueless middleman. I was convinced that I would find the answer to that question in his office files, and then, well, it would play out however it did.

I went over a wooden fence then crept around back. The moon hadn't risen yet so that helped. A neighbor's window glowed above the fence line, casting a column of yellow light, which I skirted with my back against some garden shrubs. I made out a faint silver glow and pushed through the shrubs. This was it, Preston's office window, no screen, the blinds drawn, dark beyond them except for that little bit of silver light leaking through from office equipment. I used my LED to examine the window frame, and there it was, the alarm sensor. This was where I used the magnet, fixing it in place with duct tape. Then I put a patch of duct tape on the window glass just this side of the latch. I put the barrel of the BB pistol right up against that patch of duct tape and pulled the trigger.

The impact was muted, no more than a small limb snapping in a tree, but I dropped to my knees anyway, kept quiet and listened. The night was warm and expectantly still. All I could hear was a distant TV coming from someone's house, no other sounds, no doors creaking open, no one bumbling out to investigate.

Robbie boasted once that breaking and entering for real wasn't like a TV show at all. He claimed that he'd once taken out a window with a baseball bat while people were sleeping elsewhere in the house, and none of them had awoken. It was too easy, he said. Easy pickings. They should have put newspaper in their windows the way Mama did, not that it would have stopped him but it would have given him second thoughts, that maybe he ought to just move on to a place less weird.

The BB pistol made a perfectly round little hole in that window. I took my wire and used the multitool to bend a shallow hook on the end. I fed this through the hole, hooked the latch and pulled it open. That was it. Too easy. Robbie was right. Now, however, I had to lift the window and pray that the magnet worked, that the alarm wouldn't go off. I lifted slowly, although that didn't make any difference. I could have just yanked that window up. If the alarm was going to go off, it would either way.

It didn't.

I felt for the cord, pulled the blinds, then shinnied over the window sill. I was in, navigating around Preston's desk with my LED, where I sat in his chair and pulled out his filing drawer. There were a lot of files, organized alphabetically. I thumbed through and found *Riley Skye*, tugged it out and opened it in my lap, bent over with the LED between my teeth while I flipped pages. There was nothing in that file except the contract

I'd signed and those photos he'd taken. Nothing out of the ordinary. Nothing incriminating.

I stuffed that file into my daypack, then thumbed through the *B*s, hoping and not hoping, and when I found it I let out a little squeak of breath. He'd changed her name to Barrett, Sherri Barrett. She was wearing a denim vest over a black top in her photo, and she looked so excited, it was so crushingly evident in her eyes. They sparkled. In one photo she was biting her lip in a tentative smile that said she couldn't believe that she was finally on her way.

So Preston was involved.

My heart pounded and my nostrils flared just at the thought, and I pictured flinging myself across that desk to tear out his throat and even that wouldn't be enough to make up for what he'd done. I had to calm myself. I had to breathe. This wasn't the time for heat. That would only slam uselessly against the first person who got in my way, leaving those men free to keep on doing what they were doing. This required cold, the calculated cold of dispassion, the kind of biting winter cold that spills through cracked windows and oozes across floors like an invisible predator, pitilessly searching out pipes to burst and toes to freeze.

I returned Sherri's file to the drawer, then retreated through the window, putting everything back the way it was. The little hole would never be noticed. Robbie gloated more than once that he'd actually used the same hole when he'd hit a place a second time, a third time. I wasn't worried anyway because whatever was going to happen, this would be the least of it.

There was a public park nearby. I went there to pass the night.

And it was a long night, resting against a tree, a pandemonium of mosquitoes buzzing my ears. My thoughts wouldn't allow me to sleep anyway. They pestered me worse than the mosquitoes, coming unbidden just as I might be drifting off, jerking me back again and again to rehash what I'd already rehashed to death, the what-ifs of every possible outcome, including the very real possibility that I might wind up being powerless to do anything except fall victim myself.

I spared a thought for Willie. Would he come in to find me on one of his embalming tables, gaunt, a white cloth over my privates, my arms tracked and horrible? He wouldn't make jokes about it, my naked body lying there, the Y incision desecrating the place where Chris had traced patterns in my sweat. No, he would be beyond consoling. He might actually have that heart attack. The thought made my lip tremble.

And what about Chris? I ran my fingers over my stomach where he'd touched me, imagined the Y incision there, like a wide welt of a scar. Chris would be inconsolable too, but he would storm out to do something, roaring away on his motorcycle, throttle all the way open, weaving recklessly through traffic, mile after mile until he finally accepted that there was nothing he could do. At least he would be saved in the end, as long as he didn't crash, because I hadn't told him enough to even know where to begin.

And then this recurring thought, the sneaky saboteur that struck each time sleep came near: Could I kill someone? Could I really do it?

The answer always came back with a cold resolve that sent chills up my spine. Men like these? Absolutely I could. I thought about Tommy over in Afghanistan. He wouldn't be wondering if he could kill people. He wouldn't moralize or tie his conscience in knots. He'd kill, and he'd keep on killing because the enemy left him no choice. He was only doing what he had to do.

It would change him, though. I understood that, and I feared the stranger he might be when he came home—if he came home. How would Mama handle that, her boy who'd seen real carnage, not the self-inflicted kind? She wouldn't be able to stare that down. It would be the best and worst sort of revenge.

Tommy wanted to join the Army ever since the attacks of 9-11, which affected him more than me because he was a little older, and the attacks were so close to his birthday. To me, the attacks were something bad that happened far away. Mama was too high to even know what was going on, Tommy punching holes in walls or high-rise towers falling in New York City—but Tommy...he seethed. Barely thirteen years old, and now he saw something worse than what we had to live with. That's what he told me when the time came.

Tommy was so handsome when he turned eighteen, tall and muscular and with those clear blue eyes and confident smile. He could have had any girl he wanted, even girls from the better families. Sometimes I would catch Mama gazing at him, her beautiful boy, and I would feel a stab of jealousy. All that went away when he told Mama that he'd enlisted. Mama and I both erupted, and for a short time we were hysterical allies in a futile fight. Tommy was going. Nothing she said or I said had any effect. Mama felt as if she'd been betrayed by her boy. I felt the same.

"You're still my princess," Tommy said to me during his last evening in the trailer, using all the nostalgic charm he could churn up in his attempt to calm me down. I was too old to be called princess by anyone, but that didn't prevent me from retreating to that time when Mama was a granite guardian and it was just Tommy and me. We went for a walk in the woods, taking a seat on the bench in the clearing. The fireflies were just coming out to do their ghostly show, and the air held the musty smell of rain.

"I always thought we were freaks, you know?" he said, looking down at his clasped hands. "I was ashamed. Even before Mama and Aunt Joss got so bad, I knew something was wrong. I knew we weren't normal."

"You and I were normal, though. Weren't we?" I asked my big brother, desperate for him to lie. Tommy just chuckled darkly.

"As much as we could be, I guess."

"I hate her so much," I spat out.

"No you don't. You know that."

"Yeah, I do, and so do you."

"No, I don't hate Mama. I'm mad at her all the time and I think she screwed us over pretty bad, but I don't hate her."

"Then why are you leaving?"

"Because this isn't everything, Ridley. I thought everything bad in the world happened to us. I wanted to call Mama out for it but I knew I wouldn't win. But over there," he looked off as if he could see that distant place, "they've really got it bad, like they'd think we were just weak and whining all the time. So if this is what it takes to be normal, to maybe win for once, I'm doing it."

"But it's dangerous, Tommy."

"So is meth, Ridley, but we made it, didn't we?"

I had to cough and clear my throat. We'd made it, but we were wounded and would probably always be.

"What'll happen if you don't come back?" I pleaded.

"What'll happen if I stay?"

"I don't know."

"Well I do. Nothing, that's what. Nothing." He ground his teeth and spat those words.

"That's not true! Your grades are as good as mine. You can go to college."

"I still can after I serve. They'll even pay for it. Maybe I will, but right now I don't care." He turned to me. It was getting darker, the fireflies flickering in his eyes. "But you can go to college. And you should. Mama wants you to even if she won't say it."

"How do you know?"

"Oh, c'mon, Ridley." He rolled his eyes in that firefly light. "Think about it. Through everything, did you ever miss even one day of school? When Mama was so stoned she could hardly walk, she still got us there. So don't you think she'd like to see at least one of us go to college?"

"It's not my job to make her like anything."

He shrugged. "Not mine either."

"And I don't know what I'd study anyway."

"You could study music."

"No, I just do that for me."

"Then what *do* you want to do?"

"I don't know. It's like...I want to do everything but they want to make you only do one thing."

"You can study more than one thing."

"Yeah, but that costs a lot of money and I'd be older than Mama before I got anywhere."

"Mama's not that old, you know."

"She's old to me."

He stood, but I took his hand and pulled him back down.

"Tommy," I said, beseeching now. "Don't leave me alone with her."

"I have to, Ridley. I'm sorry, but I have to. And you're old enough now to hold your own against Mama. I know I don't have to worry. You'll be okay."

Tommy said he'd email me every day but he didn't. First it was basic training and they weren't allowed. Later, when they sent him over there, he would at least email a couple of times a week. He would attach photos of him and his squad, toothy wide smiles behind dark sunglasses so that it was hard to tell them apart, all buttoned up in desert camo and bulging with gear, the air grainy, so full of sand that it made me cough just to see it.

The tone of his messages changed so subtly that I didn't pick up on it until I went back to re-read them, initially all excited by the newness of it, the exoticness of it, merging into roadside bombs, firefights and friends down, and finally targets taken out with ruthless efficiency. The enemy were targets, not people, so killing them seemed abstract.

I didn't want to kill anyone. I had enough ugliness to live with already. But I was sure that one or more of them would leave me no choice. And they wouldn't hesitate to kill me, shooting me up the same way they did Sherri and that other girl. When a wild boar charges, you leap out of the way and then shoot it in the back of the neck. You don't feel bad about it, you just do it. No, I'd never shot a boar, but some hillbilly boys at school had talked about it, grinning and proud, and I could visualize it easily enough, out in the deep woods, something lethal crashing through the brush, shotgun cocked, ready to leap aside as soon as the tusks showed themselves.

But most importantly, you did what you had to do. You took out targets and kept it abstract.

······

I WAS AT A MCDONALDS when the sun came up, my eyes heavy and gritty and the coffee wasn't doing anything to help. Their syrup came in little plastic tubs, just enough to leave me frustrated but I was too weary to go ask for more. I needed to go to the restroom to wash up and change clothes, but I was too weary to do that, too.

The new thought that wouldn't leave me alone, pestering like Robbie when he thought he was being witty, was that I didn't have to do this. Even after everything I'd purchased on Saturday, I still had enough for my bus ticket. I could just finish my little round pancakes, nibble my last sausage, then catch the next bus going downtown. An hour or so after that, we'd be heading out the interstate, the sun behind us and the world ahead, and by the time we got to Little Rock all of this would seem so long ago, a history that no one would know.

Except me.

I gobbled the last of my food, downed one of my little energy drinks, then grabbed my things and went to the restroom. Some hot water on my face would help, and not feeling sticky everywhere would help, and clean clothes would help. I splashed and wiped down, put on my denim skirt and a clean white T-shirt, stuffed Riley Skye's file into a trash can, then walked blue-booted toward the Dardanelle Agency. It was still too early but I couldn't wait. Patience was essential but I was out of patience now. Whatever was going to happen, I wanted it done before some other thought could come along to change my mind.

The office wasn't open, the Escalade wasn't there. I sat in the corner by the front door to wait, scooting over as the sun continued to rise, fanning my face with my hat.

Preston pulled in at 10:00 a.m. I was dozing by then, but the slam of his door woke me. I looked up and shielded my eyes against the sun. Preston's expression was what I thought it would be, what I needed it to be. He was grinning as if delighted to see me, but he was really grinning with glee, their loose end having delivered itself to his doorstep.

"Riley," he said, legitimately surprised. "What brings you here so early?"

I loathed the very presence of him, but I kept that hidden as well as I could.

"You said you might be able to get me another gig," I said, keeping my hand up to block the sun and whatever I might give away with my eyes. "I need to make some money."

"Well sure. Come on in and let's see what I can find."

He unlocked the door and I followed him inside. He gestured for me to sit in reception.

"I need to go make some calls for you," he said. "Just wait here. This shouldn't take long."

So far, this was going exactly as I expected. And I knew who he'd be calling. I was counting on it.

If I had been Preston, I would have waited a while longer before coming back out, to make it seem that I'd really been working the phone, but he was back in minutes. He took a seat behind the reception desk and laced his fingers, and I thought that he seemed to have only one look, one set of clothes, black slacks, white dress shirt, and glossy black shoes. Then there was the angular jaw, the perfect black hair, and the body that could set off a tingle in a woman Mama's age. All I saw now was ugliness, a sooty smear of deceit.

"So you lucked out," he said. Of course I did. "They need a back-up singer for a few tracks. The girl they hired has the flu or something, so they can use you right now. They're sending a car."

"Do I have to do videos and publicity?" I asked, because that's what I would have asked if all this hadn't been pretense.

"No, not this time. You'll just be filling in."

"Great." I tried to make that sound sincere but I'm not sure I succeeded.

We waited, Preston twiddling his thumbs. If I had been him I would have gone for coffee, or at least tried to make small talk. The silence gave me an unnerving sense that he had somehow seen right through me.

It wasn't long before the bell rang, that odd department-store chime. Preston went to answer the door. I couldn't see past him.

"Yeah, she's here," he said.

"Good," came a familiar voice, and then brow man stepped in and he had a gun. I didn't expect the gun.

"Well, look who it is," he grinned.

I wasn't afraid of the gun. It didn't really change anything, they would have had me anyway. That was the whole point. But my nostrils flared, my heat shot up, and I didn't sputter but came right out with, "Where's my guitar?"

I wouldn't have thought that his grin could go wider but it did.

"You are obsessed with that guitar." He shook his head. "I mean, stuck in a chair or with a gun in your face, that's really the first thing you can think of to say?"

"Look, Bruce, just get her out of here, will you?" That was Preston. So brow man's name was Bruce. Didn't matter. I still thought of him as brow man.

"You're coming too, Preston."

"*What?* Why do I need to be there?"

"You don't need to be there, you need to drive."

"*You* drive!"

Preston did sputter.

"Uh-uh. This girl knows kung fu or some sh—. I'm sitting in the back seat with this gun to her head and you're driving us and that's the way it's going to be."

At one time, brow man had looked like nothing more than a bored chauffeur. Now he looked like a brutish thug.

"Dammit!" Preston cursed, but he grabbed his keys and out we went, brow man keeping a cautious distance behind me.

Preston relieved me of my daypack—my *third* daypack—and steered me into the front passenger seat of his Escalade. Brow man kept his gun trained on me until I was in and buckled, then he slid into the back seat.

So far, except for the gun, everything was going according to plan. I didn't think these two had any idea that this was my plan, not theirs.

"You scream or anything, girl, and I will end you where you sit," brow man said, perhaps nervously. "You got that?"

I tried to make my voice sound shaky but it came out red anyway. "Yeah, I got it."

Preston gave me an odd look. "You know," he said suspiciously. "You never asked how much the pay was."

"Figured it would be enough whatever," I said quickly, swallowing a sudden surge of panic.

"Hmm."

The next part of the plan called for them to take me to the Gray Place, and they did—and I still had no idea where it was. I tried to follow the lefts and rights but couldn't keep it all straight, and many of the streets didn't have signs anyway. That was a setback. Not a terminal one, but not ideal either.

They walked me inside, brow man keeping his distance, back to the same dull room with the chair. My heart fell when I saw that the Martin Junior wasn't there.

"Sit and assume the posture, girl," brow man said, waving his gun. I sat stiffly. "Preston, strap her wrists with these zip ties."

Brow man was behind me, handing the ties to Preston, who was in reach of my foot but it was too soon to act. I bunched my fists as Preston pulled the ties. I could still wiggle my hands, maybe enough to work my thumbs through if it came to it.

"Okay, finally," brow man exhaled. He walked around front and holstered his gun.

"So now what?" Preston asked.

"Albert's on his way."

I needed to keep my mouth shut but I couldn't bring myself to do it. Yes, I was scared, but there was something inside me, like memories that weren't my own, and those memories spoke for me in a toothless grin, as sure of itself as summer heat.

"You know, Preston, I hate what I'm going to have to do to you."

"Girl," brow man said with a sneer, "I've got to hand it to you. You do know how to talk smack. It's not going to help you, though."

"You're the one that's going to need the help. You know what I call you, *Bruce*? I call you brow man. That's like a cave man, you know?"

"You got a smart mouth, girl. I'm going to remember that in a few minutes."

I bit my lip then, forced myself to shut up. Too much of this would make them wary. Or maybe not. Maybe I could get them so riled that they'd do something stupid. Still, it wasn't time. Just wait.

Mr. Albert came in imperiously, as if he owned the world and could spin it on his finger like a basketball.

"So here you are," he gloated. "I thought we'd never find you and then you came right to us." He paused to wipe his pate. "Where have you been hiding out?"

"I haven't been hiding."

"Well, you haven't been on Broadway either. We've been looking. It doesn't matter now, though." He considered me the way a vile king might consider an uppity peasant. "You know, you caused me a lot of trouble, and I have one pissed-off client who can't wait to get his hands on you."

"The hand that still works, you mean?"

I smiled in satisfaction when I said that.

"Don't stand so close, Albert," brow man warned. "This girl's got karate or something."

"This girl's tied to a chair," Mr. Albert snapped back. "And in a few hours she's going to be tied to a bed and getting pounded up her—" Use your imagination on that one.

I glared at Mr. Albert. He didn't seem to know what to make of that, the puzzle written clearly on his face, as if he'd expected me to be crying and begging. He shook it off.

"You know what to do," he said to brow man, and then he gave me a last puzzled look and he left.

"They're in the desk drawer, Preston. You do it."

"Why me?" Preston whined.

"Because I'm not turning my back on this b—."

Preston deflated but grudgingly complied. He went to the desk, fished in a drawer, and came back with the syringe.

"If you stick that in me, Preston," I ground out in a voice I scarcely recognized, "I *am* going to kill you. Do you believe me?"

Those words just hurled themselves onto my tongue, and they felt so good and righteous. With a jolt of awareness, I realized that I really meant them.

That rattled Preston. There was sweat on his lip.

"Just do it," brow man ordered.

Preston stooped over, felt for a vein then lowered the needle to my left arm. He wiped his lip, and then he pushed the needle in. I snarled like an animal. My wrists were tied but my elbows were free. I jerked my arm up and the needle snapped, breaking off in my arm, and blood spurted like ink from an old-fashioned fountain pen, splattering my forearm down to my fingers. Preston blanched, his mouth hanging open, some of my blood speckling his fresh white shirt. I yanked back against the tie, now lubricated with my own blood, and my left hand came free—and in one lightening motion I raised my right leg, drew my knife, and slashed it backhanded across Preston's throat.

Everything slowed in my mind. Individual dust motes stilled in the air before my eyes. Sounds muted away. In that elongated state, I had time to chuckle that they'd never thought it necessary to search a girl in a skirt. Preston went to his knees in shocked disbelief, his shirt red and dripping, his hands clutching his throat as if this couldn't be real, blood pulsing from between his fingers; then out the corner of my eye I saw the fist coming. I watched it one frame at a time, the hairs on the knuckles, a silver ring with a faceted blue gem. I braced myself as if I had hours to do it, but bracing myself did no good.

The shock of it didn't register, just my head driven backward, a searing dizziness, vision going to pinpoints, and then out.

chapter nineteen

......

I AWOKE ONCE AGAIN in the dark and my first instinct was to duck, which drove a spike of pain through my head that was so intense that I screamed.

I felt dizzy, sick at my stomach. Stars pricked at my vision. My face didn't feel right, oblong somehow. I gingerly touched skin that was hot and tender. My left eye wouldn't open. My cheek felt like a grapefruit left in the sun, and my bottom lip was fat and blubbery and dripping spit. The corner of my mouth was torn. There was something crusty on my face. I sniffed my fingers. Blood. I worked my jaw and screamed again, in such agonizing pain that I had to curl up and wrap my head in my arms.

This wasn't like that other time. I had no hazy moments where I had to work to put it all together. I clearly remembered the fist coming in, remembered the impact. I was bruised and cut and maybe worse. Broken cheek? Broken jaw? Maybe both considering how bad everything hurt. I found that if I kept my teeth together, the pain became more of an insistent throb rather than the ice pick-stabbing agony that had pierced my skull a moment ago.

And I remembered watching Preston wilt to his knees, into the spreading pool of his own blood, the disbelieving shock on his face. I did not remember seeing his last glazed moment of life, but he was dead, no doubt about it, and I had no moral qualms, no vacillating conscience. I wondered abstractly what they'd done with his body, if it was on an embalming table right now or weighted at the bottom of Percy Priest Lake.

My boots were gone—Sherri's boots—which meant they'd found the bear spray, my fallback weapon. I reached out in the dark and felt close walls. I was in a closet, possibly the same one as before. I lifted myself carefully, keeping my teeth together but not too tight. Too much bite crossed some circular threshold that sent the pain stabbing in again. I quickly learned the right balance. Pain is a fast teacher. I felt the air above me. There were no clothes hangers this time, nor the rod that held them. So there was no way out, no way to fight. This was it, then. Why was I even still alive?

That thought wound through my mind. I wasn't frightened. I didn't know what might be coming, but I wasn't afraid of it. I was more sad, sad for Chris and for Willie and for Mose, and maybe a little sad for Tommy and Timewall. I wasn't sad for Mama because I knew she would take it the way she took everything bad that happened, stiff-jawed and without the least glisten of a tear—and just thinking *stiff-jawed* made me cry out in pain.

I did know this, though, and I took some comfort from it: if Mama ever found out somehow, she'd come here and kill every one of them. I pictured it, diminutive Mama glaring up at brow man, her nostrils flaring, a rage so deep that it could explode the top off a mountain, and somehow she'd do it, she'd succeed where I couldn't.

That vision of Mama made me laugh, bringing on a cascade of pain that almost drove me unconscious. That thought of Mama, though, made me angry, that she would need to come in, full of deliberate confidence and deadly competence, cleaning up my mess as if she were always the stronger woman and I should have known it, should have just accepted it.

I scooted into a corner and kept my teeth lightly clenched, my right eye searching so hard for any point of light that the whole orb around that eye began to ache. I closed that eye and lay back, careful to lean to the right so that if I drifted off, or if my face bumped the wall, it would be the uninjured side that took the impact.

Perhaps I slept, I don't know. There really is no way to tell in the dark. I felt as if I were a veteran of this now, with enough experience to instruct others in the sensory weirdness that darkness induces, the starry lights, the colors that flow and turn like starlings, the pressure of the dark, how it folds you and compresses you until you're just a point of thought that might soon wink into nonexistence.

Light flared from under the door, slamming into me as if it were solid. I flinched, crying out against the pain.

"When I open this door, girl," I heard brow man's muffled voice say, "I'll have a gun on you. If you run, I'll shoot you in the head. Do you hear me?"

"Uh-huh," I tried to reply, but it came out so weak I could barely hear it myself. I thumped the door with my foot instead.

The door swung open and I was blinded, pushing into my corner with my hand up to shield my one good eye.

"Oh, dammit, Bruce!" I heard Mr. Albert exclaim in disgust. "Did you *have* to do that?"

"This b— killed Preston!" brow man whined defensively. "What was I supposed to do? Ask her to play nice?"

I could see them blurrily now, wavering images in the light.

"But he was already gone, right?" Mr. Albert said, disgust going to anger. "So why did you have to ruin her? She's worth nothing now. He won't want her like this."

I digested every word. It wasn't lost on me that they'd planned to sell me to someone, probably the man whose arm I broke; but what really registered was that last, *He won't want her like this*. So I must have looked bad, really bad.

"So what do you want me to do?" brow man asked resentfully. "Put a bullet in her—?"

"Not here," Mr. Albert cut in quickly. "I'll call some people. Just keep her contained. Can you do that?"

I could see clearly enough now to watch brow man bristle at that question, as if he were an amateur that Mr. Albert had to tolerate.

"Yeah, I can do that," brow man answered, glaring murder at his boss.

Mr. Albert took out his phone and snapped my photo.

"I'll send this to him," he said. "Maybe he'll want her anyway. I doubt it, though." He gave me a last look and shook his head. "Damn," he muttered as he walked away.

Now I was alone with brow man, who was eying me with enough hate to fill more than one mountain hollow.

"Did I get you in trouble with your boss?" I mocked him through closed teeth, which came out mushy, and hurt like heck, but it was worth it to see him turn so red and purple.

"You little smart-mouthed b—!" He came closer in a fury, almost close enough for me to take out his knee. I wondered how bad that would hurt. Not him, me. "You've been mouthing off since that day at the shoot, and I'm not taking any more of your sh—!"

He raised the flat of his gun, aiming to strike me in the face. I cowered back in my corner, and yes, I whimpered a little.

"Yeah, I thought so," he said smugly, lowering his gun. "You're not so tough now, are you." He pulled back with a revolted look. "And man, you stink! Get up." He waved his gun. "*I said get up!*"

My legs didn't want to obey. I rose unsteadily, pulling myself up the wall. My head swam. Brow man backed up a few steps.

"Now come on out of there. Go to the left. *Move!*"

I came out with that sinking feeling. He wasn't going to wait. He wasn't going to obey Mr. Albert. He was going to take me out back and shoot me in the head.

I went along dully. Now that I could stretch them, my legs were doing better, and if I held my head just so, it didn't hurt as much.

"Stop here," he said from well behind me. "Go through that door."

The back door, I supposed. I took a breath and tried to remember every smell, searched with my good eye for anything worth seeing for a last time. I thought about Chris, how gentle his touch was, and I smiled a little, which caused a sharp stab. "Please sink me in the lake," I mumbled to myself, blubbery lip barely moving. "Don't let me wind up on Willie's table."

I opened the door, which didn't take me out back to be shot but into an office-style restroom with double basins and three toilet stalls.

"Go in. C'mon, go in. Hurry up!"

I went inside. Brow man edged in behind me, and then I turned and saw into a mirror and I gurgled a cry. The left side of my face looked like what bursts out of a possum that's been hit in the road, hideously swollen, purple and black, my bottom lip hanging like a cartoon character. An ugly, oozing gash connected the corner of my mouth with the corner of my black and swollen eye, everything crusted in blood, so much that it was pinching and pulling the abused skin beneath. I toppled backward, felt my consciousness dimming. Brow man gave me a shove that sent me forward instead. I caught myself on the edge of the basin, hanging my head, struggling to breathe away the dizziness.

"Now wash up," brow man barked. "There's paper towels right there."

I was afraid to touch my face, fearing that the slightest pressure would set off the waves of agony.

"C'mon. Hurry up!"

What was the hurry? What did it matter?

I ran the water until it was warm then splashed it lightly at my face. Pink circled the drain and spotted the white porcelain, like the stuff you spit out at the dentist's office. I kept at it, splashing, sprinkling, the mirror revealing just how bad it was underneath all that blood.

The gash in my cheek would need stitches. A lot of them. It must have been his ring, the faceted blue gem. It slammed me in the cheek and tore its way down my jaw. Maybe Tommy could have taken a punch like that, but I always had delicate skin, like Mama's, and those fine bones beneath. Both of us could throw mean punches, but neither of us could take a punch in return, something unspoken but implicitly understood. Priscilla had hardier features. I found, in a begrudging way, that I envied her all of the sudden.

The warm water was soothing, though. In any other circumstance I could have sunk into a warm tub, dunked my head and held my breath while the water turned pink around me, dissolving every crusty scab and speck of clinging blood until my face would feel clean and renewed and in time it would heal. For now I made due with splashes, eventually patting my face ever so delicately with a wet paper towel.

The basin looked like an abattoir when I was finished. Brow man glowered behind me, catching my eye in the reflection. It still hurt, bad enough that I'd catch myself, take a sharp breath and go still, the way Uncle Bates sometimes did when he turned just the wrong way. But at least my face didn't sting anymore. The gash throbbed warmly but didn't hurt, at least in comparison to my jaw. The neck of my T-shirt was pink and stiff, but otherwise mostly clean. My denim skirt was too dark to show any stains. I adjusted it on my hips and stepped back, appraising myself in the mirror, still monstrous but not a monstrosity.

"I need to go," I told brow man, wincing and keeping my teeth together.

"You're not going anywhere," he said with derision.

I winced and swallowed before I tried to speak again, as if I were swollen with the mumps. I gave that up and just pointed to one of the stalls.

"Oh. Oh, yeah. Go knock yourself out."

I went in, and as I was closing the door, brow man kicked it back open.

"What? You gonna watch?" I burbled.

He was standing guard with his feet apart and his arms crossed, the barrel of his gun tapping his shoulder holster.

"I'm not letting you out of my sight."

I rolled my one eye, rolled my panties down and sat. Modesty is not an imperative when you're raised in a trailer with three brothers and a single bathroom. Fortunately I only needed to pee, but the tinkle sounded indecent and indiscreet with brow man standing there, his sneer going lewd. I wondered what kind of mama gave birth to a man like him.

I finished and flushed and was about to stand when brow man took out his phone and snapped a photo. I looked at him with absolute revulsion.

"Perv," I managed to get past my teeth loud enough for him to hear.

That was a last straw for brow man. Finally. His face twisted in an instant of rage. He bolted forward as I was about to pull up my panties, stomping his foot down on them and knocking my knees together. I looked up at him in clear understanding. So there it was, the inevitable outcome when a girl is compromised by a man.

We had a seminar about this at school, all us girls called to the auditorium. The boys weren't invited, although a few skulked outside the doors, peeping titillatingly through the narrow windows. Some of the girls giggled nervously as a female officer stood on the stage and instructed us about sexual assault, not a minor topic in a backward place like Fuller County.

There were different reactions, she said. Not every girl was the same. Most, however, would zone out, go catatonic, sending their minds someplace where they could pretend it wasn't happening. Others would be submissive, afraid of angering the boy—or the man—and risk bringing more harm to themselves. Very few fought back.

Afterward was the shame. Many girls didn't report their assaults because of it. I remember scowling at that. No one could shame you, only you could shame you; and if the shame was too much to bear, then get even.

The officer went on to describe support services, places you could go, people you could talk to. Right, talk to people. That always seemed to be their solution. Not go out and castrate the guy, but talk to someone. No, not Blaize's daughter.

I had pretty much tuned that seminar out by then, but one thing I caught left me practically speechless, that in most situations it was best *not* to fight back, not to enrage the man into even greater violence but to be meek and take it. It was all I could do not to jump to my feet. I wanted to holler at that lady what anyone with any sense knew, that if a black bear attacked you, you fought for your life. If you went meek, if you curled up in the leaves and the dirt, if you covered your head and played dead, that bear would kill you where you lay.

Brow man shoved me forward against the wall, pushing—I exhaled in relief—the right side of my face into the tiles.

The misconception that led to such advice, such stomach-turning timidity, was that men hold the power. But men don't hold the power, women do. They always have. Mama told me that. Where did she hear such bold words? That's another mystery I'll never know, but the words are true. Just think about it.

You see, whether they tail us or turn us—I had to chuckle for Willie. Brow man didn't like that, repaying my temerity with a savage thrust that lifted my toes off the floor—anyway, whether they tail us or turn us, what they fear losing more than their lives is right there within striking reach of a knee or the back of a heel. They are so pathetically vulnerable when they do this to us. It makes you feel sorry for them.

Brow man gave a last shuddering thrust, then leaned in close, his rancid breath on my mutilated cheek.

"Hey, you're pretty good," he whispered. "I might keep you for myself."

I whipped around through the pain and snapped his ear between my teeth, tears flooding out of my good eye but this wasn't crying, this was only dealing with the knife-twisting pain that was trying to pry my jaw apart. Brow man howled and tried to yank himself loose. The top of his ear tore away from his temple, his blood dripping off my chin—and he did what I needed him to do, he jerked away, opening himself, and I back-kicked my right heel up into his crotch with the power of a hammer to an anvil.

He let out a long blue gasp and doubled over. I gave a thought to going for his gun, but incapacitated though he was, he still might be able to fend me off. And that would use up time. Without a weapon in my hands, this wasn't enough. It wasn't permanent. He'd recover.

I ran instead, bolting through the door and sprinting down the corridor, hopping as I went to peel off my socks so that I would have better traction. I needed a weapon, a hammer, a screwdriver, a length of pipe—a stick or a rock. *Anything*!

I banged through a door and it was that costume room, clothes hanging everywhere but nothing rigid that I could hold in my hands. I quickly spun around and banged back out, numbing the pain with adrenaline. I went through another door, an empty room, chalky wallboard, dusty cement floor. I couldn't hide because my footprints in the dust would lead him right to me. I whipped out of there and tried another door, which opened as if oiled and I practically fell through it, into a room cluttered with musical instruments, mostly guitars and fiddles in their hard cases or gig bags, not props, not carefully stored for the next video shoot, but tossed in without purpose.

It took less than seconds for me to work it out, that each of those instruments represented a girl who'd come to Nashville with a dream, a dream that ended with sex and drugs or worse.

And there it was, lying against a wall, the gig bag with the Martin Junior inside! I wanted to drop to my knees and thank whatever gods there were but there wasn't time for that. Brow man could be right on me. I could picture the murder he'd have in his eyes, the enraged drive to kill me for daring to strike him in his manhood. I raced to the Martin Junior, unzipped the pouch and took out my knife, Mama's knife. What had this knife seen? What baptism of blood had it known? It felt so right in my hand, so viciously empowering, so ready to do what it was meant to do.

I raced out with the knife, sprinting onward, the fluorescent lights so slow to flicker on that I was past them before they could fully light the way. The corridor turned to the left. As I rounded it, a bullet exploded into a wall, peppering my eye with chalky grit. There was a door at the end of that corridor. I slammed through it as another bullet missed and exploded. I kicked the door closed. The lights came up. There was no lock, no way to secure the door.

I spun around to continue on. The room was large enough to echo—and there along a wall, women cowered behind their blankets, wide white eyes peering at me in terror.

"Run!" I hollered as loud as I could, trying to get that past my clenched molars. "*Run!*"

They only quailed farther back, some pulling their blankets over their faces.

I went for the door at the other end of the room which, now that I knew where I was, would soon lead me outside. Once outside I would be formidable, with room to hide and stalk. Brow man would never catch me if I could just get through that door.

The door behind me seemed to explode from its frame, slamming back against the wall hard enough to rain dust from the ceiling. I spun around. Brow man stood there, chest heaving, spit spilling between his teeth. His hair and unshaven face were matted with blood. His eyes seemed deeper and darker beneath that broad brow, cold with hate. His ear dangled like a fishing lure. He leveled his gun at my head.

The women were scuttling along the wall into the far corner, still cowering behind their blankets as if that would protect them from bullets. There was no cover, nothing to dodge behind. When you fight the bear, there's no guarantee that you'll win. The only guarantee is what will happen if you don't fight. And I'd fought. I wasn't ashamed.

I went into a stance, right foot back, toes tipped in, knees loose. I held out my left fist, elbow bent, raised the knife over my shoulder, pointing forward. Tommy taught me how to fight with a knife but he'd never shown me a stance like that, and I'm not sure why I did it. I probably saw it in a movie and it looked brave, and this was it so maybe I could show those women that you didn't have to cower to men like these—or at least I wouldn't.

I gave brow man a guttural growl and defiantly raised my chin. He only grinned, the depraved, vile grin of violence.

"Look at you," he sneered, or more like gloated. "I don't need this to finish you." He lowered his gun. "You look like a one-eyed car crash. You really think you can take me on in that kind of shape? Even if you do know karate, all I have to do is pop you in the face and you'll be screaming on the floor. And that big knife isn't going to save you. I'm going to take it from you, and I *am* going to kill you with it. Do you believe me?"

He holstered his gun, and I only just then noticed...brow man was left-handed. That's why his punch had done so much damage to the left side of my face, coming in from the side as it did, his ring cutting me upward, not downward. I adjusted quickly, flipping my knife in the air and catching it with the blade pointing backward along my forearm, a slashing position. If I could cut deep, disable his left hand, he wouldn't be able to reach his gun, holstered as it was high up into his right armpit. It was my only chance.

He came at me, running full on like a boar through the brush, closing that distance in moments but it seemed minutes in the passing, his arms pumping in slow motion, ear wagging like a lazy afternoon leaf, near enough now that I could smell the iron of his blood—and I leaped aside and slashed.

I always kept that knife sharp. What good is a dull knife, Mama would say. Brow man stumbled onto the floor in a smear of blood, his left hand half severed at the wrist. He kicked at me, spit at me, hurled impotent curses—and here I sort of stepped out of myself, watching it all from across the way, directing my hand, my knife, evading his kicks as he struggled desperately to force his right hand high enough to unholster his gun. I didn't gloat. I didn't reveal any satisfaction or hesitation, I just plunged my knife into his throat and twisted hard until the crack echoed between those walls.

chapter twenty

······

THEY WIRED MY JAW closed, which kept my teeth clamped so securely that I couldn't form any words at all, what with my lip hanging like blubber.

This wound up working in my favor because it helped me evade questions from the police, not that they'd really learn much more from me than what they already knew. The women in that room where I took out brow man were illegal immigrants who were reluctant to talk for fear of deportation, but some deal was made so they mostly corroborated my story, which I wrote out for the police. I did tell the police what brow man did to me, but only because I wanted that pill. I wasn't like Mama. I wasn't going to risk birthing a Robbie. I didn't see any need to tell them about Preston, though. Some fisherman might one day hook his body and reel it in, or else it might just bloat to the surface. Either way, it would be their mystery to solve, nothing to do with me.

What really perplexed the police, though, was that they had no record of me, no birth certificate, Social Security number, or even an online presence. I had considered telling them that I was a minor, thinking I could stay anonymous that way, but then vetoed that because it would have given them custodial power over me. So I told them that according to my mother I was twenty-one years old, and that she and I had always been alone. I didn't know where I was born. I didn't know who my father was, and there was no other family that I knew of. I'd been homeschooled because we were always on the move, busking from city to city, sleeping in shelters. I told them that my mother had died of a heart attack in Mexico last winter, in a town called Juarez, and that since then I'd been on my own. I came to Nashville because the busking was good here.

So that was it. It wasn't a crime to be free, was it? And as for the lying? Well, what choice did I have? Sometimes you just have to do what you have to do. I could live with it.

Oh, yeah, and I gave my name as Riley Skye.

The original detective who met with me was a man in his forties who looked as if he came right out of a cop show. He had that haggard, street-wizened look, the suit that didn't fit well, the gray pallor under the eyes, and the pragmatic savvy of experience. He didn't buy my story, it was obvious in his skeptical expression, but he couldn't disprove my story either. And it turned out that being free was indeed not a crime.

It also helped that I'd become a celebrity hero, the lone girl who'd taken down a human trafficking ring, and who'd done it in such a spectacular fashion. Those immigrant women spilled graphic details day after day on the news shows, broken English, making the most of their moments of fame and portraying me as an avenging angel. What cop would be stupid enough to tarnish that kind of image? Not him. He just sighed and left and I never saw him again.

The celebrity hero thing worried me. Even a month later, reporters were still camped out in the lobby downstairs. The nurses would bring me notes from them, desperate for an interview, how I owed it to the world to tell my story, to share my unique voice (laugh). A few magazines offered me money. A lot of it. But if my photo were printed in a magazine or flashed on TV, the ruse would be up. I would then become trapped in something I couldn't control, and that notoriety would reach from Bilbo all the way to California. Everyone would come. I bet even Mama. Chris would cling to my side, and while I wouldn't mind that for a while, it would become suffocating after a time. Willie would come, of course, and unabashedly tell his bawdy stories. I did smile at the thought. And Mose...I wouldn't mind Mose. He knew where boundaries lay, and which words not to speak. No, I wouldn't mind seeing Mose, but it was better if I didn't.

But my jaw was wired shut, I had screws in my cheek, and a Frankenstein scar ran down the side of my face. And I'd been sexually assaulted. They seemed to take that as worst of all, so I used it, enlisting so much sympathy that it became smothering.

The next officer to take over my case was a black woman named Bloom. Officer Bloom. She wasn't a detective, she wore a uniform, which fit her so crisply and professionally that I couldn't help but admire her, although I never dropped my guard. She was probably in her upper thirties, and wore her ebony hair in a severe wave that never got in her way. Officer Bloom had room for empathy in her serious brown eyes.

"You must come from some tough people," she commented when we first met.

"Yeah," I grunted, teeth wired together, eating and drinking through a straw.

Officer Bloom kept everyone away, guarding my privacy as if it were her personal duty.

I'd heard the term *human trafficking* before but I'd never paid it much mind. Mr. Albert ran a lucrative business. The Gray Place was a collection of storage warehouses attached to some cheap office space, which accounted for the warren of corridors and unfinished rooms, all owned by the Dardanelle Agency. The police were still trying to reconstruct the entire operation, how long it had been going on and how many victims there were. Bitter women were coming forward almost every day, piling on with their own stories of abuse and exploitation. The media couldn't get enough.

What was known for certain was that there were two operations going on at the same time. They smuggled in immigrants and indentured them to hotels and kitchens and elsewhere as cheap labor, reserving the prettier ones for paid pleasure. The Dardanelle Agency, it turned out, was a legitimate scouting firm. Someone, maybe Preston, had noticed how many pretty, young, and unattached girls were showing up to try and make it in Nashville, girls who were often living rough, and some of whom would do just about anything to make it in the business. For those not so motivated, there were always roofies and heroin.

Officer Bloom explained this to me. It was September now, still a week or so before they could take out the wires and screws. Some of the leaves were already beginning to turn beyond my window.

Mr. Albert denied any involvement. I saw him on the news. He was shocked and deeply disturbed to learn that employees of his were engaging in such a disgusting practice. He put the blame on Preston, who had disappeared, probably on the run. That photo Mr. Albert took of me was his undoing, though. They found it when they searched his phone. I laughed. Men like him, who think they're superior to everyone else, always make stupid mistakes. That photo was too grisly for publication, so I didn't have to worry that my identity would get out, if I was even recognizable anyway.

"Tell Mrs. Bowman," I said. It was easier to talk now that my lip was normal again, but having to speak without opening my mouth still gave my voice a mushy sound.

"Tell her what?" Officer Bloom asked, leaning in so I wouldn't have to strain to speak.

"Tell her that this proves Sherri wasn't a drug addict."

"I'll make sure she knows."

······

HAVING TO LIE in a hospital bed for months is its own agony. When no one was around, I'd slip out of bed and do push-ups and sit-ups. That's all I could manage. Jumping jacks or running in place would jar my jaw. Officer Bloom brought me books to read, adventure novels and the like.

"They should write a book about you," she said one day, and I thought it was a joke and laughed it off but she was serious. "It would help people," she went on. "And it might help you, too."

"I'm doing okay," I said.

"Are you sure?" And there her eyes went soft, like Mama's never did. "I should have them send a counselor in. Somebody you can talk to."

"I'm talking to you," I said, unable to inflect it the way I wanted. "That's enough."

She didn't accept that, betraying a little frustration, but then she perked up. "Oh, yeah, guess what?" she said.

"What?"

"I have something for you. I'll be right back."

She went out, and when she came back she was carrying the Martin Junior! I felt a flood of something through my chest. I don't know what to call it. Not love, but something. Or maybe love, if that's what it feels like. My eyes felt like they were crying. They weren't, of course, but they felt that way.

"I believe this is yours," she stated, beaming.

She passed the gig bag to me and I unzipped it in a breathless rush, taking out the Martin Junior and caressing it like a lover. I plucked the D string and lay back to its warm note, closed my eyes and just felt the sound.

"I'll leave you alone now," she said, but I wasn't alone. Not anymore.

······

OFFICER BLOOM CAME when they took the wires and screws out. October, gray beyond the window.

"Now I get to hear your real voice," she said, grinning and tipping up on her patent leather toes.

Those screws in my cheek had felt large enough to hold the hull plating on a ship, but what came out were these tiny stainless steel things, lying in a stainless steel pan with blood coagulating around them.

"There's recourse for your scar," the doctor said, a humorless man who reminded me of Preston. "I can call in a consult."

He gave me a mirror and I examined my face. Everything had knit well. My left eye looked mostly normal, just a little extra fold of skin that hadn't been there before. My lip looked perfectly fine. The scar wasn't as thick as I thought it would be, a thin pearly line, as if it had been painted on with a fine brush. It gave me a hardened look, a look that spoke of street experience, a look that would give pause to men like brow man and prevent a second look from men like Preston. I kind of liked it.

"No, it's okay," I told the doctor.

"As you wish," he said disapprovingly.

"They're discharging you from the hospital today, Riley," Officer Bloom said with a worried look. "But you still need time to convalesce."

"I feel fine," I said in my normal voice. It shocked me to hear that husky quality again, but now I didn't hate my voice. I was glad to have it back.

Officer Bloom smiled. "So that's what you sound like," she said. "A southeastern accent, too. So is that where you're from?"

Officer Bloom was a kind woman but she was still a cop, probing for information. I didn't hold it against her.

"I don't know," I said. "We used to busk back east, Ashville, Chattanooga, places like that. Maybe that's where it comes from."

She sighed almost imperceptibly but then smiled.

"I guess it must, then." She hesitated before going on. "So look, there's a retreat in Williamson County that'll take you. You can get yourself together there."

"I'm together right here, and I don't have money for that kind of thing anyway."

"Oh, you don't have to pay. You're their star witness. It's on the state."

"So what will I have to do if I go?"

"Anything you want. Read, meet people, play your guitar—and they have therapists on staff. You might want to talk. You never know."

I knew, but she was being kind and I didn't want to crush that. Also, I had no money, no way to buy that darn bus ticket. I needed a place to stay until I could come up with a new plan.

"Okay," I said. "Sure."

......

PEOPLE WHO WANT to help you when you're not asking for it are the most annoying people in the world. That therapist...good grief he drove me crazy. His name was Anderson. First name? Last name? He didn't say, but it wasn't mister, he made that clear while mimicking an odd stilted voice. He was too young to be a therapist, mid-twenties at most, with nothing distinguishing about him except that he was a little pudgy and a lot nosey. He was probably an intern working toward his degree. You don't expect people who don't know anything to know anything, and Anderson didn't know anything.

"I'm here to help you," he said, as eager as a puppy wanting to be petted.

"And I'm here to say no thanks."

I understood that I was being rude, but really, how many times should you have to say no to someone? He seemed sincere, though, enough that I felt bad about being so mean. At the same time, it probably wouldn't hurt his career to be able to say that he'd counseled the famous girl. He'd probably write it up in a paper, and then I'd be stuck with it forever.

The retreat was modern and bright and so far beyond Bilbo that it was a fantasy of a fantasy. The couches and chairs were of gray leather that gave off a warm smell, while the tables were of a dark wood that looked oiled. There were plenty of chrome rivets, and wall-length tinted windows. The views through those windows were expansive, of a grassy valley, horses at pasture, surrounded by poodle-cut hills that looked like dollops of autumn color dropped from the sky. My room was a comfy cubicle with built-in drawers and desk, and a soft twin bed with an ergonomic pillow. The view out my window was of deep woods. The vase just inside the door held fresh flowers that were changed daily.

So this was how rich people hid from their personal problems. It was really kind of pathetic.

I would sit in the common room with its various views, sometimes sunlit and splendid, sometimes gray and dour and looking too cold to sustain life, strum the Martin Junior and attract a gathering. One of the men—A patient? A retreatee? I didn't know what we were called—liked to sing. I asked him if he knew *What a Wonderful World* and he shook his head. Too bad. That would have done more for me than any amount of therapy.

A lawyer came to see me. It was the first of December, and the view out the windows was uniformly yuck. Allowing a lawyer to come in was like opening the gates to a Trojan horse. You can't trust lawyers. Everyone knows that. I'd never had a lawyer, but still.

We sat in the common room well away from the others. He gave me his name but I wasn't paying attention. I was instead looking for somewhere to run.

"So, Ms. Skye," he said, drawing papers from his briefcase. I couldn't make his age, but he had black hair with streaks of silver and a lot of Brylcreem. That's a nice smell, by the way. "They sent me because we need your signature to set up the trust."

"Trust?" Now he had my attention. "What trust?"

"You mean no one's told you?"

"Told me what?"

He seemed aggravated, not at me but at someone. He looked away, shook his head, then turned back to me with an intent focus. He had blue eyes, but more grayish than blue. The gold watch he wore could have fed a Bilbo family for years.

"I'm sorry, Ms. Skye. I thought you'd been informed."

"Informed of what?" I blurted in exasperation. I was starting to feel the heat, a little red around the edges.

"There were donations, Ms. Skye. People from all over. It got so big that the judge appointed my firm to deal with it."

"Donations?" My jaw dropped. "People donated money...*to me?*"

"Yes, Ms. Skye. Even from overseas. I've never handled anything like it."

"But why?"

His brow wrinkled and he looked at me closely, as if he couldn't believe what he was hearing, or else that I couldn't possibly be that naive.

"Ms. Skye," he explained with a note of incredulity, "you are famous all over the world. Surely you know that."

"*All over the world?*" I gulped against a sudden surge of panic. "They don't have my picture, do they?"

"No, Ms. Skye. The crime scene photos are sealed. But they know who you are and that you're a young woman who's had a hard life, and...I have to say, I've read the transcripts and it's all pretty harrowing. I think you're lucky to be alive."

Luck didn't have anything to do with it. I didn't tell him that, though. Instead:

"So how much money?"

He slid a paper across the table. "This is the current balance. Donations have tapered off, but some still come in."

I looked at the figure and thought I would faint. "Is this for real?"

"Yes, Ms. Skye, it is."

I couldn't catch my breath. The lawyer went on as if I weren't about to asphyxiate.

"So these papers detail the account numbers and interest rate. I have a debit card for you and a checkbook."

I understood the debit card. We bought them at the Walmart. But a checkbook? I had no idea what to do with it.

"If you'll just sign where indicated, I'll leave these with you. If you have any further questions, here's my card."

I signed the papers in a daze.

"Very well. That concludes our business." He stood and adjusted his tie. "Good luck, Ms. Skye. And by the way," he leaned in as if to whisper a secret, "if you decide to do a book or movie deal, we can help you with that, too."

He winked and went, and I sat dumbstruck.

......

CHRISTMAS WAS COMING near. I wasn't sentimental about Christmas. We did it back at the trailer, but more out of habit than anything else. Mama would put up a sad little tree, then keep herself occupied for the next two weeks sweeping up dried needles.

Anderson was adamant that I do something special. Good grief, he hounded me.

"You could use some Christmas cheer, Riley. Be with people. It'll help you heal."

"I'm healed," I grumbled back.

"Tell me about your past Christmases. Do you have good memories of them? I'd love to talk with you about it."

"I don't want to talk about it."

"You say that," he said with that puppy smile of his, "but I know you really want to. And I know it would help."

"And I really don't want to, and no, it really wouldn't help."

Nothing I could say or do would wipe that silly smile off his face. It was as if the boy had no other expression.

"Well, you'll come around." He patted my hand. He actually did that. "And I'll be here when you need me."

I wanted to stick my finger down my throat, the way some girls at the homecoming parties did to get it all out before they went home.

But Anderson's talk did give me a thought. I brought it up with Officer Bloom.

"I thought it would be nice to do some music for everybody at Christmas," I said. "What do you think?"

"I think that's a wonderful idea," she gushed. "I'd love to hear you play."

"I'd need you to help me, though."

"What kind of help?" She held her smile but with a touch of wariness in her eyes.

"There's a man who sings on the pedestrian bridge on Sundays. His name is Mose. We sang together a few times. I'd like it if he came. Do you think you can find him?"

Officer Bloom said yes a bit too eagerly. She was probably sincere in her desire to help, but I could also see those professional gears turning. Mose was the first name beyond the case that I'd ever mentioned, the first outside connection to the enigmatic Riley Skye.

"Just tell him that I'm Riley," I said. "The girl with the sweet Marin Junior. He'll remember me, I'm sure."

"I'll see what I can do."

I spent the next week berating myself for doing that. What was I thinking? One misplaced word from Mose and I would be outed. And why did I want to see Mose? What did it mean?

......

THE LAST SUNDAY before Christmas. It was cold outside. The horses were standing desolate with their tails to the wind. Word had gotten out. Not from me, but Officer Bloom must have let something slip. We were in the common room where they had a pit fire going. It was cozy, still light beyond the windows but deepening toward evening. Anderson couldn't contain himself.

"This is a great step, Riley. Great personal growth. I'm so glad I could be a part of it."

I snorted. He wasn't a part of anything except annoyance, but I'm sure his superiors would hear it otherwise, the young therapist who'd lured the famous Riley Skye out of her shell. I was wearing my third denim skirt, third T-shirt, third black jacket, and third pair of boots, which I'd sent for from the thrift store despite all that money in the trust. I felt a pang for Sherri's boots, no idea what happened to them, and the police wouldn't give me my knife back. Evidence, they said. It might be years before all the trials ended and they could return it to me.

People were gathering, taking places on the gray leather chairs and couches. Officer Bloom was there, dressed in elegant civilian clothes. Someone had placed candles on the tables. The lights were low.

Mose came in as if he were climbing the pedestrian bridge, wearing his black suit and white bow tie, grinning his grin. I couldn't tell if I was nervous or excited.

"Well, Miss Riley Skye," he boomed, bending back with his hands on his hips. When he was close enough, he leaned in, winked, and discreetly whispered, "Miss Ridley, so *you're* the girl that's been all over the news."

"Yeah," I blushed.

"That's a terrible business, Miss Ridley. Terrible."

He noted my scar and reached out with a finger, and I leaned into his hand like a child to a comforting touch, or a granddaughter to a cherished grandfather's warmth.

"You're okay though, right?" he asked, his grin slipping away and replaced with a somber expression that squeezed my heart.

"Yeah, I'm okay."

"Good. That's real good." His expression remained the same but with the suggestion of a smile. "So what would you like to play for these nice folks?"

"Can we do *What a Wonderful World*?"

"Of course we can, Miss Rid—er—Riley. I do love that one."

I threw the guitar strap over my shoulder and set up for a C chord with the quick transition to G, and Mose went into it so smoothly that it felt like warm syrup in my throat. I felt that song on my skin, in my bones, a solid comfort, and I strummed and grinned, and I was in that wonderful world once again.

We did *Mack the Knife* after that, and of course Mose made me sing. Well, he didn't make me but he wanted me to so I did, and I didn't feel self-conscious, I just bounced my shoulders to the beat and belted out lyrics with a smile, and I enjoyed it, I really did, and when it was over the people clapped and kept on clapping, and Mose turned to me, his grin wide and proud, and he opened his arms a little, and I don't know what came over me but I fell into them, his safe arms, and I shuddered and I cried, hot tears that dampened his suit and I couldn't make them stop, and I felt ashamed but also released from everything, really free for the first time, and he patted me on the back and said, "Just let it out, girl. Just let it all out."

......

MARCH IS COMING. I'll be nineteen soon. Anderson promised to leave me alone as long as I was writing in this journal, and he mostly has.

I look through the window and see that spring is on the way. The buttercups are up out there, yellow flowers wagging on their long stems as if they're in conversation with one another. I don't think there's any more to tell. I'm embarrassed that I broke down and cried on Mose, but he didn't seem to mind, and I guess I don't either. It opened me up somehow. I'm still me, I promise. I haven't changed...well, maybe a little, the kind of change that Mama wouldn't be able to stare down.

I've been thinking about Chris a lot. Not just the tingle, not just his gorgeous hair, but Chris as a person, the kind of guy who really cares. The kind of guy you can trust. People search their lives to find that, and here I had it right there in bed with me.

I still have things to do, though. But I can come back. Why not? And if he's still single then and he wants to, who knows where it might go? All I can say is that I'm not afraid of the idea. I'm not ready for him to know everything about me, but if he were here now I'd tell him a little bit, just to let him know that I trusted him. I'd tell him that my name is Ridley Speaks and I was born in the wilderness, under a tree during a howling storm. I'd tell him that I spent months doing research during my senior year. Having a brother in the Army helped.

And I'd tell him that I was going to Fort Irwin in California to meet my daddy.

finale

......

DEKE BURNET REMEMBERED picking cotton as a boy in north Texas, how the bolls cut his thumbs, deep cuts that became hardened fissures that ached and throbbed and wouldn't heal. It was the most miserable job he'd ever had, something he vowed never to do again no matter how bad things were.

And now things were that bad, and if they grew cotton in middle Tennessee he might just resort to that trade once again.

Deke was having a hard time finding work. His skills weren't in question. As a matter of fact, his skills were in high demand. His problem was that he couldn't shake the taint of his former employer. The Dardanelle Agency clung to Deke like a cow patty to the sole of his boot.

He'd only spent one night in a holding cell. The police were moving fast on that case and they cleared him early on. He was just a sound engineer. He went in to record tracks and then he went to a bar. He had no idea. None.

It was a scandal that was still rocking the industry, and he still struggled to accept it, that colleagues he'd known for years were engaging in such a crime. And worse yet, how many young and talented performers had fallen victim? People he'd recorded, watching them in the booth, urging them along, mentoring when it seemed appropriate while mentally deciding which might go the distance and which would probably flare out. Some great talent had gone through that booth. Where were they now?

And what could he do?

There wasn't a studio in the world that would employ him, not in Nashville, Los Angeles, New York, or even Berlin. He had papers from the police that exonerated him, but he couldn't get past the receptionists to show them to anyone.

Deke was fifty-five years old, too set in his ways, too late in life to start something new, and too far from retirement to keep up with the bills until he got there. His modest house in the Edgehill neighborhood was paid off. That was the only thing that kept him from having to sleep on the street with the bums and buskers, but the insurance had lapsed and he couldn't cover his property taxes. The thought of having to sell his house was grit in his coffee. He'd worked hard for that Edgehill zip code. To give it up now would erase the past decade of his life, as if he hadn't lived a day of it.

He gave a nostalgic chuckle to the old days at the Fort Worth Stockyards, and then Austin after that, halcyon days with Willie, Waylon, Kris, and Johnny, making music history and teaching Nashville a lesson. He slept mostly in bars back then, which fit the times but that was back then. There would never be another gathering of genius like The Highwaymen, and he didn't have the constitution to live that way anymore anyway.

And he thought about that girl, Riley Skye, so innocent in a tough sort of way. She had talent and didn't even know it, didn't even seem to care. In his mind, he'd pegged her as one who would go the distance. Then the story broke, unfolding in horrifying sound bites that came together to make you sick at your stomach. What they'd done to her was worse than awful, according to what was said on the news. That poor girl, in the hospital for months and then to a convalescent home. And now she'd completely disappeared. People speculated that she'd gone off somewhere to commit suicide. What a terrible, terrible waste, and a tragic loss to music.

At least it was finally warm outside. April could give you a hard freeze or eighty-five degrees. It was always a toss-up. But this was a warm April, so he had the windows up and the air conditioning off to keep his electricity bill down. He went to a shelf, rummaged for a CD then played it, the music carrying out his windows to the afternoon strollers on the sidewalks. Her voice had been unique, a husky quality like the old Country sound, not the pretty sopranos who were making the rounds now. It was her voice that made it work. Even Faith Hill wouldn't have been able to do justice to that song.

Deke sighed and put the CD in the pocket of his denim jacket. You had to surrender to days like this, times like these. Day drinking was the only way to get through them.

He hopped in his 1968 GMC pick-up and backed out of his driveway. He loved his truck. It was a real truck, a working truck, not a shiny monstrosity like what the drugstore cowboys were driving these days, the pickups that sat as high as a Caterpillar and had never carried a bale of hay in the bed, and with mufflers that blasted up and down the street muffling nothing. His GMC was a classic. Quad headlights, two-tone baby blue and white, and he'd once had the bed so full of hay that the back tires had rubbed the fenders. He was in that old Texas mood now. He put on his sweat-stained Resistol just because.

The bar he wanted wasn't far. It was a quiet place, dark, deep, and narrow. The maple bar was scratched and pitted from years of serious drinking. Christy was bartending as he'd hoped. Christy Calico. The two went way back.

"Hey Christy," Deke said, settling at the bar.

The place was otherwise empty. Christy was behind the bar polishing glasses, lit as if she were on a stage while the rest of the place was dim. She gave him a wary look, seemed about to back away but then caught herself.

"Deke," she said guardedly. "What brings you here?"

"Day drinkin', Christy."

Everything about her movements was cautious, apprehensive. She kept a distance as if he carried lice. Deke noticed and got his color up.

"Dammit, Christy. You know I didn't know nothin' about it. Mr. Albert? Preston? Shit, you knew 'em as long as I did. So cut it out, would ya?"

"Sorry, Deke, but you know how it is. If somebody sees ya then I got it on me, too. I'm still workin'. I cain't afford ta lose any gigs."

Deke sighed and stroked his wild goatee.

"Can ya at least bring me a PBR?"

Though the place was empty, Christy gave an anxious look around anyway.

"Yeah, sure, Deke."

Christy was forty-eight years old now and holding up pretty well. She was doing her hair with dirty streaks these days and she wore too much eye makeup, but her body was still tight enough to draw good tips, and her voice hadn't changed since Deke first met her in Texas all those years ago. It was her gravelly alto, pure Country, the consequence of smoky venues, hard whiskey, and hard living. She'd cut some records back in the eighties but had never progressed farther than opening for mid-level bands. The right song had just never come along. That happened sometimes. That happened most of the time. It was a shame. Nowadays she played bars and small venues, and worked part-time here to make ends meet.

She laid a wet streak on the bar and slid his PBR over as if still trying to keep a distance.

"Thanks, babe," Deke said as he tipped the bottle back.

"So whaddaya been doin'?" she asked.

"Nothin'. Not a damn thing. I couldn't find a job if it was right here in my front pocket."

"Maybe back in Texas—"

Deke shut that down in frustration. "Already tried."

"People will forget, Deke."

"Not fast enough."

He chugged that bottle.

"Give me another, will ya?"

"Sure, Deke."

Christy did feel bad for Deke, but what could she do? The business was so insular. Everyone knew everyone, and somehow that group mind made all the decisions and was answerable to no one. That something like this could just as easily happen to her was a constant anxiety.

Deke nursed his next bottle, rolling it between his palms. He had to broach the subject somehow, and he only had one shot. If she turned him down he would have nowhere else to go, no other trick up his sleeve. Thank God for day drinking. Thank God the bar was empty.

"So, Christy." He drew the CD from his pocket. "Put this on an' give it a listen."

"What is it?"

"Just a demo. Tell me what ya think."

He slid the CD across the bar before she could say no. To his relief, she picked it up. She reached down and brought out a CD player, popped the lid and put the CD in—and when the music started, Christy was transported.

She found the beat and tipped her shoulders to it, was startled when the tempo jumped in the second verse but she found that harried beat and went with it, unconsciously playing air guitar, her eyes closed so she could feel the notes. When it was over, she did a little sigh.

"So whaddaya think?" Deke asked.

"That was pretty damn good. Who's the artist?"

"That's Riley Skye," Deke said, bracing himself.

Christy's jaw fell.

"*Riley Skye?* You mean the girl—?"

"Yeah. Her."

"God damn, Deke! What are you doin' with this?"

"She cut that in my booth before—before it all happened."

"God damn!"

"Listen to her voice, Christy. Does it remind ya of anybody?"

"Yeah, Deke, it reminds me of *me*. What are you sayin'?"

"I'm sayin' you should cut that song."

"I cain't do that! It's her song an' she's disappeared or somethin'."

"She's got some lawyers over in the Pinnacle building. I gave 'em a call. They don't know where she is but they say they can work it. Somethin' about a trust. All legit. She gits credit an' they manage her royalties. It's a winner, Christy. Dammit, you have ta see that."

"But it ain't right, Deke."

"The hell it ain't! You heard that song. It's like she wrote it for ya. An' she's not gittin' ripped off. She'll git credit an' her money, an' you'll have a song with her as songwriter, an' damn, Christy, the thing'll take off. Ya know it will."

Christy went off in thought, tapping the empty jewel case with a fingernail. Deke was right. It was a great song, sweetly nostalgic at first and then angry, with a hint of redemption and a reprise to cool off with. The guitar work was acoustic and intricate, a real display of skill. But even if the song wasn't any good, Riley Skye's name would still sell it. Christy leaned on her elbows, close enough to smell the beer on Deke's breath.

"So what's the title?" she asked.

"Don't know. I guess it ain't got one."

"How about *Mama Never Told Me?*"

......

MAMA NEVER TOLD ME
Single by Christy Calico
Riley Skye, songwriter
Deke Burnet Productions

Mama told me not ta cross the street
without lookin' both ways
An' she told me ta pay attention
an' ta make better grades
An' she told me that the boys would come
an' that they'd gawk and gaze
But Mama
But Mama
You never told me how ta love

An' Mama told me
Not ta come around
When her door was shut
The towels on the ground
An' my breaths would burn
I couldn't make a sound
No food in the kitchen
No lights in the house
Winter cold inside
An' men came spellbound
An' Mama told me, look
Ain't we livin' so proud
But Mama
But Mama
You never told me how ta love

Then those better days when Mama shined
With boots and jeans dancing in time
Motors and men and braids so fine
A tooth-missed smile returned in kind
Mama told me, when so inclined
A new baby was deep inside
Mama you told me all of this
Yes Mama, you told me so much
But Mama
But Mama
You never told me how ta love

Yeah,
An' Mama told me not ta cross the street
without lookin' both ways
An' she told me ta pay attention
an' ta make better grades
An' she told me that the boys would come
an' that they'd gawk and gaze
But my mama
My mama
She never told me how ta love

Afterword

......

There is a paved bicycle path in Nashville called the Music City Bikeway, which runs roughly twenty-eight miles roundtrip between J. Percy Priest Dam east of town, and the John Seigenthaler Pedestrian Bridge over the Cumberland River downtown. This is a spirited bicycle ride, with some hearty climbs, dedicated bridges over the Cumberland and Stones Rivers, some fast, forested flats along those rivers, and side routes to various parks along the way.

I have cycled the Music City Bikeway many times over the years, always enjoyable but better during the week because the path tends to get crowded on the weekends. On an autumn Sunday not long ago, in weather too inspiring to waste, I took my bicycle and myself down to the dam terminus to brave those weekend crowds. The bikeway was indeed crowded but the ride was exhilarating nonetheless, the air crisp and clean, the sky a breathless blue, the leaves fluttering golden in the breeze.

A football game had let out just as I reached the pedestrian bridge, thousands of fans shuffling over the bridge in a mass-migration to the parking garages downtown. I had never seen that many people on the bridge, shoulder to shoulder like a zombie horde. I questioned whether the bridge could take the weight, and questioned if it wouldn't be prudent to just turn around right there at the foot of the bridge and make the fourteen-mile return trip. I always climbed to the center of the bridge before turning back, though, a tradition for me, so I sighed, dismounted, and joined the throng.

At the overlook in the center, where I usually dismount, make a photograph, drink some water and down an energy bar, an old black man, tall and erect and decked out in a black suit and white bow tie, was crooning to the passing fans in a resurrected Louis Armstrong voice and singing *What a Wonderful World*. Despite being bumped and elbowed, and my bicycle being repeatedly kicked in the back tire, I was compelled to stop and listen. This was the authentic Nashville, not the gaudy commercialism overtaking Broadway, and this was the man who would become Mose. It was too crowded and chaotic to get his name, but he's out there somewhere. I hope this book somehow finds its way into his hands.

Ridley Speaks was a special project for me, perhaps because I never had a daughter of my own. Were I to have been blessed as such, I would have wanted that daughter to be like Ridley, despite Ridley's flaws and insecurities. For readers who have become immersed in the saga, there was a Riddles on the Appalachian Trail during my 2018 thru-hike. She was an intrepid young woman from Canada who was hiking solo, and whom I passed for the last time early on a misty morning during my final thirty-mile sprint to Springer Mountain, Georgia. When I first met Riddles at Highway 19E in Tennessee, I misheard her trail name and so called her Ridley from then on. Perhaps this book will somehow find its way into her hands as well.

There was also a Cockadoodle on the Appalachian Trail, Nicholas Yanoshak of Pennsylvania. I met him during my 2021 thru-hike, and we have since become friends and trail brothers. We are *tramily*. The way I describe him in the book is pretty much the way he appeared to me when I first met him on the Nantahala River during that hike, with the heavy orange backpack, guitar neck sticking out the top. Since I possess not even the makings of a music gene, Cockadoodle's help with the music parts of the story was not inconsequential. I couldn't have done it without him. You can be sure that the book will find its way into his hands.

Also invaluable to the music scenes was another of my trail brothers, Jeff "Hoosier Daddy" Erdman of Indiana. Just imagine taking calls at all hours, being questioned repeatedly and perhaps tediously about things that music people take for granted. Exactly what is the difference between a note, a chord, and a key? Listen to this song. Which chord does it open with? What is the meter, or the tempo, or whatever you call it? Because of Hoosier Daddy's patient help, I think I do know the difference between notes, chords, and keys now, although I still stumble with beat, meter, and rhythm.

For further effusive thanks, I turn to Jacky Carver Sr. and Jacky Carver Jr., the proprietors of Sanderson Funeral Homes in Carthage, Tennessee, for taking the time to describe their procedures to me, that realm where few of us venture until the very end, and of which, as a consequence, I knew nothing beforehand.

Without the assistance of my trail brothers, as well as father and son Carver, *Ridley Speaks* simply wouldn't be. They each have my thanks and gratitude. Any mistakes, however, are mine alone.

I must also thank my editor, Amanda Valentine, for her support and dedication to this saga. We still have a way to go before we bring the saga to its conclusion, so please bear with me.

Thanks and appreciation also to Vicki Valentine, who designed the books and created the wonderful cover art and themes. I still tear up a little whenever I see her cover for *Blaize Speaks*.

Priscilla is next, possibly the most complicated character in the saga. She's going to be tough to write.

                              Kirk Ward Robinson
                              Smith County, Tennessee
                              February 2024

Look for
Priscilla Speaks
A Novel

Book Four of The Speaks Saga

From HighlandHome Publishing
ISBN: 979-8-9886815-3-3
Coming soon

ABOUT THE AUTHOR

......

Kirk Ward Robinson, a four-time Appalachian Trail thru-hiker, was born and raised in south Texas and has since lived in every continental American time zone. He is an inveterate hiker and cyclist, which is how he prefers to travel and explore the world. His wide-ranging career has included roles as a chief operating officer, bookstore manager, stagehand, bicycle mechanic, and executive director of an educational non-profit organization in cooperation with the National Park Service. Robinson has been twice named to Kirkus Reviews' *Best Books*: in 2012 for *Life in Continuum*, and in 2015 for *The Appalachian*. He earned five stars from Foreword Clarion Reviews for his novel *The Latter Half of Inglorious Years*.

These days he maintains a small ancestral farm in the hills of Tennessee.

www.kirkwardrobinson.com

www.ingramcontent.com/pod-product-compliance
Lightning Source LLC
LaVergne TN
LVHW041907070526
838199LV00051BA/2537